JERRY KENNEALY

"SCREEN TEST"

## ALSO BY JERRY KENNEALY

*Nick Polo, PI Series*

Polo Solo
Polo, Anyone?
Polo's Ponies
Polo in the Rough
Polo's Wild Card
Green with Envy
Special Delivery
Vintage Polo
Beggar's Choice
All That Glitters

*Carroll Quint Series*

Jigsaw
Still Shot

*Stand Alones*

Nobody Wins
The Conductor
The Forger
The Suspect
The Hunted
The Other Eye
The Vatican Connection
Chasing the Devil
Cash Out

Down & Out Books
3959 Van Dyke Rd, Ste. 265
Lutz, FL 33558
www.DownAndOutBooks.com

The characters and events in this book are fictitious. Any similarity to real persons, living or dead, is coincidental and not intended by the author.

Cover design by James Tuck

ISBN: 1-943402-27-2
ISBN-13: 978-1-943402-27-4

For Shirley,
my beautiful wife and amazingly patient
in-house editor.

# CHAPTER 1

The spring of 1968 was a hell of a tumultuous time in the good old U.S. of A. Martin Luther King, Jr. was shot and killed in Memphis, the Vietnam War was turning into a nightmare, the streets of every major city were filled with violent protestors, President Lyndon Johnson announced he wasn't going to stand for reelection, Steve McQueen, the hottest actor in Hollywood, the King of Cool, came to San Francisco to make a movie, and I got my hands on a priceless blue diamond.

It all started one day when Vanessa the Undresser was sitting across from me at an outdoor table at Enrico's Sidewalk Café on Broadway. Enrico's was a hot spot in the city, frequented by artists, politicians, celebrities, and hookers—such as Vanessa.

It was situated right next to Finocchio's, a nightclub that featured crossdressers—talented singing and dancing female impersonators, of which Vanessa was one. Her specialty was a strip number done to a bump and grind version of the old standard, "A Pretty Girl is Like a Melody."

"He raped me, Johnny O," she said. "He beat me up bad and raped me."

Vanessa was a transsexual, born in Dayton, Ohio, under the name Robert Alverson. She was tall and lean, with a pretty cameo-shaped face. Her hair was the color of honey, and drooped over her left eye. She pulled her hair back and showed me the purple-red bruises around her eye.

"There are more bruises," Vanessa said, fingering the pink silk scarf she wore around her neck. "I think he would have killed me if I hadn't spit out the gag he'd stuffed in my mouth

1

and screamed bloody murder."

The waiter raked his bottom teeth over his mustache as he deposited a cup of coffee for Vanessa, and a CBA—coffee, brandy, with an anisette float for me—on the table. He'd seemed upset when we didn't order some food. Sidewalk café dining might be wonderful in Paris, but there was bumper-to-bumper traffic crawling along Broadway, including diesel spewing buses and big rigs.

Once, when I was enjoying a cocktail at Enrico's, a woman at a nearby table told her husband to "Eat the soup before it gets dirty."

"When did the attack take place?" I asked.

"Two nights ago, late, after my last number. This bastard called me over to the bar and bought some expensive champagne. He was all sweet and loving, until we left the club."

"Where'd you take him?"

"The Rendezvous."

I tested the CBA. The Rendezvous was a small Basque hotel located on a steep alley a block away from where we were sitting. It had a restaurant at street level and three floors of rooms that were rented to merchant seaman by the week, or hookers by the hour.

"What do you want me to do?" I asked.

"Find him. Arrest him," she said angrily.

"Did you report it to the police?"

"You're the police, damn it."

It was an unseasonably warm spring day. I leaned back in my chair and focused on the tourists strolling along the street, stopping to peer in the doors of the seedy topless joints that took up much of the real estate space. "Did you talk to the beat cops at Central Station?"

"Right after I got free and cleaned up. They more or less told me to get lost. Then yesterday I met with an inspector in the Sexual Assault Detail. He told me the same thing. Said there was nothing he could do."

"What was his name?"

"Cornell. He smelled like he'd slept in his clothes all week. I got the feeling that if I gave him a blowjob, he'd find a way to do something."

Ed Cornell was not one of my favorite people, but he had a point. "Vanessa, you're a man, a crossdresser, and a hooker. If I found the jerk that roughed you up, it would be his word against yours. And, it's not fair, but it's a fact—the district attorney would never prosecute the guy."

Vanessa pulled off her gloves, white cotton ones, the type they give to pallbearers at funeral parlors. She could easily pass as a pretty girl even in the bright sunlight, but once the gloves were off they exposed the big knuckled hands of a man. She picked up a spoon and rapped it against the rim of her coffee cup. "You owe me, Johnny O, so find him. If you can't arrest him, then rough him up, like he did to me, or tell me where he is and I'll have some friends beat the hell out of him. This kind of guy, he doesn't do this just once. He'll do it again. You're the fixer, right? That's what they call you, so fix this bastard before he kills someone."

Vanessa was right. The bastard probably would do it again. And I did owe her. A couple of months ago a man, after a few too many drinks at Finocchio's bar, had stormed into the dressing rooms, donned a wig and demanded things he shouldn't have. He happened to be a United States Senator from Vermont. It would have made a great media story.

One of the bartenders called me. Finocchio's was a CFP, cop friendly place. The owner fed uniformed cops in the kitchen, donated to all of the police charities, and off-duty cops seldom had to pay for a drink at the bar. But if Vanessa hadn't hidden the senator in a closet, he would have been in a paddy wagon and en route to the Hall of Justice jail.

Vanessa showed me a back way out of the nightclub and I dragged the senator back to his hotel. When he sobered up he was begging for forgiveness, and for me not to let the story get in the papers. It would ruin him, his family, etc., etc. Now he owed me a *big* favor. And cops like me could make good use of favors like that.

"Do you have a name for this guy?" I asked Vanessa.

"Boris."

"A last name?"

"No. But I've got something better." She snapped open her silver-colored vinyl purse and extracted two glossy black-and-white six-by-eight photographs and slid then over to me.

"Trixie took the pictures," Vanessa said.

Trixie was Finocchio's photographer, a pint-size crossdresser with a wig like Harpo Marx's, who snapped photos of customers without their permission and then asked, "Would you like me to print that up for you, sir?"

The man sitting at the table with Vanessa was wearing a single-breasted suit. He appeared to be in his late thirties. His shirt was buttoned at the neck. No tie. He had thick dark hair with a ruler-straight part on one side. In the first photo he had a boozy smirk on his face, in the second he was scowling.

"He spoke good English, but he had an accent," Vanessa said.

"What kind of an accent?"

"Russian, I think. He kept calling me '*Golobee by yard,*' or something like that. And he said that this was better than freezing his ass off in Moscow."

"How tall was he?"

"About your size, but he had narrower shoulders. No fat on him. He had muscles, especially on his arms. And tattoos."

"What kind of tattoos?" I asked.

"Knives, stars, and spider webs. Crazy stuff like that. "

"Was he with friends?"

"No. All by himself. We discussed money, and he showed me a roll the size of my fist. Twenty-dollar bills, at least on the outside of the roll."

"Did he pay for the drinks in cash, or with a credit card?"

I asked.

Vanessa peeled the wrappings from two sugar cubes and shook them like dice in her hand before dropping them into her coffee. "Cash. He was a big tipper before we got to the room. After that I never got a single dollar off the bastard. And he took my purse. I had a couple of hundred bucks in it."

"Was your driver's license in the purse?"

"No. I never carry any ID on a date. The son of a bitch was going to kill me, Johnny. He slapped me around and then used a knife to cut up the bed sheets. He gagged me and tied me to the bed. While he was doing me, he was choking me."

She deepened her voice and put on an accent: "I going to break your neck like a chicken."

"Where'd he get the knife?"

"His pants, I guess. His gun must have been in his jacket."

"He had a gun? What kind?"

Vanessa shrugged her shoulders. "What do I know? It was black. And after, after he did me, he screwed one of those barrel things on the end of the gun and—"

"A silencer? He put a silencer on the barrel of the gun?"

"Yeah. He was laughing. Said he was going to shove it up my butt and blow my brains out." She made the sign of the cross against her chest. "I had chewed the gag loose and I started screaming. Whoever was in the next room was pounding on the wall, saying he was going to call the cops. So Boris took off. He's crazy, Johnny. You've got to find him."

If Vanessa was telling the truth, the silencer made a big difference. Villains in James Bond movies had silenced pistols, but rapists, drunks, and everyday criminals did not. I couldn't remember ever handling a case involving a silencer.

"I'll do what I can," I told her.

Her face formed a disappointed frown.

"I mean it, Vanessa. You're right. I do owe you. And I want to protect you, so be careful. Ask Trixie if she has any more photos of the man. Maybe he'll show up in the background of shots she took of other customers. That could help."

I took a business card from my wallet and wrote down the number for the Communications Division on the back of the card.

"If you can't reach me at my office, call this number, day or night. Tell them it's an emergency and they'll find me, okay?"

"Okay," Vanessa said, with little enthusiasm.

I finished the CBA, got to my feet and dropped some money on the table.

Enrico Banducci, the owner of the café, was a burly, soft spoken man who always wore a beret. He was famous for launching the careers of entertainers like Lenny Bruce, Bill Cosby, Barbara Streisand and Woody Allen on the road to stardom from the stage of his brick-walled *hungry i* nightclub.

He caught up to me as I was walking to my car.

"Inspector, I got a call from Alan Rickeby, a Hollywood producer working on the movie Steve McQueen is shooting in the city. He told me you recommended that they film a scene here, at my place."

"McQueen wants the film to show the real soul of the city, not just tourist spots. I thought your café would be perfect."

Banducci moved in close. "I appreciate your help. Come for dinner. Bring a friend." His eyes wandered over to Vanessa who was stirring her coffee. "My treat."

# CHAPTER 2

My unmarked police car was parked in front of a nearby fire hydrant. I sat behind the wheel and went over my conversation with Vanessa. Boris. A nasty Russian with a semi-automatic pistol that could handle a silencer. It had to have been a semi-automatic; silencers won't work on a revolver.

Vanessa was scared, and rightly so. I believed her. Now I had to figure out what to do about it.

I had started my career as a policeman at the tender age of twenty-two and at first worked out of the busy district stations. But not for long. I had what was known as "juice" in the department, thanks to my father, "Roaring" Rory O'Rorke. Pop had been a police captain, the head of what was then known as the Chinatown Detail. Besides policing Chinatown, the Detail was known for its rough ways in discouraging members of organized crime from taking up business in San Francisco. As the story goes, Mickey Cohen, the notorious Los Angeles Mafia thug, had shown up in town, along with a couple of muscle men and a toothsome young blonde. Shortly after they had settled into a suite at the Mark Hopkins Hotel, there was a knock on the door. It was my father and his partner, Jumbo Flagg. They took out the muscle and then my father slapped Cohen around. Cohen was a former boxer, but he was no match for my father, who had a record of seventeen wins, all by knockouts, in the ring, or Jumbo, who was built like a gorilla and had a face that looked as if it had been hit by a frying pan—for the simple reason that it had been hit by a frying pan. They dragged Cohen and his two stooges down to the train depot and sent them back to Los Angles.

Pop had used his juice to get me into the Bureau of Inspectors, plain clothes cops—the best jobs in the department in my view. It was an appointed position, no civil service test involved. You had to know the right people. I worked the Burglary, Homicide. Fraud and Armed Robbery Details before I landed the plum job as the Department's Executive Protection Officer. I'd also picked up an unfortunate nickname—the Fixer.

Visiting high power politicians and entertainers were given special treatment, and it was often my job to set them up with bodyguards and to recommend quiet hotels and restaurants where they wouldn't be disturbed.

The actors and performers were seldom a problem—the politicians were always a problem.

The City picked up the tab for protection on many of the visiting celebrities. When the City didn't pay, the celebrities or their studios did, directly to me. I farmed the jobs out to guys I trusted in the department. They worked for me on their off-duty hours. It was good for them, good for me, and the brass didn't care, as long as I threw them an occasional perk, like tickets to a play, or an invite to a bigwig cocktail party.

The filming of *Bullitt* was considered a high priority item by the powers that be: Mayor Joe Alioto, Chief of Police Thomas Cahill, the Chamber of Commerce, and several local banks were involved in financing the flick.

There were high hopes that the film would be successful and that it would lead to San Francisco becoming Hollywood North.

The cast and crew of *Bullitt* were to be given carte blanche in regards to traffic control and, since it was basically a cop story, access to police personnel.

Each of the main actors, along with the director, had a plain clothes inspector at their beck and call. That could have been a problem, but it turned out just fine.

The cop that got the best of the deal was Inspector Gus

Korereis, who was assigned to Jacqueline Bisset, the female lead, who, Gus assured me, was every bit as sweet and pleasant as she was drop-dead gorgeous.

I drew Steve McQueen.

McQueen had a reputation as a cop hater, possibly because of his alleged fondness for smoking dope, but during our first meeting, when I drove him around in my unmarked car for a night of prowling, I explained we really didn't give a damn what he drank or smoked, as long as he kept it out of our sight. He was fine with that. Better than fine. The only thing I ever saw him smoke was a filter-tipped Viceroy cigarette. McQueen wanted his character to act like a real cop—the gestures, the wordage. He noticed things, asked a lot of intelligent questions, and didn't have a "reach impediment." He was quick to reach for his wallet and tipped well.

After leaving Vanessa, I drove over to Leavenworth Street, in the posh Nob Hill area of the city, where McQueen had rented an apartment. Alan Rickeby had called the office and said McQueen wanted a meeting. His unit was on the eighth floor. The stairways were too narrow for the pool table he'd wanted installed, so a crane had been hired to lift it up the outside of the building and through the windows that had to be removed to maneuver the pool table indoors.

There were several production people in the apartment, some I knew by sight. Alan Rickeby, the production manager, was a sharp-witted man with wheat-colored hair and over-sized tortoise-shelled glasses that magnified his pale gray eyes. We had hit it off at our first meeting several months earlier when he came to the city to scout things out. He was a reasonable guy with no ego.

During a lunch at Doro's restaurant on Montgomery Street we went over a rough draft of the script and mapped out spots that would look good in the film. There were several no-brainers: the Mark Hopkins hotel, the Hall of Justice, and the gloomy Victorian, smudged red brick buildings that housed the San Francisco General Hospital.

If you catch a cold, the flu, suffer from stomach problems, or were having a baby, you avoided SF General, because it was a petri dish of infectious viruses and an assortment of nasty bugs.

But if you'd been shot, beaten with a baseball bat, been on the losing end of a knife fight, or in a major traffic accident, the hospital's Trauma Center was the place to go. The doctors and nurses were all first class. It's where I'd met my wife. She'd been a nurse in the Center before moving back home to Jamaica.

Rickeby wanted local color—places that hadn't been used in other films.

"I mean, the Golden Gate Bridge is great, but it's in every flick ever filmed here."

I showed him Enrico's, which he liked, an old rundown hotel on Embarcadero, and a Pacific Heights mansion on Vallejo and Divisidero Streets.

There was going to be "the chase scene of all chase scenes in the movie," according to Rickeby. We drove around town for two days checking out possible locations, and then one morning Steve McQueen showed up in the green 1968 Mustang GT fastback he would use in the film, and took us for a ride—Rickeby sitting nonchalantly in the front passenger seat and me in the cramped back seat, cringing and saying Hail Mary's as McQueen barreled the car around town.

Rickeby wanted a place for Bullitt to live. "Not a house, nothing too fancy, somewhere on a steep hill."

Rickeby loved steep hills, and the city had more than enough to satisfy him.

I told him I knew just the spot, a flat on Clay Street, right across from a neat little Mom and Pop grocery store. It was my flat, and we worked out a deal where they had two weeks to do the filming there and I had a nice rental fee.

"Steve wants to see you," Rickeby said, pointing to the room with the pool table.

It was a large room, probably originally designated as a dining room. The pool table, with teak railings set in a stainless steel base, took center stage. There was no furniture, just barbells, a weightlifting bench, and a lemon-yellow Westinghouse refrigerator.

McQueen was wearing a black T-shirt, khakis, and brown suede desert boots. In person he looked pretty much as he did on screen. He was of medium height, wiry; his brown hair was cut short and finger-combed. His eyes were a shade of blue that stood out against his tanned skin.

He pointed a cue stick at the refrigerator. "O'Rorke. Want a beer?"

"I'm fine. What's up?"

He gave me one of those cool, squinty smiles of his. "I noticed you wear a turtle neck sweater. No other cops, just you."

Believe it or not, turtlenecks were somewhat of a daring fashion statement back then—for cops. Hippies and poets wore them. My interest was that they kept the icy city winds off the back of my neck.

"During the day the department likes a suit and tie, but off duty, or at night, you can go casual."

McQueen leaned his cue stick against the pool table. "You wear a shoulder holster." He patted his hip. "Every other cop I've seen has his holster on his belt."

I unbuttoned my sport coat. "I've got no hips, no butt. I wear the gun on my belt and my pants fall down."

He laughed and said, "I've got a gaffer, a lighting technician, Russ Cortig, who ran into a problem. He got busted early this morning at a party in the Haight-Ashbury District." He gave me that smiling squint again. "He's a good kid, not a doper—just likes to party."

"Where is Cortig now?"

"He was bailed out of jail at ten o'clock. He's staying at the Sheraton Hotel out by Fisherman's Warf. A lot of the crew is staying there. I'd appreciate anything you can do for him; we like to think of the crew as family. Full name Russell A. Cortig, twenty-eight, date of birth is May sixth. Lives in Venice Beach. I can get you his social security number if you need it. I was hoping you could fix things so he wouldn't have a record. Having a record makes it tough to get a job in this business."

I took out my notebook and wrote the information down. McQueen was a quick learner—talking like a cop, giving me the guy's ID info. "I can't promise you anything."

McQueen picked up the cue stick and lined up a shot. "Do what you can do, that's all I ask."

# CHAPTER 3

I drove back to the Hall of Justice. *Hall* is really not an accurate description. Think of a giant shoebox shaped mass of concrete blocks with no redeeming architectural charm. I had to admit, it was functional. Inside were the superior and municipal criminal courts, a district station, the Chief's office, all of the Inspector Bureaus, and on the top floor, a city jail. In the basement was a cafeteria of sorts. Bad sorts. I went directly to the Crime Lab and handed one of the photographs Vanessa the Undresser had given me to Walter Ito, a technician who could do wonders with photographs.

"Can you crop the head of the man, Walter? Make me a dozen or more pics of his face, and then some full body shots."

Ito brushed his hands across his white lab jacket before examining the photo. "You don't want the lady in the pictures?"

"No, thanks." There was no sense in telling Walter that there was no lady in the picture.

Next I headed to the Records Room, slipping through the "Police Personnel Only" marked door. I knew most of the civilian clerks by their first names, and made small talk with my favorite, Linda Ricca, a plump, always smiling mother of five with huge brown eyes.

"Whacha need, Johnny O?"

"A guy was busted last night out in the Haight." I gave her Russell Cortig's full name and date of birth.

The reports were typed at the outlying stations, and then delivered to the Records Room, where they were copied and filed away in banks of five drawer metal filing cabinets that had been made in San Quentin.

Linda did some digging. She glanced at Cortig's mug shot. "Oh, he's cute," she said, before handing me the file. The mug shot showed a man with a mop of curly brown hair and scared-rabbit eyes.

The report on Cortig's arrest was five pages long and listed fourteen names in addition to Cortig, including Rudolph Nureyev, the great Russian ballet dancer.

Among those arrested was someone I didn't know and didn't pay attention to—Charles Manson, who, in a year's time would become world famous for his part in the bloody Helter Skelter murders involving the beautiful and very pregnant actress Sharon Tate and five others in Los Angeles.

Life is filled with strange coincidences. Steve McQueen was a friend of Tate's, and his name was later found on Manson's celebrity hit list, along with Elizabeth Taylor, who was going to have Helter Skelter carved on her face with a hot knife before Manson and his drugged out family of misfits gouged her eyes out. Richard Burton was to be castrated, Tom Jones, his throat slit, and Sinatra was to be skinned alive while he was forced to listen to his own music.

Luckily, Manson was arrested and put in prison for life before he could carry out his plans.

The gist of the report was that there had been a wild party at 532 Clayton Street, the police came and, as Fats Waller's song so aptly put it: "We're all bums when the wagon comes."

The Park Station uniformed cops had thrown as many revelers as could fit in the back of the paddy wagon and hauled them off to jail.

What caught my eye and gladdened my heart was the name of the officer in charge at the bottom of the report: Sergeant Fred Breen.

"There's no criminal record for Mr. Cortig prior to last

night," Linda told me. "I'll run him statewide and through the FBI, if you want."

I wanted.

Park Station was one of the department's ten district stations. It was located at the edge of Golden Gate Park and close to Kezar Stadium, where the 49ers played their home games. It was originally the quarters used by the Mounted Unit, and on a rainy day you could still get a whiff of the horses. The building is a two-story Mission style with a tile roof and barred windows. It was once considered to be out in the boondocks and a good spot for a cop who wanted to coast out of the job without working too hard. That all changed when the "Flower Children" invaded the Haight-Ashbury, just a few blocks away. In 1970 the Weatherman Underground tossed a bomb through the window, killing one sergeant and seriously wounding eight other police officers.

Three bedraggled bums—I know that sounds politically incorrect now, but that's what we called them—all in their twenties and dressed in dirty jeans and ripped windbreakers, were standing fifty yards from the station's entrance, holding hands and chanting: "Ess Eff Pee Dee, why you gonna beat on me!" over and over in hoarse, rusty voices.

I nosed my unmarked car in between two black-and-whites and made my way inside, holding up my badge so that the uniforms would know I was friendly.

"Fred Breen in back?" I asked a sergeant with a telephone jammed against his lumpy jowls.

"Yeah, I guess so," he said with little enthusiasm.

Breen had his admirers in the department, but they were in the minority. Fred was also known as "Sergeant Sunflower," after a cute hippy girl pinned a flower on his police uniform in front of a waiting newspaper photographer.

When the droves of drugged-out kids started arriving in the Haight, Fred kept track of them, and when the concerned parents came to town to search for their missing sons and daughters, Fred gave them a hand. Quite often that hand ended up being filled with wads of cash.

He was sitting behind a desk littered with manila files. The walls were covered with thumbtacked photographs of kids taken before they ended up in the Haight.

Breen leaned back in his chair and smiled, showing his sparkling white teeth. He was a handsome man, with a thin nose and square jaw. His thick dark hair was razor cut, a day or two from the barber's chair. He worked out in the gym several times a week and always had a suntan. His blue uniform shirt was starched like a plank.

We had gone through the police academy together, and he quickly picked up the title "Freddy the Fox" for his ability to ease his way out of difficult assignments.

He'd never met a mirror he didn't like, and one morning I'd asked him: "How'd you get that pimple on your nose, Fred?"

There was no pimple, but after a day of staring at himself at every opportunity in the academy bathroom mirror, a pimple appeared. Mind over matter, and it really mattered to Fred. He was off sick the next day.

"Johnny O. The Fixer. What brings you out to my neck of the woods?"

"I wanted to talk to you about a report. This one. A bust out on Clayton Street."

I dropped the report in front of him and he took his time going through it, his forehead wrinkling as he tried to figure out what my angle could be.

"You representing Rudolph Nureyev in this?" he finally asked.

"He's of no interest to me, Fred."

"Who then?"

"Russell Cortig."

He went back to the report. "What's so special about Cortig?"

16

"He works with Steve McQueen. Steve says he's family. I'm thinking that we could scratch Cortig from the report. Make it like he was never there."

Breen bounced to his feet and took a quick glance at his profile in a mirror near the door. "Are you and McQueen tight?"

"We get along, Fred. Can you fix the report?"

It was a silly question. Of course he could fix it, but first he'd want to find out just what he would get out of it.

"How's this movie of McQueen's going?" Fred asked. "I hear they're hiring cops for stand-ins and bit parts."

"That's right."

He gave me a full front assault with his teeth. "I always wanted to be in a movie."

"You're made for the movies, Freddy. I'll talk to the man. I'm betting he can find a spot for you."

Breen sat down and pulled a blank report form from a desk drawer and rolled it into his typewriter. "Just one speaking line, Johnny O. One line would be okay with me."

"I'm sure you'd do just great in a screen test, Fred."

While he typed out an amended report, I studied the photos on the walls, a somehow sad mixture of family portraits mixed in with snapshots of young boys and girls swimming, playing with Frisbees, and petting shaggy dogs.

"It was a big party, even for the Haight," Fred said. "Janis Joplin was there, a guy from the Rolling Stones, the tall ugly one, I can't think of his name. Of course we let the heavy hitters go, but Nureyev, the ballet guy, he jumps out a window and starts dancing across the roofs. Man, it was crazy. When we finally caught up with him and brought him back here, he was great. Signed autographs for everyone. Charming guy." Fred looked up from the report and gave me his teeth again. "Funny thing, he said he wasn't running away from us. He was running from a Russian who wanted to break his legs."

"Russian?"

"Some KGB guy, Nureyev said."

Breen ripped the report from the typewriter, signed the bottom, stood up and handed it to me.

"Mr. Cortig's name was placed in error in the original report, Johnny O."

"Did you see this Russian?"

"Nah. You know how it is. Everybody's running away, bumping into each other. I did see a guy in a suit, figured he was FBI. Never saw his face."

Fred peeked at the mirror again. "Those federal jerks just don't have a clue of how to blend in. A suit! He might as well wear his badge on his lapel. Let me know when I go on camera."

# CHAPTER 4

I decided to give Russ Cortig the good news in person, because I wanted to question him about the Russian who allegedly wanted to break Rudy Nureyev's legs.

I used the desk sergeant's telephone, called Steve McQueen's number and was connected to Alan Rickeby. I passed along the information about Cortig, and my meeting with Sergeant Fred Breen.

"You promised the guy a speaking role in the movie?" Rickeby said with some heat in his voice.

"No. I told him you might find a spot for him in the movie, and then he mentioned that one line would be okay for him. All I said was he would look good in a screen test. I made no promises, Alan. Hell, a screen test that lands on the cutting room floor isn't much in order to get Cortig's record completely squashed, is it?"

"I guess you're right. McQueen will be happy, and that's the main thing. The line crew is finished shooting for the day. I'll get a hold of Russ and make sure he's waiting for you at the Sheraton Hotel."

"Tell him I'll meet him at the bar in an hour," I said.

I then called the office. My desk was situated in the back corner of the Fraud Detail. Gina Abbott, the detail secretary, said I had a pair of calls to be returned: Doctor Hester, which was the code name for Charles Ledegue, an FBI agent, and Francie Stevens, an attorney for the D.A.'s office, a lady with whom I had a romantic interest.

I called Francie first, hoping she was in the mood for a late dinner.

"Johnny. How's your father doing?"

My dad was in the Laguna Honda Hospital, a city-owned acute care and nursing facility, suffering from what was known as dementia back then. Alzheimer's wasn't a buzz word yet. In fact, many people just called the victims crazy.

"He's hanging in there, Francie. Thanks for asking."

"I'm not just being polite, Johnny. Danny Flagg was his old partner, right?"

"That's right. Why the interest?"

"Three days ago Daniel J. Flagg made a deathbed confession, stating that your father murdered Willie Mar, a Chinatown gangster, in June of 1951. Shot him to death in a night club in Chinatown, and then they buried him in the Chinese cemetery in Colma."

The phone suddenly felt slick in my hand. "You're kidding me."

"I wish I was. Flagg was living up in Lake Pend Oreille, Idaho. He was in the hospital, had bone marrow cancer and knew he only had a few days to live. So he called in the Bonner County Sheriff's office and gave them the confession."

Jumbo Flagg was a quart of vodka a day man at the end of his career, and, after retirement, had moved to Idaho to fish and drink the rest of his life away.

"This is crazy, Francie. Flagg must have been out of his mind. I mean, literally out of his mind."

"Maybe," she said. "He seems to have gotten very religious late in life." Francie's voice lowered. "Johnny, according to Flagg's confession, after your father shot Mar, they took some gold coins and Chinatown gambling chips from Mar's safe. He still had two dozen of the gambling chips and four gold coins, United States Liberty Head twenty-dollar gold coins, each one a little more than an ounce of pure gold."

"I can't believe it, Francie," I said.

"Well, I hope you're right, because Mike Rhodes says he's

going to have Roy Creely investigate the matter. They're taking it very seriously."

I groaned out loud. Mike Rhodes was the head of the D.A.'s Special Prosecution Unit and Roy Creely was an ex- SF cop, who had worn out his welcome in the Internal Affairs Unit and switched over to being an investigator for the D.A. They both had something in common—they hated cops.

"Why are they wasting time on something that may not have taken place all those years ago? What's the sense in it?"

"Willie Mar's son, Henry, is a powerful man in Chinatown. He's in the same rotten business his father was, and he's politically connected with the crowd that runs city hall."

I knew all about Henry Mar. "My dad is in no condition to talk to anyone. Half the time he doesn't know who I am."

"I understand, Johnny. Creely is off duty until Monday, so nothing will be done until then. I just wanted to give you a heads-up."

I calmed down and thanked Francie, but I was in no mood for a late dinner.

I hung up, took some deep breaths, and then walked out to my car.

The protesters were still protesting when I drove out of Park Station. They all gave me friendly middle-finger waves.

There were no cell phones, no pagers, so a lot of my time on the phone was spent in phone booths, and the best of those were in the lobbies of the city's major hotels.

I parked in a red zone a block away from the Clift Hotel on Geary Street, a short stroll from Union Square. The Clift's phone booths were as big as some of the rooms in the cheaper nearby hotels. I settled myself onto the cushioned chair and called Dr. Hester.

Agent Charles Ledegue's half-whispered voice answered the phone.

"It's Johnny. I'm at 931-0770."

"Ten minutes," Ledegue said before breaking the connection.

It would take him at least that long to get to a payphone in the federal building, so I wrote "out of order" on one of my business cards and jammed it into the phone's coin slot.

I wandered into the hotel's famed Redwood Room, a classy bar with ten-foot redwood walls and a long, lavish bar supposedly carved from a single redwood tree.

There were several businessmen in suits at the bar and one young, cooing couple holding hands, gazing into each other's eyes at a table by the fireplace. The man was wearing a flowered shirt, the girl a canary-yellow scoop neck dress. Both were pink with sunburn.

The bartender looked familiar, a tall guy with dark hair, the hairline only inches from his brow, and droopy eyes.

"Vodka up, please."

"You got it, Inspector."

He put the drink together with practiced hands. "You don't remember me, do you, Inspector? Dick Lenahan. I went to school with your brother, Ron." He slid the glass over to me. "I was sorry to hear that Ron bought the farm in Vietnam."

My one and only brother had chosen a military career in the United States Navy. Lieutenant Commander Ronald O'Rorke was one of the first pilots lost in Vietnam, in August of 1964; his A-1 Skyraider was hit on a mission over Nam, and splashed into the water while he was trying to make it back to the U.S.S. Constellation aircraft carrier.

Lenahan poured himself a drink and raised it in a toast. "Ron was a good man."

"He was that." I drained the drink in one gulp, a tip from actor Richard Burton, who I had the pleasure of driving around town one weekend when his wife was shopping. He had a well-deserved reputation as a hard drinker. We had stopped for a "libation on the altar of friendship," at a financial district bar, and in that marvelous voice of his he said, "An ice-cold vodka martini, the glass fogged with condensation. Straight up, straight down, the warm painkiller hitting the stomach, then the brain, and then an hour of sweet melancholy euphoria."

There would be no euphoria with the Clift's vodka. I hadn't thought of my brother Ron in a long time. Too long a time.

I took three dollar bills from my money clip and dropped them on the bar. Lenahan pushed them back. "Drink's on the house today, Inspector."

"Use it to buy something for that couple that can't keep their hands off each other," I said, reaching out to shake his hand.

The payphone was ringing when I got back to the booth.

"I thought you gave me the wrong number," FBI agent Ledegue said, when I picked up the phone. "I called three times."

"Trip to the men's room, Charlie. What can I do for you?"

"I need some non-pubs."

He read off a list of telephone numbers, three with area codes from Nevada, and one local number.

I copied them down, and then Ledegue said, "The concourse? Tomorrow morning, ten o'clock? I'll bring the donuts you bring the coffee."

"That's not much time, Charlie."

"I really need them, Johnny."

I made grunting mewing noises for a few seconds and then said, "Okay. I'll do my best," then hung up.

Now you might be wondering why a highly placed FBI agent would call an SF cop in order to get the addresses for non-pubs, unlisted telephone numbers.

It goes back to 1965 when Robert Kennedy was a crusading U.S. Attorney General. He went after the Mafia and Teamster boss Jimmy Hoffa with a vengeance, including

23

tapping the phones of the major gangsters running the casinos in Las Vegas. The Mafia knew a little about vengeance, so they went after Kennedy—with attorneys, suing the FBI and the phone company over the wire taps. The phone company, caught with their electronic pants down, paid off big time, leading to their turning off the taps regarding phone records to the FBI, unless there was a federal subpoena involved, a time consuming process.

The SFPD had some of the same restrictions. A subpoena was needed, unless there was an emergency such as bombs about to go off.

Of course there was always a way around restrictions. I dropped two dimes in the phone and spoke to Lou Papas, a network technician at Pacific Bell, and in five minutes, had the addresses for all of Ledegue's numbers.

I thanked Papas, and said, "How are we doing, Lou?"

"I've got you down for twelve non-pubs so far this month."

I paid Papas two dollars a number—not bad, since I charged Ledegue ten.

"You want to meet?" I asked him.

"No hurry, Johnny. We'll settle up at the end of the month."

I thanked Papas. It was nice to deal with an honest man once in a while.

# CHAPTER 5

Russ Cortig was waiting for me at the bar of the Sheraton Hotel. The room was jammed with a mixture of the *Bullitt* film crew, the hotel's regular guests, and a gaggle of tourists seeking shelter from the winds whipping through Fisherman's Wharf.

Cortig looked much better than he had in his mug shot. His hair was brushed, his face freshly shaven and he was wearing a clean shirt.

"You O'Rorke?" he asked as I approached the bar.

We shook hands and he signaled to the bartender. "What are you having? It's on me."

This was turning out to be a day when people wanted to buy me drinks.

I ordered vodka up and sat on the stool next to Cortig.

"I really want to thank you, Inspector. That was stupid of me, getting busted like that."

"Tell me about the party," I said.

Cortig shook a Lucky Strike from its pack and lit it with Zippo lighter while we waited for the bartender to finish his production of placing a napkin and a small cocktail glass in front of me.

"It was a hell of a party. Chicks, booze, lots of drugs, which I didn't touch. I'm strictly a booze man. I was talking to this really cute blonde chick when the fuzz showed up and I ended up in a patrol wagon."

He raised his arms in a gesture of mock surrender. "End of story."

"Did you see anyone you knew at the party?"

"Recognized, but didn't know. Mick Jagger, Janice Joplin,

25

Brian Jones, and Dennis Wilson, from the Beach Boys. There was a guy in a suit, who I thought was a cop, but he turned out to be a foreign prick."

"Foreign. Could he have been Russian?"

"Yeah, I think he was."

On a hunch, I took the photograph of Vanessa the Undresser and the Russian from my coat pocket and laid it on the bar. "Were either one of them at the party?"

Cortig blew out steams of smoke through his nostrils as he studied the photo.

"Didn't see the woman, but the guy was there."

My shoulders gave a quick, involuntary twitch. "Are you sure?"

"Yes, I was talking to Nika and was trying to get her to—"

"Nika?"

"The blonde chick." He made smacking sounds with his lips. "What a doll. Tight red sweater and a really mini-mini-skirt. And she was wearing one of those ladies Rolex watches with all the diamonds. Said she was twenty-one, but I was thinking more like eighteen, nineteen."

"Was Nika alone?"

"There was another girl with her; she was probably twenty-five or so. Dark hair. Pretty, but nothing like Nika. Nika called her Polina. I remember, because I never heard that name before. I had Nika talked into leaving with me, but she had to go to the bathroom first."

He took another drag on his smoke then tapped his index finger on the photograph. "That's when this joker came over and began asking all kinds of questions. Did I know her well? Where was she going? He started acting rough; put his hands on me. I knocked them away and was ready to throw a punch when the sirens and whistles went off and everyone starting running."

"Did you get his name?"

"No. He spoke broken English. That's why I figured he was Russian, like Nika."

"Was he alone?"

"As far as I know," Cortig said.

"The man in the photo uses the name Boris. Did that name come up during your conversation?"

"No."

I took a sip of my drink. It was half water. "Nika told you she was Russian?"

"I said I liked her name. She said she was from Russia."

"What's her last name?"

Cortig ground out his cigarette in an ashtray. "I didn't get that far."

"What about where she lives? Works?"

"She didn't say. I mean, we were only together about ten minutes. I told her I was working on the Steve McQueen movie." He rubbed his chin and smiled. "She liked that. She wants to be in the movies."

I suggested to Cortig that we sit at a table.

I found one with good overhead lighting, and then picked up the cocktail menu. The back of the menu was blank. All I needed now was a pencil with an eraser.

A friendly cocktail waitress supplied me with one, and then I started asking Cortig questions as I sketched.

"Nika. What was her face like? Round? Slim? Oval?"

"Uh, oval, I guess."

I made an oval outline on the back of the menu then placed dissecting lines where the eyes, nose and mouth should be.

It took about fifteen minutes, and quite a bit of erasing, but in the end, the drawing showed an attractive young woman with dark-lashed, almond-shaped eyes, a pert nose, bow-shaped lips and a rounded chin.

Cortig said, "Hey, you're pretty good. That's Nika. It's not exact, but it's close. Her eyes are a light brown color and her blonde hair looks natural, not dyed."

"There was a famous Russian ballet star at the party, Rudy Nureyev. Did you see him?"

"No, but Nika told me he was around. She said he was cute, but then she said something in Russian that sounded like 'pie dick.' I asked her what she meant and she kind of giggled and said he was gay."

"Does Nika have an accent?"

"Yeah, but not real thick, like the guy in your picture."

"How about the other girl, Polina?"

"She had some kind of an accent, not like Nika's, a little different."

"Do you think Nika knew the Russian guy who questioned you?"

Cortig tugged at an earlobe. "I don't think so, but I can't say for sure. I'll tell you one thing: I'd sure like to run into Nika again."

I handed him one of my business cards. "If you see Nika, Polina, or the Russian, give me call. Right away."

He took out his wallet and slipped my card inside. "Thanks for fixing the arrest record for me."

"It's what I do, Russ," I said. "But if you get busted again, I won't be able to help you, so keep it slow."

# CHAPTER 6

I arrived at the Hall of Justice early the next morning. Walter Ito from the crime lab had left two dozen photographs of Boris on my desk, ranging wallet-size to eight-by-tens. He wasn't handsome, wasn't ugly, but he was definitely an interesting character. The slick hair, the slightly sunken eyes. He gave off a whiff of violence, along with a mixture of intelligence and cunning.

I wandered down the hall to the Sexual Assault Detail, to talk to Inspector Ed Cornell about Robert Alverson, aka Vanessa the Undresser.

"He's a fruitcake, Johnny," Cornell said. "One of his sick customers wanted to leave without paying, so he makes up this fairytale."

There were four other Inspectors in the room, all busy on the phone or typing out reports.

Cornell was in his early-fifties, stocky, balding, with a knocked-about face, and a basic-training haircut. His forehead and cheeks pitted with acne scars. He was wearing a gray herringbone polyester sport coat and a wide brown tie speckled with orange flowers. He was one of those guys who believes the bottle is either half empty or its broken. And he had no sense of humor, which is rare in cops. Despite what you see on screen, most cops are funny—it may be dry humor, wisecracks, clowning around, telling jokes. I know a couple of cops who could be stand-up comedians. You have to be able to laugh at the job, and yourself, or you'd go crazy.

"What's your interest in this faggot, anyway, Johnny? Is Alverson bitching that I gave him a hard time?"

29

"Nothing like that, Ed. There's no problem with the way you handled the case, and I'm not butting into your business. Alverson did me a favor a while back. He called to show me these photographs of the man who roughed him up."

I dropped one of the photos of Boris that Trixie had taken at Finocchio's onto the desk. Cornell gave it a cursory look. "This guy could be anyone. Alverson's jerking you around, pal."

"Did he tell you about the gun with the silencer?"

"That and the bit about he's going to break his neck like a chicken were the best parts of the story. It's all bullshit."

I picked up the photo. "Have you had any other cases involving transvestites being roughed up after sex lately?"

"No. But you know how it goes with these dairy queens. Half of them love being slapped around, the other half hates our guts. They keep it inside, and let their pimps handle the dirty work."

"Okay, Ed. Thanks."

Cornell struggled to his feet and put his hand on my shoulder and squeezed it hard. "Hey, Johnny O. The favor Alverson did for you. It wasn't for a blow job, was it? You're not going gay on us are you?"

I pushed his hand away. "No, Ed. And say hello to your wife and my kids for me."

I was halfway to the door when the coin dropped and Cornell yelled out, "Fuck you, O'Rorke."


I stopped at the Flying Saucer, an open-around-the-clock diner at 27ᵗʰ and Geary. There were three uniformed SF cops in the booths, along with two highway patrolmen sitting on the stools facing the kitchen. Edie, the owner, loved to have cops hanging around. "I've been here six years and have never been robbed," she liked to say.

I picked up two large coffees and drove over to the Golden Gate Park Music Pavilion, an oval shaped bowl with a regular grid array of pollarded Scotch elm trees nestled between the De Young Museum and the Academy of Sciences.

On weekends as many as a thousand people showed up to enjoy the free band concerts in the pavilion. That morning there was just one man sitting on a bench near the band shell—FBI agent Charles Ledegue.

For some reason Ledegue always picked a place in Golden Gate Park for our meetings. I had the feeling that he'd read too many books about clandestine British spies rendezvousing in dark, tree-filled settings while they tried to identify a mole in the Secret Service.

Ledegue went against the image the Bureau liked to project of their agents: tall, lean, square jawed—a cross between Superman and Cary Grant. He was a short, thickset man in his mid-forties, with rounded shoulders, a beer-barrel stomach and thinning sandy-colored hair.

He had a Bachelor of Science degree in Criminal Justice from Illinois State University, along with a handful of forensic science and behavioral science honors from the FBI academy, which sounded very impressive, but somehow all of that training had drummed out his common sense.

"Hi Charlie," I said, dropping down on the bench alongside him.

He jumped a bit, causing his pipe to drop onto his lap.

"Damn it, man. You startled me."

He brushed ashes from his gabardine raincoat and jammed his pipe back between his teeth. He puffed hard to get the pipe going again, sending up plumes of sweet, cheery-smelling smoke.

I passed Ledegue a cup of coffee. The names and addresses for the unlisted phone numbers he'd requested were on a sheet of paper rubber-banded around the cup.

"Thanks for the quick service," Ledegue said, his pipe dancing between his teeth as he bent over and picked up a paper bag from between his feet. The bag was filled with glazed jelly donuts and paper napkins. Mixed in among the donuts was a white envelope, the paper so thin I could see the outline of the ten dollar bills inside.

I took one of the head shot photos of Boris from my coat and handed it to him. "Ever run into this guy, Charlie? He's Russian. Uses the name Boris when he's drinking and chasing sex."

"What's your interest, Johnny?"

"He assaulted a Finocchio's entertainer, beat her up pretty bad."

"Finocchio's? You mean a...crossdresser?"

"That's right. Boris packs a semi-automatic with a silencer."

"A silencer? How did you happen to come by his picture?"

"The club's photographer took it. Do you recognize the man?"

I munched on a donut while he took a pair of reading glasses from his jacket.

"Ummm. Not familiar."

"Someone told me that there was a possibility that this character is KGB, and is in town to try and bust up Rudy Nureyev."

Ledegue's eyes narrowed. "Who told you that?"

"Nureyev, after he was arrested at a dope party in the Haight."

"I read about the incident in the paper." Ledegue took a long look at the photograph. "Do you know who Yuri Andropov is?"

"A Russian big wig. Head of the KGB, isn't he?"

"He's a long time communist nemesis. He's started a program to defend the Soviet government from dissidents— those being anyone who disagrees with them. The program involves shoving these people into state run psychiatric hospitals. You can imagine what happens to them. The repression of dissidents includes plans to maim Mr. Nureyev. They don't like defectors."

"So Nureyev could be right about Boris being after him."

Ledegue swiveled his neck around searching for prying eyes or surveillance cameras. "He could be, but I don't think a ballet dancer is at the top of their hit list. The Cold War is colder than ever, Johnny. There are a total of fifty-six high ranking KGB agents in California."

"What are they doing, Charlie?"

"Doing? Well they're spying of course. They're interested in American technology. We just bagged one of them for trying to bribe a metallurgist from Stanford University."

I took a final bite of the donut. It was greasy, overly sweet, and filled with sticky raspberry jam. Perfectly delicious. "What did you do with the Russian?"

"Kicked him out of the country. Believe me, I could tell you stories that would curl your hair."

"Where do all of these KGB agents live? At the Russian Embassy?"

"Yes. Out in the Marina District, on Green Street. At least the ones we know of."

"Could you ask your people if they've ever seen the man in the photograph?"

Ledegue tapped the stem of his pipe against his teeth. "Well, I don't know—"

"The next three unpublished numbers will be freebies, Charlie."

He nodded and slipped the photo of Boris into his raincoat pocket.

It's amazing what the promise of a few freebies can do. I was certain that the money that Ledegue passed out to me didn't come from his own wallet. All police agencies had slush funds under various names: bag money, dole-dough, confidential fees, milk money, vacation funds, or just "jack."

It was cash that often had been confiscated in drug busts or other illegal activates and was used to pay off informers, or in sting operations where the department buys drugs from a dealer, or purchases stolen property in order to make arrests. Or to entertain visiting cops.

Whatever the terminology, the FBI had boatloads of it. That was why you never wanted to mess with the feds—they had the money and the manpower to make life miserable for anyone.

I reached for another jelly donut. "Heard any good gossip lately, Charlie?"

Cops love to gossip.

Ledegue said, "Bobby's coming to town next week."

"Bobby, as in Kennedy?"

"The very same. The Secret Service is handling his protection. He's running for president, and will be making the rounds of the deep-pocket contributors. And the Boss is coming to town."

"Your boss? Hoover? What's the big occasion?"

"He's forming a joint crime committee with big city police chiefs. He and your boss seem to get along well."

J. Edgar Hoover and Chief Tom Cahill—a dynamic crime fighting duo if ever there was one.

"You leave first," Ledegue said.

"Okay." I leaned over his shoulder and whispered in his ear. "That guy with the long-lens camera in front of the Japanese Tea Garden looks a little suspicious, don't you think?"

His neck swiveled so fast he dropped his pipe again.

"Where?"

"He's behind those blooming cherry trees. Probably just another tourist, Charlie. Call me if you come up with anything on the Russian."

It was a bit of a cruel thing to do to Charlie, the non-existent guy with the camera, but maybe it would prod him into scheduling our next meeting in a warm restaurant or a dark bar.

# CHAPTER 7

It took two stops before I found a phone booth that had not been vandalized. I called Glen Eshmont, the police department union's attorney and filled him in on my father's ex-partner's accusations regarding the murder of Willie Mar.

"Jumbo Flagg," Eshmont said. "Who would have ever figured him for something like this? I'll get right to work on it, Johnny. No one from the D.A.'s office is going to talk to Rory unless they contact me, and then I'll make sure that won't happen. I wouldn't put it past that asshole Roy Creely to sneak into Laguna Honda Hospital and record a statement before I get the word out. Tell the people at Laguna that except for you and me, your father will have no visitors—period. And, Johnny, think about Henry Mar. When he gets this news he may take some action. You know what I mean?"

I knew exactly what Eshmont meant. My father could be a target for Mar, and so could I. I doubted that Mar had read the Old Testament, but I was sure he knew all about *an eye for an eye.*

In some ways Henry Mar was a more dangerous character than his father, Willie. Henry was the West Coast leader of the bing kong tong, an offshoot of the powerful triads in New York City, and as such, he was the chief West Coast importer of China White, a pure form of heroin smuggled in from the Golden Triangle in South East Asia. He was also involved in prostitution, extortion, and of course gambling dens in Chinatown. Like all criminal organizations, the tongs and triads ruled by violence. Their signature method of torture and execution involved a kitchen meat cleaver.

I touched base with the office. There was a call from

Marlene Matson, Frank Sinatra's secretary. Sinatra would be in town for three days next month and wanted *the usual security.* Which I would be happy to provide. Like McQueen, Sinatra had a hard to get along with reputation, but he was a pussy cat when he came to San Francisco. Every one of my contacts wanted to be on his security team, because as soon as Sinatra got off the plane, he shook each cop's hand, leaving a fifty dollar bill behind. Fifty bucks was a *lot* of money at the time. And when you worked Sinatra, you went where he went, and no waiting in the car. Whatever restaurant he ate at, you ate at, and it was an open menu—you ordered whatever you wanted. You opened a car door and he slipped you a five or ten dollar bill and another fifty-buck handshake when he left town. And his secretary would send me a check for the security detail the day after she received my invoice.

I had the feeling that even if FBI Agent Ledegue came up with something on Boris, he was going to hold back on giving it to me. It's the way the feds work—take but don't give—unless they absolutely have to.

I decided to check out Boris with "The Swine," Alex Zek, a Russian born hoodlum who had a justly earned reputation as being the biggest stolen property fence in Northern California. He described himself as an Importer-Exporter, and about half of his deals were legitimate—but it was on the other half where he made most of his money.

He was also an out-and-out snitch, ready and willing to dish out the latest dirt on his competitors and the activities of the new breed of Russian gangsters who were getting a toehold in California criminal activities. Activities he wanted to keep to himself.

It was like dealing with the devil, but by playing to his ego and making him think we were buddies, I'd been able to put away some very bad criminals. Sooner or later Zek would make a mistake, and I'd be able to send him to prison where he belonged.

Zek had been given his nickname by "Driller" Malloy, a fence who was no longer in business, having been run out of town by Zek. "He's a swine—big, fat and ugly and he takes everything he sees, and kills anyone who gets in his way."

Malloy got the "Driller" nickname due to his fondness for using a Craftsman half-inch drill-set on clients who were reluctant to pay their bills. Rumors were that Malloy left town with several half-inch holes in his arms and legs, thanks to Zek.

Zek's warehouse was four stories of weather-stained concrete with iron-barred windows and a curling tar paper roof located at the corner of 22$^{nd}$ and Vermont. I parked in front of a fire hydrant that had been graffitied with F-bombs.

A carbonized-steel bulletproof door guarded the front entrance. There was a slide-back peephole the size of a deck of cards at head-height in the door. A voice reverberated through the opening.

"Who you?"

"Johnny O'Rorke to see Mr. Zek."

"He know you come?"

I pushed a business card through the peephole. "No. But he'll want to see me."

It took several minutes before the door rasped open and there stood a gangling, giant of a man. He had to be close to seven feet tall and had an Abe Lincoln beard, with no mustache. A Russian AK-47 rifle with a wooden pistol grip and a banana-shaped extended clip hung from a canvas strap around his shoulder.

"I veel show you up. Valk dis vay," he said.

We *valked* down a narrow corridor bordered by stacks of cardboard boxes that reached the ceiling until we came to a wood-slatted hoistaway elevator.

The giant raised the wooden gate with his foot and gestured me inside, then backed away and slammed the gate down.

The elevator wheezed and coughed its way to the third floor, where I was greeted by Zek's secretary, Lidiya. She was in her early twenties, a Russian immigrant with chestnut-colored hair that reached down to her waist. She was wearing a rhinestone-studded blouse and a mid-thigh miniskirt.

"Nice to see you again, Inspector," she said.

"Your English is improving, Lidiya. And you look great."

She accepted both compliments with a bow of her head. "He's in his office."

Zek's office was filled with crates and boxes of all sizes and shapes. There were a couple of pistols and a long-barreled rifle lying on a football-shaped mahogany table that was surrounded by metal folding chairs. Zek always liked to have guns nearby, and he liked to have them loaded.

"Johnny O. Why are you such a stranger?" Zek asked.

Zek was in his early-fifties, a self-proclaimed former member of the KGB. Every Russian crook I'd come across claimed the same thing, but about this—and little else—I believed Zek. He was of medium height, thick through the shoulders and stomach, with an Elvis-style pompadour. He had whiskey-colored eyes that he often popped when he was emphasizing a word, a phrase, or beating on someone's hands with a hammer.

He was dressed as if he'd just stepped off a disco dance floor: a saffron-colored three piece suit, a white long-collared shirt opened to show off his chest hair and a lion-head gold medallion hanging from a gold chain around his neck. The suit pants were skin tight and there was a noticeable bulge in the crotch area. A bulge brought on by the insertion of a sausage-size piece of hard black rubber, not by any natural endowment.

You might be wondering how I knew of this, and the explanation is that during a strip search at the Hall of Justice prison the damn thing fell out of his pants—much to Zek's embarrassment.

"Who's the giant you've got guarding the door, Alex? I haven't seen him before."

"Viktor. A good boy. He was a basketball player for Soviet Union Olympic team. Not good enough to become a professional, so he came here and I, what do you say? Took him under my wing."

Viktor struck me as a man who would be more comfortable with an AK-47 than a basketball.

Zek plucked a bottle from a wooden box, placed it on the table, and then said, "Try this. Remy Martin XO Cognac. You'll love it, Johnny O. I'll deliver a case to your place."

A few years ago, when I was working Homicide, Zek was arrested on a murder charge. The body of a Ukrainian Mafioso had been found in the hull of an old fishing boat that was about to be cut up for scrap. The victim, Georgi Styov, had been beaten, stabbed, and had had his penis hacked off. Witnesses testified that Zek and Styov were sworn enemies, and that they'd had a major falling out a week before Styov's body was discovered. Zek pleaded his innocence, tears running down his blubbering face.

I started digging around and learned that Styov had been in trouble with a Russian gang in L.A., a gang whose modus operandi for eliminating their enemies included the removal of their penises. Zek claimed he'd been in Seattle at the time of the killing. I found two witnesses—neither of which were pillars of the community—who backed him up. So Zek was released, and he thanked me. And thanked me, over and over again. Cases of whiskey, vodka, and expensive wine began arriving on my doorstep. When I tried to return them, Zek waved his hands in innocence. "Not me. Must be *Ded Moroz.*"

*Ded Moroz* is the Russian Santa Claus.

Zek opened the bottle, poured a stream of the brownish-gold Cognac into two balloon-shaped snifters and then dug his fingers in another box for cigars.

He clipped the end of a cigar with a fingernail, then slid it and a Dunhill tortoise shell lighter across the table.

"Is the best cigar in world. Havana wrapper, hand rolled on the sweaty thigh of young Cuban girl. Sit. Drink. Smoke."

President John Kennedy had placed an embargo against Cuba in 1962, but that hadn't bothered Zek. Not much did. I dipped the end of the cigar in the Cognac before lighting it up.

I'm not much of a cigar smoker, but this one was first class. Zek lived well. Crime was paying better than ever.

"I'm looking for a Russian, Alex," I said.

"Well, if it's a woman, make sure she's under thirty. Russian women are beautiful until the day after their thirtieth birthday, and then they get fat. Overnight. It's amazing."

I took one of the cropped photographs of Boris and passed it over to him.

"I'm looking for this man."

Zek studied the photograph for several seconds, and then placed it on the table next to his Cognac glass.

"Who is he, Johnny?"

"He told someone his name is Boris, and he could be KGB, like you."

Zek thumped his thumb against his chest. "I used to be KGB. No more. I am a proud American now."

A fellow I knew in the U.S. Customs Agency told me that Zek had been granted his citizenship after he'd dumped everything he knew about the KGB to the Central Intelligence Agency.

"Well, when you weren't so American, did you ever run into this man?"

He fingered the photo of Boris. "Never. What is your interest in him? Who told you he was KGB?"

After a great deal of observation, I'd discovered that Zek had a *tell*. Whenever he was lying, his lips tightened and he drew them in against his teeth, just a fraction of an inch, and it caused his normal brash, gregarious voice to soften a bit. He was lying to me.

"Rudolph Nureyev said he was KGB."

Zek's eyes popped. "Nureyev?"

"He thinks Boris is out to break his legs."

"You're joking. Why would KGB waste time on a silly dancer? Is crazy."

More lies. If the FBI knew about the KGB's order to maim Nureyev, then Zek would know about it.

"Then tell me why this clown is in town, Alex. He assaulted a transvestite," I said. "Threatened to kill her by putting the silenced end of his pistol up her butt and pulling the trigger."

"Transvestite. You mean—"

"Boris called her something that sounded like *Golobee by yard*"

"*Golubaya b'iyad.* Fucking gay whore. This whore, she is a friend of yours, Johnny?"

"You could say that. She helped me once. I owe her a favor. You know all about those kind of things, don't you, Alex?"

He pocketed the photograph. "And she tell you Boris man had a silencer on his gun?"

Zek seemed as surprised about that as I had been.

"That's right. And he had tattoos all over his arms; knives, stars, and spider webs."

Zek bent his eyebrows together. "Not good, Johnny. Dagger tattoo means he is killer, hit man. If there were drops of blood by dagger, each drop would be for someone he killed. Stars show he tough guy, will bow down to no one. Spider webs can mean many things: that he is thief, has been in prison, takes drugs."

Zek took off his suit jacket and rolled up his shirt sleeve.

"Look. No tattoos. Not one, anywhere. Police catch you, read your body. Tattoos tell them what crimes you commit. I will have my peoples ask around about this Boris. KGB not send man stupid enough to kill whores to America. You like the cigar? Take more."

"One. For my father."

"Sure and take the lighter; I just got in a shipment of them. And I have a refrigerator. Brand new. One little scratch only. A stove, too. Double-oven."

"No thanks, Alex. Just find Boris for me."

Lidiya rode down in the old ratty elevator with me. It seemed to take a long time to get to the ground floor.

Viktor, the giant, was waiting by the trunk of my car, a case of Cognac and several boxes of Cuban cigars at his feet. He loaded them into the trunk, and then slammed down the lid hard enough to rock the whole car.

The cigars meant one less shopping stop for lunch. I picked up two cold bottles of beer, a pint of Jim Beam bourbon, a flask of Old Spice aftershave lotion, and a corned beef sandwich, and then drove to the hospital for lunch with my father.

# CHAPTER 8

The Laguna Honda Hospital was a sprawling Spanish Revival style building with decorative Mediterranean tile work.

There was an entertainment hall frequented by the likes of Bing Crosby, Bob Hope, Phil Harris, and other top-notch entertainers who stopped by to bring a little cheer to the elderly residents. Crosby had once quipped that "It was impossible to get a standing ovation, because most of the audience were in wheelchairs."

I parked, picked up the bag holding lunch, and as I approached the main entrance I noticed a vehicle very similar to mine, a beat-up Ford sedan with a whip antenna and a spotlight. The sun visor had been pulled down in front of the driver's seat in order to show off a block printed placard that identified the car as belonging to the San Francisco District Attorney's Office.

I placed a palm on the hood—it was warm.

I raced up the stairs, through the front door and hurried past the receptionist and fast-walked toward my father's room, my crepe-soled shoes making kissing sounds on the cool tile floors.

When I reached my father's room the door was open and I could see he was in his wheelchair. A man in a dark blue suit was hulking over him. It was Roy Creely, the District Attorney's investigator.

I eased the lunch bag onto the floor and then snapped my right hand around Creely's neck, and tightened my fingers so that they pinched his internal carotid arteries.

"Get out of here," I hissed into his ear.

Creely wrestled his neck free of my grasp and turned to face me.

He had dry, curly brown hair, a mottled red face centered by a sharp, bony nose and teeth that could eat an apple through a tennis racket. He was about my age, and my height, but he had thirty pounds on me.

"What the hell do you think you're doing," he rasped. "I'm going to have you—"

"You're not going to do anything but get out of here. Call Glen Eshmont, the union attorney. No one talks to my father without Glen's say so."

Creely brushed his hands down the front of his suit jacket. "You're being stupid, O'Rorke. I'm here on official business and—"

"Did you check in at the registrar's desk? Did you receive permission to visit my father?"

He rocked back and forth on his heels for a few moments, and then said, "I'll have to report this to my boss, Mike Rhodes. He's not going to like it."

"Which part? You abusing your authority by ignoring the hospital's visiting regulations or your molesting and accosting a helpless elderly patient?"

Creely rocked back on his heels again. He had a reputation as a "Sunday Artist." Someone who liked hitting a man with a sneak punch when he wasn't ready for it. He'd needle some guy until a brawl was about to start, then say something along the line of, "Hey, I don't want to fight." Then he'd take a coin out of his pocket. "I'll flip it in the air. Heads we fight, tails we don't." While his unsuspecting opponent followed the flight of the coin, Creely would punch him in his throat. That was the end of the fight. One blow to the Adam's apple rendered a man helpless. Then Creely would go after him, like a cat playing with an injured mouse.

He was thinking about making a move on me when the door swung open and Alisi, a sturdy Samoan nurse who always had a calm demeanor and a ready smile strode into the room. For all her sweetness, I figured she could have handled both me and Creely if the need arose.

She planted her hands on her ample hips and said, "Is everything all right in here?"

"This man is an investigator from the District Attorney's office, Alisi. There's a court order barring him from bothering my father."

"Well then, you'd better leave, sir," she said in an authoritative tone.

Creely pointed a finger at me, said, "Next time, O'Rorke. Next time you won't have a skirt to hide behind."

"Use the time to practice falling to the floor, Roy."

Creely tried to slam the door shut, but it had one of those pneumatic closing devices and it barely moved.

Alisi nudged the paper bag with her toe. "I assume this is one of your usual lunches for your father."

"You assume correctly," I said with a grin.

She made grunting noises then took off to help those in real need.

Through all of this, my father sat slumped in his wheelchair. In the last year he'd had several slips and falls. His right leg was now in a full cast, from ankle to hip. Couple that with crippling arthritis, along with Alzheimer's, and you know that he was not a happy camper.

He had retired from the police department seven years earlier, and wasn't handling retirement well. The department had been his life, night and day—every day.

He coped by reading everything from poetry to thrillers to history books, and drinking too much bourbon and Rainer Ale, known to its admirers as "green death."

"Pop," I said. "Are you okay?"

Not a muscle moved. I edged close to him. His iron-gray hair was still thick, and there was one lock that insisted on hanging over his brow. His lean, handsome, weather-damaged face now resembled an eroding rock formation. His eyes were slits that looked as if they'd have to be pried open with a screwdriver. There was a fresh bandage on his neck covering a recent skin cancer surgery. I placed a hand on his shoulders and was saddened by how frail he felt. His hands were still huge, his fingers twisted by the arthritis into the kind of tree roots you see breaking through concrete sidewalks.

"It's Johnny, Pop. Your son."

His right eye creaked open and he stared at me for several seconds.

"Of course it is. Don't you think I'd recognize my own boy?"

Unfortunately, that's exactly what I thought. Or feared. There were days when he was full of stories about the old days, or reciting the poems of the hard-drinking, hard-living Welshman, Dylan Thomas.

Then there were days when he just sat there, lost, frightened, and with no idea of who I was.

"How about lunch, Johnny?" His denim-blue eyes twinkled a bit. "You brought it, didn't you?"

"I did. Let's go find a nice spot for a picnic."

As I was pushing his wheelchair out the door, he said, "Who was that asshole who woke me up before you came?"

"Roy Creely, from the D.A.'s office."

"What the hell does he want from me?"

"That's what I want to find out, Pop. This is important. Did Creely ask you any questions?"

"I think so, but I couldn't hear what he was saying."

"Did you tell him anything?"

"Fuck off."

# CHAPTER 9

I found a table shaded by a green umbrella in an isolated section of the hospital grounds. There were poppies all over the hills and a row of flowering plum trees nearby. Blossoms were scattered everywhere, like dirty confetti.

While my father nibbled away at his corned beef sandwich and drank Rainer Ale, I filled him in on Jumbo Flagg's deathbed confession.

"They're going to try and come after you, Pop."

"Who's they?"

"The District Attorney for one. There could be others. Tell me what happened that night." I hated having to ask the question. "Did you shoot Willie Mar?"

He crumbled the sandwich wrapping paper into a ball and threw it at a squawking blue jay perched in one of the plum trees.

"Jumbo and I paid Mar a visit to that damned dungeon of his. Mar was a strange bugger. One day he'd be polite and bowing his head at you, the next time he'd be high on something—not whiskey I'm sure, some of those drugs he was importin'. Mar ran a string of whore houses in Chinatown, and he was well connected to the power brokers at city hall, so I couldn't shut 'em down, but he'd started bringin' in kids, wee ones." He held a gnarled hand out. "Six, seven, eight years old. Disgustin'. I wasn't puttin' up with that."

I took out one of the cigars that Alex Zek had given me from my coat pocket, bit off the end, lit it up with the Dunhill lighter and handed it to him.

"Disgusting enough for you to shoot him?"

He studied the cigar before sticking it in his mouth and

taking several long, luxurious puffs. "Where the hell did you get this beauty, Johnny?"

"Alex Zek."

He barked out a laugh. "The Swine. That villain is still around is he?"

"Why'd you shoot Willie Mar, Pop?"

"I told him I wasn't puttin' up with him using the children. I made my point clear to the bastard. He didn't like it.

"Jumbo started slappin' him around, and Mar came out with a knife; wicked lookin' thing with a curved blade. He sliced Jumbo pretty good on his arm and was goin' for Jumbo's neck, so I pulled out my gun and plugged him."

I breathed a slow sigh of relief. He'd shot Mar to save Flagg's life. Something I could live with. And I was certain he was telling me the truth. My father had many faults, but lying to his son wasn't one of them. I brought out the pint of Jim Beam bourbon and poured a shot into a paper cup. His doctor had told me that the whiskey wouldn't harm him. "It's as good a pain killer as any for your father right now."

I handed him the whiskey. He swallowed the drink and wiggled the cup for a refill.

He downed the second shot, smacked his lips and said, "Jumbo should have been more careful. You hit a man, you got to figure he's going to fight back."

"Did you use your service revolver, Pop?"

"It's all I had. One shot in his stomach, the second right in his heart. He dropped to the floor like a ton of bricks."

"Try and remember. Be sure about this. Did the bullets stay in Mar's body? Or did they go right through him?"

"He was a fat little bastard. They stayed where they belonged."

"Then what happened?"

He leaned back in the wheelchair, closed his eyes and worked the cigar from one side of his mouth to the other. I was afraid that I'd lost him that he was back in that never-never land he sometimes drifted off to, but I was wrong.

"We wrapped Willie in one of his carpets, one of those fancy Oriental things he liked, and took him out to the car. No one saw us. It was about three in the morning. I was for dumping him in the bay, but Jumbo said he had a better idea. Bury him at the Chinese Cemetery down in Daly City."

Daly City was then a small bedroom community just south of the San Francisco border.

"So off we drove," he said. "Mar bleeding into his expensive rug in the trunk, and Jumbo whinin' about the cut on his arm."

"Do you remember where you buried him in the cemetery?" I asked.

He wriggled the cup again and I filled it to the top.

"In a freshly dug grave. Didn't have to go to deep. Good thing. Jumbo was no help with a shovel."

I took a slug of the whiskey right from the bottle before asking, "Do you happen to remember the name on the grave's tombstone?"

"Woo, Hoo, some damn name like that. It was dark, son." He chuckled. "The dead of night. It was no loss. I hope the devil swallowed Mar sideways."

A freshly dug grave. If Jumbo Flagg had spilled that information to the police, all they had to do was check for who had been buried around the time of Willie Mar's disappearance and start digging.

"Jumbo said that you and he took gold coins and gambling chips from Mar's safe."

Some cigar ash fell onto the lap of his white robe and he brushed it away, leaving a gray smear.

"I remember there were some chips and coins. Jumbo grabbed them, and stuffed a few in my pocket."

"Where are they, Pop?"

"Where the hell was I goin' to spend Chinese gamblin'

chips? I can't remember where I put them or the fuckin' gold coins. "

He moaned and scratched at his cast. "Damn thing itches like hell, and I can't get to the itch. I never thought Jumbo would turn rat. What the hell was he thinkin'?" He eyed the level of whiskey in the bottle. "How's the Darkie, Johnny?"

The Darkie. That was the name he'd pinned on my wife—ex-wife now—Dashay McKay, who had worked as a nurse at the San Francisco General Hospital.

It was a simple boy meets girl story, except that the boy, me, was Irish, and the girl was a beautiful, mocha skinned Jamaican. I had been nervous about how my family would react to our getting married.

Brother Ron told me I was dumb, stupid, crazy, and then later on asked me if Dashay had a sister.

My sister Peggy turned whiter than the Holy Ghost when she met Dashay.

My mother, Mary. Let me tell you about my mom. A few years back I had shot and killed a man in the line of duty. He was a serial rapist, a particularly cruel one. There had been a stakeout, and I saw the guy climb out of an apartment window and go up the fire escape. There was a rooftop chase. He had a gun—he fired at me—I fired back.

The department put me on leave, and I had to be cleared by a psychiatrist before I could get back to work. He was a clever guy, who asked a lot of clever questions—ones that could be picked apart no matter how I answered them.

One question was, "What would you do, Inspector, if you had to arrest your mother?"

"Call for backup," I'd told him.

My mother Mary was a woman who walked down a steep, ski slope of a hill from our home on Diamond Street to Most Holy Redeemer Church every single day for mass and Holy Communion, and then she'd walk back up that toothache of a hill. She gave Dashay a limp handshake and then quickly drew me into the kitchen and told me, "Johnny. She's a nigger. A nigger!"

My father deepened his brogue and turned on his charm button to full blast while he told Dashay that without a doubt she had a lot of Irish blood in her, "Thanks to that bastard Englishman Oliver Cromwell, the bloody-handed Lord Protector of the Commonwealth of England, Scotland and Ireland, who, among his many sins, sent thousands of Irish slaves to Jamaica in 1652."

His advice to me was "She's a jewel, Johnny. But tis trouble you're asking for."

He was right. Mixed marriages were rare at that time. Dashay's parents were none too happy that their daughter had married "white trash." But in the end it wasn't the families that caused the marriage to break up—it was the day to day grind, the actions of those we thought were friends, but who'd stopped inviting us to dinners or parties, the cold shoulders from cops and their wives at police functions. The reactions in restaurants and bars—openly hostile looks from strangers. I was called a nigger lover, Dashay "Aunt Jemima," and much, much worse. I'd lost count of the times I'd lost my temper and gotten into fights.

Our work schedules only added to the problem—I'd work nights, she'd work days, then the schedules were reversed.

Finally Dashay suggested a break. She'd go home to Jamaica and visit with her parents for a month or so. She never came back. The divorce was final fourteen months later.

"She's fine," I told my father. "The last I heard she was the head surgical nurse at St. James Hospital, in Montego Bay."

Dad puffed on his cigar, tilted his head back and closed his eyes. "Tell me what you're working on, Johnny. And how you got the Swine to give up this fine cigar."

So our roles had reversed. I used to love to listen to his cop stories, now it was my turn to spin the yarns. I told him all about Vanessa the Undresser and the Russian, Boris, along with Rudy Nureyev and Steve McQueen's gaffer, Russell Cortig, and Nika, the beautiful young Russian girl.

His eyes stayed shut, his breathing deepened, and, when the cigar fell from his hand to the dry brownish grass I got to my feet and put my hands on the back of the wheelchair.

His head snapped up. "You brought the Old Spice didn't ya, son?"

I pulled out the red topper on the white bottle of aftershave and handed it to him. He splashed it over his hands, all around his face, and then took a swig of the stuff, which was mostly water and alcohol, and squished it around his mouth before spitting it out. It was known as an Irish Shower, and he'd used over the years to get rid of the stink from observing an autopsy, or going through the pockets of a long dead murder victim. Or when coming home after being on a run, a two or three day drinking marathon, which he poetically described as "Chasing rainbows in the bottom of a glass."

"You're not fooling the doctors or nurses with that," I told him.

"No doubt, but they probably appreciate the effort. This Boris—did Zek know anything about him?"

"He said he didn't, but he was lying."

Pop slipped the bourbon bottle into his robe pocket.

"Vanessa. Boris used her for his perverted kind of fun. If that old madam Myra Favre is still in the business, ya might think of talking to her. If anyone knew of a scum pervert like Boris beatin' up on street muffins, it'd be Myra.

"But the pretty little girl, Nika. He's not after her for sex— she's work for Boris. A Russian with a silencer on his gun is a serious man. Why is he after Nika? What could this young lass have that he wants? You better find this Boris before he gets to her, Johnny."

# CHAPTER 10

After getting my father back to his room, I went directly to the see the hospital's administrator and explained the facts about his situation. No visitors unless they were approved by me or attorney Glen Eshmont.

I then drove to the family home on Diamond Street. I'd been staying there while the *Bullitt* crew was renting my flat.

My mother had died two years earlier, the result of injuries suffered when a Wonder Bread bakery truck hit her on her way back from morning mass.

It was a two-story house with an English entrance. I opened the door and stepped inside. There was the clean smell of laundry soap and lemon oil.

I'd hired a wonderful woman, Fiona O'Day, a widow in her sixties, to come to the house four hours a day to cook and clean for my father. She quite often stayed over an hour or more to throw back a few highballs with Pop.

As wonderful as she was, I was going to have to find a full-time facility for him when he got out of the hospital.

I trudged up the steps to my father's bedroom—they'd had separate bedrooms for as long as I could remember. I was partly to blame for that. I'd been what the Irish call a "Guinness Gayla" an *unexpected* baby. Unwanted, I found out later.

According to my brother, Pop hinted at a "termination" and my mother screamed and shouted and damned him to hell for weeks. It had been a difficult birth that had affected her health. "It was a save you or her proposition," my father told me. "And you know Mary. She'd rather die a saint than risk the chance of offending the main character in the Bible."

No matter how hard Fiona O'Day worked at cleaning my father's room, there was no way she could have gotten rid of the lingering scents of tobacco and spilled whiskey.

The bed was made up military-style; you could bounce a quarter on it. I dragged a chair to the seven-foot tall oak armoire. It had an arched pediment that nearly touched the ceiling. I stood on the chair and saw my father's revolver on the top of the armoire. It was coated with dust—probably the one place in the house that Mrs. O'Day couldn't reach with her dust cloth.

I moved over to the bed and examined the gun. It was a Smith & Wesson model 10, the grips cracked and scratched, the four-inch barrel worn down to bare metal in spots. I swung the cylinder open and shook the bullets loose. They fell like lozenges onto the bed. Though the revolver was a "six-shooter" there were only five bullets. One of the first things they taught us at the firing range was that you never kept a live round under the gun's hammer.

I reloaded the bullets and shoved the gun into my waistband.

I searched for over an hour for the gold coins and the Chinese gambling chips that Jumbo Flagg had sworn on his deathbed had been taken from Willie Mar's office, but didn't find them.

Every so often, San Francisco's famed newspaper columnist Herb Caen would write about the perfect time and place for a true San Franciscan to meet his maker: At age ninety-nine, in the back seat of a Cadillac limousine, sitting next to a beautiful young woman, a martini in hand, in the middle of the Golden Gate Bridge when "The Big One" hits. The earthquake that everyone knew was coming sooner or later. Much later I hoped.

I parked alongside a California Highway Patrol car in the employee lot at the south end of the bridge, across from the toll plaza, and made my way to the pedestrian path on the west side of the bridge—facing out to sea. If you happen to have the need to drop something off the bridge, you never use the east side—facing the city. That one gets all the action: bikes, tourists, and jumpers. For some reason jumpers always take flight from there. Perhaps it's a need for a final glimpse of the city's skyline before plunging into the cold, unforgiving salt water 245 feet below.

The wind was blowing hard enough to knock your hat off, if you happened to be wearing a hat, and it was driving in a high bank of wispy gray fog that had a bite of salt in it. My only fellow bridge walker was a woman dressed in a heavy black cloth coat walking a good-sized Airedale. She gave me a sad smile, then dropped her chin to her chest and hunched her shoulders to fight the wind.

I leaned over the railing, made sure that there were no ships passing below, and dropped the Smith & Wesson. It spiraled down, disappearing from sight before hitting the ocean.

It was deep water at that point under the bridge—three hundred plus feet. No one would ever find Rory O'Rorke's service revolver. As I walked back to my car I wondered how many more incriminating weapons were buried in the mud and muck of the ocean floor.


I was back at my desk kicking around ideas for my next move when Larry Candella, the Captain of Detectives, knuckled the top of the desk to get my attention. Candella was a slender man, with an olive complexion and a full head of dark hair with precise comb tracks showing in the gel. He always wore well-tailored ivy-league style four-button suits and solid-colored silk ties. He could pass for a banker, or worse, an attorney. But he was a cop, and a damned good one.

"I heard about Jumbo Flagg's deathbed confession,

Johnny. Roy Creely was in to see Chief Cahill. He claimed that you assaulted him at the Laguna Honda Hospital."

"It never happened," I said. "Alisi, the floor nurse will back me up on that."

Candella patted his hair without disturbing the wave.

"Did Creely interview Rory?"

"No. I got there just in time to stop him from doing that."

"From what Creely said, Jumbo claimed that Willie Mar was shot and killed with your father's gun. Henry Mar knows all about Jumbo's death bed confession. He wants his father's remains found and the killer punished. I'm going to do everything I can to protect Rory, but I wouldn't want that gun showing up anywhere."

"It won't. You don't have to worry about the gun."

He locked his eyes on mine for a moment and then grinned.

"Good. Just how bad is your dad's health?"

"One day he's fine, the next he doesn't know who I am. He's liable to say anything, Cap. That's why I don't want the D.A. or his staff anywhere near him."

"I'll talk to them, Johnny. How's the Steve McQueen movie going?"

"I'm keeping them all happy, boss."

Candella started to leave then turned back to face me. "I hear they're using a lot of cops as extras. If they need someone to play a captain, or a commander, I'm available, you know what I mean?"

I knew exactly what he meant. *Everyone* wanted to be in the movie, even if it meant just being an extra. At least Candella had some standards. He wouldn't want to be seen as a plain old uniformed cop.

The only people I'd met with bigger egos than actors were cops. Which in a way made sense. To be a good cop you had to know how to act—how to play good cop one time, bad cop the next. How to use body language to get your points across without saying something that could be considered perjury in a court room, and how to finesse testimony so that it's not an out and out lie to a judge or jury. And believe me, everyone lies in court—especially a criminal court: big lies, little lies, white lies, evasions, outright whoppers, half-truths. The judge lies pompously, the attorneys lie constantly and cleverly, the defendant lies robot-like, because he has rehearsed his lies in front of his attorney, or, if the case warrants it, a trial consultant. The witnesses lie in order to help their buddies. There are the jurists that lied unsuccessfully in order to get off the case, and then the ones who lied in order to get picked for the jury—the professional jurists, the most dangerous people in the court room.

They call the witness seat in a trial the hot box for good reasons. No matter how certain you are of your facts, no matter how well you prepared the case, no matter how scrupulously honest your investigation was conducted, a good attorney—good as in ruthless, relentless, viscous and vindictive—can make you sweat bullets as he tries to tear down your investigation, your reputation, your very existence—carve you up like a Christmas turkey.

I was in court when my former Homicide partner Bob Schultz was testifying on a case involving a husband who had brutally beaten his wife to death in front of their three-year-old child.

It was as close to an open and shut case as we could have hoped for.

But Schultz had made a mistake, one that had nothing to do with the case. He'd worn a belt that his son had given him as a birthday gift. The belt buckle was a big hunk of stainless steel that formed the numbers 187.

187 of the penal code indicates criminal homicide—murder.

The defense attorney noticed the buckle and went after Bob for ten minutes: "You must be proud of your job,

Inspector, wearing that belt, helping to send innocent people to the gas chamber." On and on it went.

The jury loved it. The defendant was convicted of involuntary manslaughter, rather than homicide—all because of a lousy belt buckle.

# CHAPTER 11

It was getting late, and most of the cops, the judges, law clerks and civilian personnel had left the building and were heading home or to a favorite saloon. I took the elevator down to the Hall of Justice garage, walked out to the parking lot, popped the trunk of my car and picked up one of the Remy Martin Cognac bottles that the Swine had given me, along with a Cuban cigar, and then rode the elevator up to the fifth floor.

All of the detective bureaus were on the fourth floor. The fifth floor included the Chief's Office, Administration, and Operations. At the far end of the building there was an unmarked door, behind which lurked the Intelligence Unit, known simply as "The Unit."

The Unit operated in its own little world, with little attention or interference from the brass. It dates back to the 1930s, and was said to have some one hundred thousand files on individuals: actors, actresses, union leaders, and political figures. The current people of special interest included war protestors and civil rights activists. There was a "Red File" with up-to-date data on local communist activities, including a stakeout on the Russian Embassy from the windows of a terraced mansion nearby. No one I knew could figure out how the Unit had wrangled this plush surveillance spot, but the FBI, CIA, and the whole alphabet soup of government agencies wanted a piece of it.

The Unit wasn't about to give it up. They logged a lot of lucrative overtime keeping tabs on the Ruskies.

The members of the Unit also did a lot of sting operations, so they were given wide latitude as to what they could wear.

Most had beards, long hair, and dressed in old, beat up clothes. They did their wardrobe shopping at the Salvation Army.

The door was locked. I pounded on the glass. The Unit wasn't a nine to five operation. They kept their own hours, and most of those hours took place when it was dark. I heard heavy footsteps, and then a thick voice called out: "Who is it?"

"Johnny O'Rorke."

The door opened a crack and a beady coal-black eye over a lavender-tinted nose appeared. "The Fixer. What do you want?"

I waved the Cognac bottle. "I just felt like having a drink with you, Bob."

The door snapped shut, then opened wide and Lieutenant "Bogus Bob" McCard eased his head out wide enough to make sure I was alone, and then waved me inside.

McCard was tall, bulky, and had thick straw-colored hair that looked as if it had been attacked by sparrows for nesting material. He was dressed in faded jeans and a black hooded sweatshirt.

McCard was originally from Iowa, and people who were foolish enough to want to give him a hard time brought up stories of Iowa farmers and their love of pigs.

The reception room was dark. McCard nodded his head in a gesture for me to follow him down a narrow hallway to another dark room. A 16mm movie projector was throwing out images of a three-story apartment building on a busy street. There were cars whizzing by and a good deal of pedestrian traffic.

McCard snapped on the overhead fluorescent lights and turned off the projector.

"What's up, Johnny O?"

I settled the Remy Martin bottle onto an open spot between the files, cardboard coffee cups and still photos that covered his desk.

"I need your help in tracking down a Russian, Bob."

I handed him a photograph. "This guy uses the name Boris. He worked over a transvestite, and then threatened to shove a silenced pistol up her butt and blow her away."

McCard made a grimace, dropped the photo and picked up the Cognac bottle. He examined the label carefully. "What does big dirty old Boris have that you want?"

"He was at a big bust out in the Haight the other night. Nureyev, the ballet dancer was there, and—"

"Yeah, I know all about that. I had a couple of my people out there. We were picking up some nice stuff on those left wing pinko rock stars when that goddamn clown Fred Breen shows up, Sergeant Sunshine, in all his glory. The jerk threw one of my guys in the wagon, though I have to admit, he was dressed as scummy as the rest of the crowd."

McCard rummaged around in his desk drawer and came out with two fairly clean shot glasses. He cracked open the Cognac and poured us both a drink.

He was on his second drink when I'd finished telling him of my interest in Boris.

McCard made faces, squirmed in his chair as if he had a cramp and then got down to bargaining. "I'd like to help you, pal, but we're busy as hell; the demonstrators, and the—"

"J. Edgar Hoover is coming to town, and Bobby Kennedy will be here next week, Bob."

That got his attention.

"Cary Grant and Kirk Douglas are staying at the Mark Hopkins Hotel for a few days."

McCard grimaced. "Jesus, don't tell me that Grant and Douglas are—"

"No. Grant had a minor medical procedure at the U.C. Medical Hospital. Douglas is shacked up with a movie producer's girlfriend. A well-upholstered redheaded starlet."

McCard edged forward in his chair. "Which producer?"

"Darryl Zanuck," I said, wondering why all of this was of so much interest to him. Almost every major hotel in the city had a security detail manned by retired or off duty cops. They kept me informed on the comings and goings of celebrities, a few who wanted police protection, others who wanted nothing to do with the police.

Still, it was my job to see that celebrities were kept "comfortable" in the Chief's words.

I'd met both Grant and Douglas before. One of the Top of the Mark's cocktail waitresses described them perfectly to me: "Kirk Douglas, always trying to be perfectly charming. Cary Grant, always perfectly charming without trying."

I plopped a Cuban cigar down in front of McCard. Again, he took time to read the label.

"Okay, Johnny. I'll look into it. But I can't promise anything."

"There's one more thing, Bob. A young girl, Russian, speaks English, I think she lives in the city or nearby." I showed him the sketch I'd made. "She was at the party. Her name is Nika. I want to find out everything I can about her."

"Give me a break," McCard said. "There were probably a couple of dozen young girls that fit that description that were smoking pot and snorting coke. No way my guys would remember her."

"She's cute, blonde hair, wore a tight red sweater and she had a Rolex on her wrist."

McCard waved a hand angrily in the air and said, "So, she's a rich bitch out slumming. I can't waste—"

"Sinatra is coming to town next month, Bob. I'm going to need another man for the bodyguard team."

Bingo! McCard's cheeks bulged out like a trumpet player.

I'd used him on a Sinatra job six or seven months earlier, and he'd loved it.

"Okay, Johnny. I'll do what I can for you." He pushed himself to his feet. "What's going on with the Steve McQueen flick?"

God, please, I pleaded. Not another wannabe actor. "Nothing special, Bob. Everyone seems to get along."

"Good." He walked me to the door, and after I stepped outside, said, "This isn't your usual turf, Johnny. Why are you putting all of this effort into a case of some tranny getting roughed up? Let Sexual Assault handle it."

I didn't have a good answer, so I just shrugged my shoulders. It would have been easy to kiss Vanessa off, say that I'd done my best but couldn't find anything on Boris. But I didn't want to let go of it, didn't like having someone who'd helped me being assaulted, no matter what their sexual make-up. After a while you get a sense, a feel about a case. And my feeling was that Boris was into something big. I also had a feeling that it was time I did some real police work for a change.

# CHAPTER 12

Francie Stevens placed her hands in a prayer-like position and said, "*Mea culpa, mea maxima culpa.*"

Francie had that sleek, sophisticated seductress coolness that Alfred Hitchcock liked to use for his movie heroines. Great cheekbones, great legs. Her flaxen colored hair was cut in a style that caused a lock to fall in front of her eyes at the merest shake of her lovely head.

She was single, just having gone through a nasty divorce, and in no mood to get into anything serious at the moment—which suited us both just fine.

We were having dinner at the Blue Fox, one of the city's poshest spots at the time that billed itself as the "restaurant across from the morgue" because the entrance was located in an alley just across from the morgue in the old Hall of Justice. It had gold leaf walls, crystal chandeliers and red carpets, as well as a room where wine bottles, salamis, and prosciutto hams hung from the ceiling.

Francie said, "I had no idea that Roy Creely was coming back to work so soon. I think Mike Rhodes must have called him and told him about your father and Creely just couldn't wait to get into the case."

"That's okay. I was able to catch Creely at the hospital before he could do any damage."

Francie took a dainty sip of her drink, and then said, "Creely was furious when he got back to the office. He and Rhodes had a long meeting. I couldn't get the gist of their conversation, but I did hear your name shouted out a few times. When Creely came out, he made a couple of phone calls, and then left in a hurry. I asked his secretary what was up, and she said that he was going to Chinatown to meet with Henry Mar."

In 1968 there wasn't a glass ceiling holding back female assistant D.A.s, there was a concrete roof. I didn't want Francie jeopardizing her job on my behalf, and I told her just that.

"Don't worry about it, Johnny. I've given my notice." She smiled widely. "I'm going to work for Tim Riordan next week."

I smiled back. Riordan was a flamboyant, top notch criminal attorney, who was always vying with fellow attorney Melvin Belli for headlines in the newspapers.

"Congratulations. I hate to see you go over to the dark side, but it's a hell of an opportunity for you."

Andre, the restaurant's maître d', came over with a bottle of red wine cradled in his arms.

"The gentleman at the table by the piano sent this over."

There were seven men sitting at the table, all of whom seemed to be having a good time. One gave me a friendly wave, and then went back to chatting with his buddies.

"Who's that?" Francie asked. "He looks familiar."

"It's Don Gordon, an actor. He plays Steve McQueen's sidekick in *Bullitt.*"

Gordon was a likeable, unpretentious guy who liked riding around town with real cops.

"Ummmm," Francie said. "Tell me all about McQueen."

I did just that while we enjoyed our veal marsala.

"Johnny, even though I've only a few days left as an assistant D.A., I've got to be careful. If Mike Rhodes found out that—"

"He won't," I said, trying to sound confident. As much as I liked Francie's company, we'd have to keep our distances for a while.

Her foot sneaked across the floor and her toes started dancing on my ankle.

Starting tomorrow we'd keep our distance, I decided.

"So what's your next step?" she asked, her toes moving upwards. "About your father, I mean."

"Good question."

"Your dad's house. Creely will start digging there."

"I'm not worried about it."

"You should be, Johnny. I read Daniel J. Flagg's statement and it's pretty strong stuff. Strong enough for Creely to go after search warrants, as well as getting a court order to exhume Willie Mar's remains. I haven't had access to the Sheriff's reports. They interviewed Mr. Flagg pretty extensively before and after he gave the statement."

"The reports would make interesting reading," I said, being about as subtle as a sledgehammer.

"You think?" she said, sounding sweet and sarcastic at the same time. "Obviously, the first thing they'll be searching for is your father's gun. Flagg was definite about that—your father shot Mar with his police revolver."

*His* revolver was the key word. The city didn't start supplying officers with weapons until the 1990s. Prior to that, a cop bought his own gun with his own money. So the department would have no records of my dad's revolver as to ballistics from the firing range. Those old movies you see where the malcontent hero cop turns in his badge and gun are just that, old movies. The gun is his, and, if he'd been promoted beyond patrolman, so was the badge. They made us pay for those high-rank badges.

"I'm not worried about the gun, Francie."

"What if they do find Mar's grave and there are still lead bullets in the remains? You know better than I do how easy those could be traced back to the weapon they came from."

"I'm not worried about the gun," I repeated.

Francie opened her mouth to say something, and then snapped it shut. "I think we should change the subject."

We ordered coffee and then Andre came over with the bill.

He took a coin from his pocket and said, "Feeling lucky, Johnny? Double or nothing?"

"Why not?"

He rolled a quarter between his fingers, then slapped it down on the top of his left hand and covered it with his right palm. "Heads or tails?"

"Tails."

He took a quick peek at the coin, sighed, tore the check in two and said, "You win."

"What was that all about?" Francie asked, after Andre had backed away from the table. "Almost every time you take me out to a fancy restaurant, you flip a coin for the bill and you always win."

"I'm just a lucky guy." Actually, I had done Andre a small favor. His wife worked for a food broker who specialized in imported French wines and cheeses. Her boss was giving her a bit of a hard time. There was no such phrase as sexual harassment at that time. It was considered the norm for horny bosses to make jokes and suggestive comments to their women employees. I had stopped by the joker's office and tactfully scared the hell out of him.

The secret to these free meals was to always leave a heavy tip for the waiter and maître d'.

Francie stirred her coffee and watched the cream swirl around. "Do you feel like stopping at my place for a drink?"

"Nothing would please me more," I said, meaning every word.

"We can play that coin flip game, only I get to flip the coin."

"And what are we betting on?"

"Who makes the bed in the morning."

# CHAPTER 13

The first thing in the morning, I dropped Francie off at the Hall of Justice, and then headed to my father's house for a change of clothes. Though it was early, I wasn't alone. Fiona O'Day was in the kitchen, listening to Don Sherwood, San Francisco's self-proclaimed "World's Greatest Disc Jockey."

"Good morning," she said cheerfully, a dishrag in her hand. "I thought I'd just do a little cleaning before Rory comes home."

"That might not be for a while, Fiona. A few weeks, maybe longer."

She rubbed her arms as if she suddenly felt cold. "Then I better be giving you the house key."

I was glad she suggested it, because if she hadn't, I was going to have to ask her for it.

She hung her apron up neatly on the cupboard door, plucked the key out of a crocheted red purse that I had a hunch she'd made herself, passed the key over and then gave me a big hug. "Sure and you be callin' me. Anytime you need me, Johnny."

I shaved, showered, changed clothes and then went hunting for those gold coins and gambling chips again.

This time I got lucky. They were hidden in the basement, a vast concrete floor affair that was as cold as an icebox in the winter. There was room to park four cars, with space left over for a full-sized boxing ring and a sand-filled leather two hundred pound punching bag.

I'd spent hours pounding into that bag under Pop's watchful eye. "The left, son, a jab or a hook, that's how you win fights. Punish him with the left, finish him off with a right."

He'd been a good enough boxer as a young man to catch the eyes of several promoters, but had dropped out after he was told he'd have to throw a fight.

Pop taught me how to handle myself in the ring, and then showed me the secrets of *Bataireacht*, the Irish version of martial arts.

The gold coins and gambling chips had been wrapped in handkerchiefs and stashed in an old metal fishing tackle box in the basement, secreted under a bunch of fishing flies and jars of salmon eggs that hadn't been opened in fifteen years.

There were eight gold coins and six red, octagon-shaped plastic chips with an embossed dragon's head in the center that were called *dayang*, and could be used all over Chinatown: in an *Ngao fong*, an illegal gambling den, or to buy food, clothing, whatever. They came in different sizes and colors, and were stamped with the equivalent dollar amounts: five, ten, twenty-five, fifty and a hundred. These chips were the size of a silver dollar and were worth fifty dollars each. A total of three hundred bucks.

Also in the tackle box I found a wrinkled yellowed envelope that held three small black-and-white photographs, the old type with scalloped edges, of a happy couple: my father, young, tan and dapper in a dark bathing suit and a woman wearing a two-piece outfit that must have been daring at the time. They were at the beach, smiling at the camera. There was a roller coaster in the background which I remembered well, and a long wooden boardwalk leading to a wedding cake of a building that housed a fabulous arcade. The Santa Cruz Beach Boardwalk.

I studied the woman closely. She had short-cut curly hair, long legs and an all-around good figure. She had a high forehead, a turned up nose and ears with long lobes. In one photo they were holding hands while running into the surf. In the third photo my father's hand was draped over her shoulder, bordering on touching her left breast. She was looking up at him with her tongue stuck out.

I had no idea who she was, but she had obviously been someone special to my father, who was definitely married to my mother at the time the photos were taken.

Santa Cruz was probably the perfect spot for their lovers' tryst, some sixty miles from San Francisco, and my mother avoided the beach and sunshine with a passion.

I pocketed the photos and carried the coins and chips up to the kitchen and washed them with a bar of Lifebuoy soap to get rid of any fingerprints. The gold coins were still bright, shiny, and unblemished. The gambling chips had seen a lot of use, but would still be as good as cash in Chinatown.

While I tried to figure out what to do with them, I called the office. There was just one message of importance, from Dr. Luceti, at the Laguna Honda Hospital.

I called the good doctor, fearing the worst, and I got it.

"I'm afraid that the biopsies taken from your father's neck and shoulders have come back positive Mr. O'Rorke."

"Skin cancer"

"Melanoma. And there is reason to believe that the cancer has spread."

"Is there a way out of this for him, doctor?"

"I wish I could be more optimistic, but, coupled with his other medical issues, I'm afraid that there's not much more that we can do for him."

After we hung up I sat in a kitchen chair staring blankly at the wall. I felt depressed, sick to my stomach, my mind whirling with memories of Pop. He wasn't the perfect father or husband, but I loved him dearly. He was so strong, so full of life, so much fun to be around as a child, to reflect in his power, charisma, presence, whatever it's called. *He'd* walk into a room and all noise would hush for a bit, whether it be a bar, a church dinner, or a funeral.

Being Irish, we attended a great many wakes and funerals. He often spoke at these affairs, usually quoting from Dylan Thomas.

> Now I am a man no more
> And a black reward for a roaring life
> Tidy and cursed in my dove cooed room
> I lie down thin and hear the good bells jaw

I finally got to my feet, washed my face in the sink, put the coins and chips in a brown paper shopping bag and decided to go visit a certain madam—knowing that Pop would approve.

# CHAPTER 14

I called Pete Kissel, a buddy in the Vice Squad, and asked if Myra Favre, the lady of the evening my father had suggested I talk to, was still in business, and if so to get a current address.

"Yeah, Myra's my grandmother's age, but she's still working," Kissel told me. "She never gives us any trouble, so we don't bother her. What's your beef with her?"

"No beef. I'm looking for a witness in a case I'm working on."

"Hold on, Johnny. I'll get her address and give her a call to let her know you may be visiting."

The house was one of San Francisco's famed "Painted Ladies," located on Steiner Street, across from Alamo Park. It was a three-story peaked-roof Italianate-style home built in the late-nineteenth century, with symmetrical bays featuring curved glass windows, rows of gingerbread moldings and fish-scale shingles. It was painted in hues from vibrant purple to pale lavender. There were large, cone-shaped wicker baskets filled with freshly cut flowers framing the stained glass front door.

I pushed the scalloped brass doorbell. The door was opened by a real painted lady. I guessed she was in her mid-seventies. She had bright henna-red hair with corkscrew curls. Her face was soft, heavily rouged and featured battle-aged hazel-colored eyes canopied by long eyelashes that pretty near closed completely when she smiled. She had a turned-up nose like the woman in the Santa Cruz photos. Purple-stone earrings that resembled small chandeliers dangled from her long-lobed ears. She smelled as if she'd just gotten out of a bath full of floral scented perfume.

She was wearing a leopard-print silk robe and lavender ballerina-style slippers. One hand held a cane with a handle in the shape of a horse's head.

"I'm Myra Favre and you must be Inspector O'Rorke," she said in a well-modulated, velvet-toned voice. "Pete Kissel called and told me to expect you."

She opened the door wide and waved me into the house.

I followed her into a high ceiling room with flocked red velvet wallpaper. Favre pointed the tip of her cane at the envelope tucked under my arm. "If that's a search warrant or some other disgusting legal document, I'll have to contact my attorney before we proceed."

"Nothing like that," I assured her. "Just a photograph that I'd like you to see."

Favre settled into a high-backed chesterfield with a black background, covered with embroidered playing cards: aces, kings, queens, jacks and tens. She patted the cushion next to her and said, "Sit next to me, please. My hearing is not what it once was."

I sat down, my knees bumping against a claw-footed mahogany coffee table. There were two antique crystal decanters on a revolving silver stand, and two spindle stemmed glasses on the table.

She reached for one of the decanters. "Can I offer you an aperitif?"

"No thanks."

The tip of the decanter made clinking sounds against the glass as the ruby red liquid was poured.

"When you drink as much as I do, Inspector, you have to start early."

Favre took a dainty sip. "Port. Purely for medicinal purposes, of course." She sighed and leaned back against the cushions. "My doctor has prescribed a mélange of vile prescriptions for all the aches and pains of this aging body. Have you ever read the cautions that come with those medicines? My God, the possible side effects would scare the knickers off a ninety-year-old nun." She took another sip of the wine. "No, a bottle or more of this every day is more to my liking. Now tell me, how I can help you?"

"It's about Robert Alverson, Vanessa the Undresser, I was wondering—"

"My, you certainly work fast. I just heard about Vanessa less than an hour ago."

"What did you hear?"

"That the poor dear was murdered. At her cottage, in Sausalito. Have they caught the killer?"

I tried to keep the stunned look off of my face. "I hadn't heard about it. When did it happen?"

"Some time last night."

"And who informed you? The police?"

"No. Ronnie Tremaine. You might know her as Trixie. She worked with Vanessa."

"How was Vanessa killed?"

"Trixie found her sitting in her hot tub. Her neck had been broken. Trixie was scared silly, but she had the sense to call the police right away."

I handed her the envelope containing the photo of Boris and Vanessa. "Trixie took this. I'm interested in finding this man. He met Vanessa at Finocchio's, took her around the corner to the Rendezvous Hotel, and beat her up."

Favre's peaked eyebrows rose toward her forehead. "The Rendezvous. I warn my people not to go there; it's not a very clean establishment."

"Vanessa screamed and the guy in the next room threatened to call the police. Do you recognize the man in the photo? He's Russian. He told Vanessa his name was Boris."

"These creatures seldom give their real names; however, maybe he did in this case. Who would make up a name like Boris?"

Favre slipped a pair of pink framed reading glasses from a

robe pocket and studied the photo carefully. "M-m-m-m," she said softly like a cat. "Not a bad looking man, rather brutish, but a lot of Russians are like that. His hair is well cut, and neatly combed. His suit is expensive. Did you notice the working button holes on the jacket's sleeves? The buttons weren't just sewn on. That tells you that the suit didn't come off a rack; it was most likely tailored for him. His shirt has a spread collar, which best fits his long face and thin neck. And you can just make out what appears to be a black-onyx cufflink on his French cuffs. Your Boris spends time and money on his appearance."

I took the photos and stared at them intently. "You seem to know a lot about men's clothes, Ms. Favre."

"I know a lot about men, in and out of their clothes, Inspector."

"Vanessa told me that Boris roughed her up, tied her to the bed and threatened to sodomize her with his gun, which had a silencer on it. I'd like to know if you've heard of assaults like this happening to any other..."

"Whores, Inspector? Call girls? Hookers? I used to like the term harlots when I first started my business. No, I haven't heard of any such things, but I will ask around. This Boris, do you think he lives around here?"

"No. He spoke English, but with a thick accent. I have a feeling he's either Russian Mafia or KGB."

"Was he drinking heavily when he was with Vanessa?"

"Yes, he was."

She took a deep sip of her port, and then set the glass down carefully. "If the man was new to San Francisco, there is the possibility that he was unaware of just what he was paying for. Years ago I operated a *maison de a'mour* in Sausalito. It was a full-service establishment with young ladies of all races and creeds. There were some customers who much preferred boys dressed up as girls. 'Pussy-on-a-stick' was the term often used. I made sure I provided them with the very best makeup, wigs and lingerie. School girl outfits over garter belts were very popular. Gloves and a turtleneck sweater, or just a bandana around the neck, usually did the trick if the poor dear's manly Adam's apple was too obvious. There were a few times when things were very busy. The customer wanted a girl, and was put into a room with something else. Once the little darling dropped her knickers and the truth was revealed, the customer became upset. One of them came close to killing a lovely boy named Ramona. Do you think that could have happened with Vanessa?"

"It's possible, but I doubt it. You'd have to be pretty dumb to go into Finocchio's and not know what was going on."

"Ah, Inspector. A man who is liquored-up and has a hard-on is capable of anything. May I keep the photograph?"

"Absolutely."

"Good. I will definitely ask all my sources if they've seen Boris."

I thanked her for her time and got up to leave.

She fluttered those eyelashes at me and said, "O'Rorke. Could you by chance be related to Rory O'Rorke?"

"He's my father." I studied her face, with its turned up nose and long earlobes and tried to roll the clock back to the day in the Santa Cruz photographs I'd found in Pop's fishing tackle box. "Is he a friend?"

"Oh, yes. He was a gentleman of the best kind. Is he well?"

"I had lunch with him yesterday," I said. "In fact, he suggested I talk to you."

Favre smiled widely, sending waves of cracks across her makeup. "How nice. Give him my love would you?"

I fingered the envelope with the Santa Cruz photos of Pop and Favre in my coat pocket and thought of bringing them out. But then I thought better of it.

"I certainly will."

# CHAPTER 15

The Marin County Coroner's office was located at the Hall of Justice in San Rafael, just a few miles from Vanessa the Undresser's cottage in Sausalito.

You can't miss seeing famed architect Frank Lloyds Wright's Civic Center from the freeway. It's a dramatic, futuristic grouping of two long horizontal buildings with cantilevered walkways and a ribbon of decorative archways running along the outside of its four floors. Wright designed it to blend in with the beautiful surrounding hills: the walls are painted sand-beige, and the barrel-arch roof a shade of sky blue. It has its admirers and detractors. It reminded me of Ming the Merciless's palace in the Flash Gordon serials.

Flash Gordon too old for you? Then how about the Macau Casino where James Bond tangled with a komodo dragon in *Skyfall*?

The coroner's clerk was a man in his forties who told me his name was Luther, in a tone that indicated he was proud of that fact. He had a jaw that was wider than the top of his head and was wearing thick glasses that had been mended with Scotch tape. He studied my badge and ID card for longer than was necessary, and then led me into a chilly hallway that led to an even chillier room that held rows of body storage coolers.

Luther checked the index tabs on the coolers and rolled out one that was at knee height. He then unzipped a bleach-stained canvas body bag to reveal the remains of Robert Alverson, aka Vanessa the Undresser.

His neck had been twisted to his left. My guess was that the killer had come from behind, grabbed Alverson's head and did his work. I moved the zipper down and examined his hands. His fingernails were long, painted pink, and well cared for. Not a single nail broken. He hadn't put up any kind of a defense.

"Death obviously resulted from cervical fracture," Luther said. "The assailant had to be quite strong, in my view."

I asked to talk to the operating coroner, but he was unavailable according to Luther. He promised to send me a copy of the autopsy as soon as possible.

"We're very busy at the moment, Inspector. You know how that is."

I really didn't know how that was, but I had the feeling that if I pushed for the report, Luther would have taken delight in misfiling it.

I used a Thomas Brothers Map book to find my way to Alverson's place in Sausalito. Remember, no Google computer maps, no GPS systems.

Sausalito's a beautiful little town with a bawdy past. It had been a haven for mob-backed gambling halls and bootleggers during the 1930s. None other than notorious bank robber Baby Face Nelson had hid out in town while J. Edgar Hoover's boys were scouring the Midwest states for him.

In the early-sixties it was a hot bed—hot waterbed actually—for hippies who used the houseboat communities for sex, drugs, and rock and roll.

For a while, hotshot high school kids from San Francisco, after a night of guzzling beer, would brag about going over to Sausalito to "roll a couple of queers." Beat them up and take their money. This came to an abrupt end when they found that their victims weren't the limp-wrist sissies they were hoping for, and that they were the ones who ended up with busted noses and broken teeth.

The map took me along a twisting, cracked pavement road. A bright pink post-mounted mailbox with the name VANESSA stenciled in white block letters pointed the way to

Alverson's place. The dirt road kept narrowing until it was barely wide enough for a car to squeeze by.

The road ended abruptly in front of a vine-crusted cottage with a cedar shake roof. A bubblegum-pink MGA convertible with a white top was protected by a tin-roofed carport.

A Sausalito PD black-and-white was parked facing the road, which meant I'd have to back out when I left.

The detective handling the Alverson case had told me he'd meet me at the address at three p.m. I was twenty-five minutes early, and so was the detective.

He was leaning against the car, a ginger-haired, freckle-faced man in his early-thirties. He was of medium height, and had a neat, compact build. He looked athletic—nothing like weight lifting or football. Swimming? A runner? He was wearing a brass-buttoned blue blazer, tan slacks and a vanilla-colored shirt with a muted striped tie.

I climbed out of my car and enjoyed the view for a moment. The side of the hill leading down to the waterfront was upholstered with lupine and poppies, and Angel Island, Alcatraz, and the Bay Bridge were strutting their stuff under a chalk-colored sky.

"Hi, Inspector," Freckle Face said, as he walked over to greet me.

We shook hands and he gave me a shy smile. "You don't remember me, do you? Duane Garant. I took several of your classes at the police academy five years ago."

He was right. I didn't remember him. When I was working Homicide, I gave classes on Arrest and Control techniques to new members of the SFPD. Sometimes members of smaller departments around the Bay Area joined the sessions.

"I hope I did you some good," I said.

"Oh, you did, sir. It helped me get promoted to detective. Are you ready to check out the crime scene?"

I was. Garant escorted me past the cottage's front door and around the back to an L-shaped deck constructed from terra-cotta colored tile.

There was a redwood hot tub at the far end of the deck that looked like an oversized wine barrel.

"You've seen the body?" Garant asked

"I have."

Garant took a chrome pencil-shaped expandable pointer from his coat jacket and pulled it out all the way to its five-foot length and started to tell me his theory of how the murder took place.

He put the tip of the pointer on the tubs edge. "The victim was in the tub, he was taken from behind, and his neck broken. There was no sign of a struggle. We found the body floating in the tub. Simple as that."

Garant glanced over at me with puppy-like eyes waiting for my approval.

"Sounds good," I said. "What's the time frame?"

"I don't have the coroner's report yet. The time of death is going to be difficult to determine due to the fact that the body was in the warm hot tub. Their best guess is that Alverson was killed between four and ten o'clock last night."

Durant pointed to a coiled black rubber garden hose at the end of the deck. "The killer apparently used the hose to clean up his footprints. The hose was lying on the deck when we arrived."

"How about his access? Any tire tracks out front?"

Garant coughed and cleared his throat. "Yes. Most belong to the MGA convertible Mr. Alverson parked in the car port. We have castings of all the others."

"Let's go inside," I suggested.

The bedroom had a cottage-cheese acoustical ceiling. Two of the walls were mirrored-door built-in closets that held an array of clothing, approximately half of which had been torn from their hangers. There were a dozen or more wigs on the floor. A dresser had all of its drawers open and lingerie was sprinkled around the room. The king-size waterbed was half-covered with a faux fur ermine bedspread. The tangled pink silk sheets had been put to hard use and there were traces of lipstick and makeup on the pillow cases.

There were four plastic vibrators spread across the foot of the bed, varying in sizes from a finger to a bright red one the size of my forearm.

The dressing table was one of those ones with light bulbs all around its mirror. Makeup jars were overturned and a bottle of Chanel No.5 perfume had been opened, the contents spilled across a tray holding dozens of lipsticks.

A door on the far wall led to a small bathroom with a shower over a tub. The plastic shower curtain featured red valentine's hearts.

The medicine cabinet door was wide open and the usual aspirin, mouthwash kind of things had been dumped into the sink.

"I've heard that homosexuals have a history of being violent when it comes to killing one of their own," Garant said.

It was a popular myth—gays being exceptionally viscous—and that's all it was, a myth. Husbands, wives, children, any and all of them could get whipped up into a blood-letting orgy.

"Do you have someone in mind, Detective?"

Garant flicked through the pages of a spiral notebook. "A Mr. Ronald Tremaine, who also uses the name Trixie, reported the crime. He claims he stopped by to see Alverson a little after two in the morning. Said that he was worried when Alverson didn't show up for work at Finocchio's, which is a gay establishment in San Francisco."

"I know all about Finocchio's," I said.

"Tremaine is also a—"

"Crossdresser. Yes, I know Trixie. I don't want to tell you

how to work your case, but I wouldn't consider him much of a suspect."

Again Garant coughed into his hand. "We found one of your business cards on the victim's dressing table. With a handwritten phone number on the back."

"I gave it to him a couple of days ago. Alverson was an informant, and a good one. Is the crime lab finished in here?"

"Yes, sir."

I handed Garant one of the photographs of Boris and told him what I knew of his connection to Alderson as I poked around the room, stressing the point that I considered him a prime suspect. "He assaulted Alderson, and threatened to kill him, first by 'breaking his neck like a chicken,' which is just what happened, and then by shoving a pistol with a silencer up his butt and blowing his brains out."

We toured the rest of the cottage: there was a room that was filled with luggage and boxes of clothing, and a pint-sized bathroom off the kitchen. The kitchen had a pink built-in stove and oven, a pink refrigerator, a Formica table, and a set of white fiberglass tulip chairs. Everything was spic and span.

"Is the crime lab finished here?"

"Yes," Garant said in puzzled tone. "Why?"

"I'm hungry."

The refrigerator was well stocked. I slapped together a sandwich of sliced salami, Swiss cheese, and rye bread and washed it down with a bottle of Heineken beer.

Garant said, "If what Alverson told you can be believed, this Russian had a weapon with a silencer. Why wouldn't he have used it to kill him?"

"Bullets can be traced to a gun, and Alverson was alone in the tub, helpless; it was easy for a KGB trained assassin to simply break his neck."

Garant was shaking his head slowly from side to side. He wasn't buying into my theory.

"Then why the thrashing of the bedroom?"

It was a good question. "Boris may have been looking for something, maybe the photographs that were taken of he and Alverson at Finocchio's, or maybe he just wanted it to look like a lover's quarrel had taken place before the murder. It could be that there had been some kind of an altercation before Boris showed up. Was anything stolen?"

"Not that I'm aware of. I still think that we have to consider the homosexual angle, sir."

"Not *we*, Detective. You. It's your jurisdiction, your case. Boris is a KGB agent who doesn't want it known that he's into kinky sex with men, and he's quite willing to kill anyone who could let that information get out. Why he's here, what he's planning to do next is what I've got to figure out." I reached for the pink wall phone. "I'm going to check in at the office."

# CHAPTER 16

There was only one message for me, but it was a welcomed one. Russell Cortig had called saying he had some important news. I contacted him at his room at the Sheraton Hotel.

"Nika rang me, Inspector. The cute Russian chick. She's hot to see us filming a scene with Steve McQueen, so we made a date for tonight. We'll be working at the old hotel on Embarcadero from midnight to four or so."

"Did you get her last name? A phone number?"

"No. She was acting kind of funny—talking really low, whispering. But she said she'd be there."

"Good. So will I."

I asked Detective Garant for Trixie's home phone number and address and then headed back to San Francisco. The fog was rolling in like dry ice as I crossed the Golden Gate Bridge.

Trixie's home address was in the Sunset District, a two-story flat, positioned on the corner of 42nd and Taraval that had been painted a milk-chocolate color. A Sunshine Cab was idling in front.

I parked across the street and approached the cab driver. He was in his fifties, with thinning dark hair shellacked against his scalp, a drinker's nose and a toothpick sized gap between his front teeth.

I showed him my badge. "Who are you waiting for?"

"Some broad named Trixie. Why? What's the beef? I'm just trying to make a living, man."

"I'm not stopping you. Did Trixie say where she was going?"

"The dispatcher said the airport." He glanced down at the watch on his hairy wrist. "I been waiting five minutes already.

In my business, time is money."

As if on cue, Ronald Tremaine, in full Trixie-mode, clattered out of the lower flat. She was wearing her Harpo Marx wig, a polka dot scarf around her neck, a white vinyl coat and high heeled shoes. She was carrying two orange-colored suitcases and had a Pan Am canvas flight bag hooked over one shoulder.

She skidded to a stop, nearly toppling over when she saw me.

"Hi, Trixie," I said, reaching out for the suitcases.

"You can't stop me. You can't!" she said in a squeaky, frightened voice.

"I wouldn't think of it."

She dropped the suitcases to the street and held the Pan Am bag across her chest. "I didn't tell them about you. I swear!"

"Tell who?"

The cabbie beeped his horn and said, "Come on. Let's go."

Trixie backed away from me. Her eyes were wide with fear and her lips were quivering.

I took a dollar bill from my money clip, leaned in the cab and tossed it to the driver. "Put the lady's bags in the trunk."

Trixie was moving sideways, and looked as if she would break out into a run at any moment.

"Easy," I said. "I'm not going to hurt you. Nobody is. Now what did you mean when you said you didn't tell them about me?"

"The police," she blurted out. "I didn't tell them anything about you."

She really had me confused. "Trixie, start talking or I'm going to send the cab away and take you down to the Hall of Justice."

She continued backing away from me, her eyes darting left and right. "Okay," she said after taking in a deep breath.

"Vanessa told me about you coming over to her place yesterday, and—"

"Vanessa told you *I* was coming over?"

"Well, she said the San Francisco cop she'd talked to, so I figured she must have meant you."

"When was this?"

"Yesterday. In the afternoon. It wasn't you?"

"No," I assured her. "Now relax, I'm on your side. Tell me just what Vanessa said."

"Just that a cop was coming to see her." She patted her wig with one hand, licked her lips, and then continued. "'He probably wants a blow job.' Those were her exact words."

"What else?"

"Nothing really." She smiled shyly. "I mean just stuff, about work, clothes, and those kinds of things. She didn't sound upset, or scared, nothing like that."

"Listen, Trixie, a cop may have gone over to see Vanessa, maybe it was about the assault, but he didn't kill her. I think that Boris, the man who was with Vanessa in the photos you took at Finocchio's, is the killer. How did he find out where she lived? Did she ever mention giving him her address?"

"No. Vanessa was too smart for that."

"Then how did he get her address? Vanessa told me that she didn't have any ID in her purse when she went to the hotel with Boris. Could it be someone from Finocchio's?"

"No, no, no. That would never happen. Maybe...maybe he just followed her home. In her pink MGA. It's easy to spot. She always parked it in the lot next to Finocchio's. She...kept the parking attendant happy. It was always right up front, by itself, away from the other cars. She loved that convertible."

Could it be that simple? If Boris was KGB, he would know how to follow a car, especially one as distinctive as Vanessa's.

"The Sausalito police told me that you were the one that found the body, Trixie."

She started shaking, like a dog trying to get rid of the

dampness. "God, yes. It was horrible. I've never seen anything like that." She blinked some tears away. "Never. You're not going to arrest me?"

"No. You've done nothing wrong, and I don't blame you for wanting to get out of town." I handed her one of my cards. "If you can think of anything that might help me catch the killer, call me. Even if you don't, call me and let me know where you are."

I opened the cab door and slammed it shut after she was settled in the seat.

She gave me a sad little smile before the driver stabbed the accelerator and surged away from the curb.

I inhaled deeply and blew my breath out as if it were cigarette smoke. I had that queasy, uneasy, guilty feeling in the pit of my stomach. My mind was whirling with "I should haves." I should have figured that Boris might go back after Vanessa. I should have warned her to be careful. I should have put more effort into finding Boris. I should have done a lot of things, but now Vanessa was dead, and I couldn't shake the feeling I was partly responsible.

But why had Boris felt the need to kill Vanessa? Why wouldn't he just forget about her? Was there something she hadn't told me?

I needed a drink, and I needed to talk to a cop, and I knew just where to go.

# CHAPTER 17

There were some good cop bars in San Francisco, and one great one, Cookie's Star Buffet, a saloon on Kearny Street across from Portsmith Square. It was narrow and dark—the walls covered with photos of old politicians, gangsters, sports immortals and police memorabilia from around the world.

The clientele was a mixture of cops, firemen, lawyers, judges, teamsters, bookies, gamblers, reporters, private eyes, a few white collar executives from nearby skyscrapers, and guys who sold things that fell off the backs of trucks.

Not many of the fair sex frequented Cookie's—there was too much cigar and cigarette smoke and swearing going on. When a woman or two did make an entrance, Cookie made sure that the swearing stopped. Francie Stevens loved Cookie's.

A high-stakes Liar's Dice game was taking place at the far end of the bar when I arrived, the sound of the dice cup slamming against the bar top rising above the chatter.

Cookie was a lean man with strong features who always seemed to have a twisted rope of an Italian cigar clamped between his teeth. He poured me a Jack Daniel's and water without being asked.

"Thanks, Cookie. Is Ed Cornell around?"

"Playing dice. And winning for a change."

I worked on my drink and kept an eye on Cornell. He was in the middle of a pack of suit-and-tie businessmen. Someone tapped me lightly on the shoulder and I swiveled around to see a small, wiry guy with foxlike features wearing a checkered tweed jacket and a wide brim brown fedora with a colorful feather in the band. He was jockey size, thus his nickname, the Jockey. Danny Higgins was an all-around-crook, who among other things successfully worked the old *tens-for-five* scam at crowded bars, cigars stores and restaurants. While the person handling the cash register was busy, Danny would hurry up to them with a five dollar bill in hand and say, "Hey, can you give me two tens for a five?" A quick fifteen-dollar profit. He was also an excellent pickpocket and an accomplished burglar.

"Do you remember me, Inspector? You busted me about three years ago on a burglary rap. No hard feelings. You caught me fair and square and you treated me real good. No rough stuff. And you put in a word for me with the judge. I always appreciated that."

"Good to see you, Danny. I hope you're being a good boy."

"Got out of San Quentin eleven months ago; got a good job, driving a banana. Everything is great."

By saying he was driving a banana, Danny was telling me he was working for the Yellow Cab Company.

"I saw you walk in here and I just wanted to say hello. Are you still fishing, Inspector? I remember you told me you and your dad liked to go fishing together. Fly fishing, if I'm remembering right."

"You've got a good memory, Danny." There was a time when our family took a yearly vacation to Ireland, my mother catching up with relatives while my father took us kids fly fishing on the Bandon River in County Cork.

Danny tipped his hat and backed away. "Okay, Inspector. Nice running into you."

I picked up my drink and carried it down to the end of the bar. Inspector Ed Cornell was joking and laughing. Winning in a game of Liar's Dice does that to a man.

I tugged at the elbow of his suit jacket. "We have to talk, Ed."

"Not now, pal. I'm busy."

I tugged harder. "Right now."

Cornell lit a fresh cigarette from the dog-end of his old one, and said, "Let's go outside."

I steered Cornell to Dunbar alley, which was bordered by a stand of chain link fencing.

"What the hell's going on, Johnny O?" Cornell said. "I was cleaning those guys' clocks. What's the big deal?"

"Robert Alverson. Vanessa the Undresser. You went to his house in Sausalito, Ed. For a blowjob, right?"

"Bullshit. I got better things to do than to—"

"Alverson was murdered, Ed. Sometime yesterday evening. He had his neck broken while he was in the hot tub, and then his bedroom was ransacked."

Cornell shut his eyes, took a hit on his cigarette, coughing at the first inhale.

"The Sausalito cops are handling the murder investigation. They dusted the whole place for prints of course, Ed."

"Who...who told you I was there, Johnny."

"Alverson talked to a friend who said that a San Francisco cop was coming over for a blowjob. It was you, Ed."

Cornell gave a listless shrug. "Bullshit, no one can prove that—"

I grabbed him by his suit's lapels and threw him against the chain link fence.

"Don't fuck with me, Ed. You were there."

"You're choking me," he said, slapping his arms against the fence.

I pulled my hands back and gave him some room. He bent over and went on a coughing spree for several seconds, then took some deep breaths. "Did you squeal to the Sausalito cops that I was there?"

"Not yet."

"Listen, Johnny, after you talked to me I realized that I hadn't done a real good job on the case, so I called Alverson, went over there to see if he had any more information on this supposed Russian guy with the silencer."

"Did he?"

"No. He said he had friends looking for the bastard, but nothing had come of it. I never even saw a hot tub or a bedroom. Alverson greeted me at the front door. We sat in the kitchen, had coffee and talked for about fifteen minutes. That was it. "

"So you didn't get a blowjob?"

"I don't swing that way."

"Okay, Ed. If Sausalito does pull your prints, I'll back you up. Let's go back to Cookie's; I'll buy you a drink."

I was nursing my second drink when someone tapped me politely on the shoulder. It was a grinning Danny Higgins, holding an eight-foot bamboo fly rod in his right hand.

"This is for treating me right, Inspector. Thanks."

He slapped the rod in my hand, and then ran out of the bar.

There was a price tag tied to one of the rod's wire loops. It was from the Abercrombie & Fitch store on Post Street, some six blocks from Cookie's. Danny's life on the straight and narrow had taken a slight turn. The Jockey rides again.

After finishing my drink I drove over to Abercrombie & Fitch. No one questioned me as I entered the store, carrying the fishing rod. I walked over to where dozens of beautiful rods were on display.

No sales people approached me. There were no security guards in sight. I leaned the rod against a display case and left, and again no one paid the least bit of attention to me. Danny could have walked out with the cash register.

My next stop was at Old St. Mary's Cathedral, on the corner of Grant and California Streets.

The inside of the church was just a notch above dark, and had that wonderful smell from years of burning candles. I found the poor box and slotted the gold coins my father had taken from Willie Mar into the box one at a time, listening to the clinking sound as they hit bottom.

What would the priest think when he opened it up in the morning? A gift from a repenting gambler? Alcoholic? Prostitute? Murderer? Thief? Certainly a sinner of some type. He'd be right about that.

I hung around the front of the church for a couple of minutes before spotting an elderly Chinese woman with a severe case of kyphosis, her spine curved dramatically, her head pointed down at the sidewalk. She had a wooden cane in her right hand which she stabbed against the sidewalk with every step. A large woven shopping bag with celery and carrots peeking out of the top was looped across her left shoulder.

I edged up beside her when she stopped for a traffic light and dribbled the Chinese gambling chips into her shopping bag.

She took no notice of me, and I wondered what she'd do when she unpacked the bag and found the chips. Celebrate with a dinner out? Buy more food? A new coat? Or, more likely, head directly to a gambling den.

# CHAPTER 18

It was nice to get back to my flat. The *Bullitt* crew had left it in great shape; everything clean, fresh vacuum tracks in the rugs—the refrigerator stocked with Old Milwaukee Beer, Bollinger Champagne, a crisply roasted chicken and a deli platter filled with cold cuts and various cheeses.

I took a short nap, showered, changed clothes and headed down to the Embarcadero, a major boulevard that borders the city's waterfront, where Steve McQueen was shooting a scene at the Kennedy Hotel, which had been rechristened the Hotel Daniels for the film. It was a grim, rundown six-story building across from Pier 18, in the shadows of the Embarcadero Freeway—a ribbon of ugly concrete that was taken down after the earthquake in October 1989.

So, sadly, had the hotel, which was not the type of place that attracted jewel thieves, but it had its uses. It housed a group of needy seniors on welfare, addicts of all kinds: drugs, alcohol, gambling, and the poor devils who spun in and out of the revolving doors of mental health institutions every few months.

The street was roped off. There were cop cars, an ambulance, a group of crowd extras, and some folks who had just shown up to see what was going on, only to find out that they were going to be in a movie! That and the tented cafeteria filled with coffee, tea, donuts, and sandwiches kept them happy.

The weather was cooperating—a clear, star-filled sky, and no wind at all. A fire engine was parked behind the ropes, at the ready to hose down the street so that it looked Vaselineshiny on film. There was a commotion as McQueen came out of the hotel's front entrance.

I caught his eye and he gave me one of his squints, and a thumb's up.

I wandered around until I spotted Russ Cortig. He was wearing an orange fluorescent vest and had a pair of over-the-ear headphones with a small microphone positioned in front of his chin. He was checking out a spaghetti nest of electrical cables connected to lights, reflectors, and generators.

"Has Nika shown up?" I asked.

"Not yet." He gave a long sigh. "I don't know if I'll be able to see much of her. We're running behind schedule. We'll probably be here until six in the morning."

"You see her or that Russian, you tell me right away, okay? I'm going to stick close."

And that's what I did. For more than two hours, as the slow, painstaking process of working all night to get a couple of minutes of film in the can took place.

I was on my second cup of coffee when I spotted Nika talking to Russ Cortig.

It had to be Nika. The girl was young, beautiful, and bore a good resemblance to the sketch I'm made from Cortig's description.

She was wearing faded jeans stuffed into knee-high suede boots and a tight fitting suede jacket with laces across the bosom. Her blonde hair was tied back in a ponytail.

Cortig was making apologizing gestures with his hands.

Nika pushed her lips out in a pout. I moved in close enough to hear her say, "You said you'd introduce me to Steve."

She had a slight accent, but I couldn't pin it down as being Russian.

"I will," Cortig said. "It's just that we're having trouble with the lighting. Can you stick around for a couple of hours?"

"Hours?" she said.

A slim brunette wrapped up in a Burberry trench coat, the belt dangling from its loops, and opened just enough to show the distinctive plaid lining, approached them and said something in what I guessed was Russian. She was attractive, in her twenties or early-thirties, with short straight hair. Polina? The woman Cortig had seen with Nika at the Haight-Ashbury party? The two of them got into an argument, the brunette rolling back the sleeve of her coat and pointing at her wrist watch.

Cortig stood by helplessly, then pushed the headphones closer to his ear and said, "Right away, Steve."

He gave Nika a feeble wave. "Call me, later. I promise I'll get you to meet McQueen."

Nika tapped her right boot on the street for a few seconds, then whirled around and stalked off, the brunette at her heels. They walked a full block before stopping in front of a two-tone, cream-and-dark-chocolate colored sedan with the distinctive Rolls Royce Flying Lady hood ornament sitting atop the car's massive grill.

The driver slid out from behind the wheel. He was a big man—big all over. Head, shoulders—six feet plus of meat and muscle decked out in a leather coat with sheepskin lining. He had dark, oily hair brushed back without a part and a Zapata mustache that curled around his lips and reached his jaw.

He moved around and opened the door for Nika and her companion, and then his eyes swept the street. I was partially hidden by a parked ten-wheel dump truck, but I got the feeling that he'd spotted me.

My car was too far away to get back to and give chase, but it didn't matter. I had the Roll's license plate number: EGB826.

When I got back to the unmarked I radioed the Rolls Royce license number in to Communications. It must have been a slow night, I received the information in less than two minutes. The Rolls was registered to a Dimitri Vanel at 68 Westbury, Hillsborough, California. Hillsborough was an enclave for the ultra-rich some fifteen miles south of San Francisco.

The Vanel name rang a slight bell, but I couldn't quite place it. But I knew someone who would probably know a great deal about Mr. Vanel.

Bright and early that morning I called Alex Zek. Lidiya, his sexy secretary, told me he was going fishing. "On his boat. You know where it is? He wants to see you."

"Call him and tell him I'll be there in twenty minutes."

Zek kept an eighty-two-foot converted tugboat tied up at the wharf of an abandoned shipyard by Pier 70.

I pulled up behind Zek's car, a shiny black Cadillac hearse. The Swine was many things—but subtle he was not.

Zek had named the boat *Krùto,* which literally translated to sharp, but in common Russian slang meant cool, awesome, kickass.

The *Krùto's* white-and-red trim painting was faded and chipped. It had a string of old tires for bumpers and the rounded rear deck was rusted and stained. It had a big galley, and, according to Zek, a large bedroom that "Sleeps four, fucks eight." While it looked bulky and awkward, Zek had installed powerful twin diesel engines that gave it a lot of pep.

I paused before jumping on board. There were two nervous stub-horned goats tethered to the rear gunwale. Alongside them was a pair of large plastic containers.

Zek strolled out of the cabin door, a wide grin on his wide face. He was wearing a dark heavy wool shirt and a red knit watch cap.

"Come aboard, Johnny O. I making us breakfast."

"What's with the goats?" I asked.

"They're bait, for the fishing."

"What the hell are you fishing for?"

"Sharks. Out by the Farralone's."

The Farralone Islands were a group of desolate, rocky islands thirty miles west of the Golden Gate Bridge populated by colonies of seals and sea lions. The seals attracted all kinds of sharks, including great whites.

The goats backed away when I approached. I nudged one of the plastic containers with my foot. It was filled with chunks of dark, bloody meat.

"Anyone I know in there, Alex?"

"Hah. Funny man. Is chum. My butcher supplies me with cow and pig meat—their heads, guts, and blood. The sharks love it."

"So what do you do? Try and catch the sharks?"

"Catch? No. I shoot them. The small ones first, who get eaten by the bigger ones. Those I shoot too. There is blood everywhere. That when the great whites show up." He nestled an imaginary rifle to his shoulder and pulled the trigger. "Boom. Bye-bye shark."

Besides being cruel and inhumane, this also sounded illegal. "Why? What are you getting out of this?"

Zek spread his arms wide. "I'm a sportsman, like your famous writer, Hemingway."

I followed him to the galley, a messy affair with a restaurant style stainless steel stove and refrigerator. He was frying *weslena* on the stove: thick veal and pork stuffed sausages the size of my old nightstick.

"Good to see you, Johnny O. Have a seat. Put mustard on bread, please."

The table had been set with plates, knives, forks, a basket of bread slices, three jars of mustard, and two opened bottles of *Spaten*, a strong German beer.

There was also a Luger pistol and a short-barreled side-by-side double barrel shotgun with a gleaming walnut stock.

"Have you got licenses for all of these damn guns of yours, Alex?"

Zek tore off his cap and sent it sailing across the room. "Of course. I am a collector."

"Lidiya said you wanted to see me."

Zek laid the hot frying pan on the table. "Maybe I have good news for you. I showed picture you gave me of the man you call Boris to people I know. He is Russian. And he was KGB. Works private now, for important man in Moscow."

"Which important man?"

"High ranking Russian official who has business on side." Zek rubbed his thumb and forefinger together. "Big money business. You know what I mean?"

"Mafia?"

"*Russkaya Mafiya, Bratva, Gazprom,* there are dozens of names, but this man, he is *zapoldo*, someone who is well connected politically but deals in shady business." Zek gave a wide grin. "Is still Cold War, but lots of people making lots of hot money."

"What's his name, Alex?"

"It would do you no good to know. He is in St. Petersburg one day, Moscow the next. Has houses all over, never sleeps in same house two days together and never come to America. When he needs something done here, he sends people like Boris."

Zek settled into a chair, picked up a beer and said, "Eat. Is good."

I was tired of sparring with Zek, and all of that talk about killing sharks had ruined my appetite.

"I need names. For this important Russian thug, and for Boris. I tell you what, you give me their names and I'll give you one that you'll find interesting."

"You making game with me? Fooling me?"

"No."

He sawed off a chunk of the sausage and chewed it slowly, and then his voice dropped down a level or two. He picked up a fork and pointed the tongs at me. "You my good friend,

Johnny O, but this is business. You go first."

Zek was not the kind of guy you let push you around, because once he started, he'd never stop. The secret to keeping any informant in line was to make sure that he was afraid of you. Even better was to have him think you were a little bit crazy.

I stood up and moved toward him. "Fuck you, Zek. I'm not one of your flunkies."

They say timing is everything. If so, I had picked the wrong time to challenge Zek. Viktor, his giant bodyguard bumped his way into the galley. There were two long-barreled rifles hanging from their straps draped around his left shoulder, and monster of a revolver, the biggest one I'd ever seen, in his monster of a right hand.

"Viktor," I shouted. "Are you left handed or right handed?"

He stared at me as if I was crazy.

"Me? Right handed. Why you—"

"Because after I take that gun out of your hand, I'm going to break one of your arms, and since I'm a nice guy, I'll pick the left arm, that way you can still wipe your butt."

Viktor's face went through a range of emotions: puzzlement, disbelief, and finally anger.

He was raising the barrel of the revolver in my direction when Zek said, "Viktor, my friend is just teasing you. Go feed the goats. Keep them happy." He turned his attention back to me.

"Sit back down, please. I forgot you have such a temper. Relax. We talk."

I took a notepad and pen from my jacket pocket. "Names, Alex. Who are these guys?"

He put his hand in front of his mouth to cover a loud belch. "Important man is Arkadi Kusmenko." He spelled it out slowly. "Very powerful, very rich. Now, Boris man you want, he was KGB. Now he works for Kusmenko."

"So you know him."

"I knew him long ago. When he was young boy, had spiked hair and pimples. That's why I didn't recognize picture right away. He used last name Jakov back then, but could be anything now. They change names more often then they change underwear." Zek leaned his elbows onto the table and stared into my eyes. "Boris very bad man, Johnny O. You see him, you be careful, okay?"

"I will. Now here's a name for you. Dimitri Vanel."

Zek went back to work on his sausage, taking his time. He swilled some beer around in his mouth and swallowed. "How you come to know this man?"

"I don't know him. Yet. But somehow Boris is involved with him."

"Involved!" Zek let out a belly rumbling laugh. "Vanel's real name is Vanelnikov. He's Russian. Very rich, very powerful businessman, with big friends in politics, Central Committee, everywhere."

"He's living in Hillsborough" I said. "What's the connection between Vanel and Arkadi Kusmenko?"

"They were once friends and business partners—drink vodka from same bottle, sleep with same women. Make fortunes smuggling drugs, alcohol, Western jeans, books, movies, whores, weapons. Then something happened—I don't know what, but they become rivals, hate each other. Each has a gang, and there are killings on both sides. Vanel move to France takes family with him. He always spent much time in France. Sister live there. Now he pretends that he *is* French. Changes name to Vanel, buys big house in Paris, place for skiing in the French Alps, buys yacht so he can keep it in the marina at St. Tropez on the Riviera and throw fancy parties."

"That takes a lot of money," I said.

"Vanel left Russia, but he didn't stop being in business; he still had connections in Moscow, and he did business with French Mafia—same shit as in Moscow: drugs, whores, stolen paintings, statues. Vanel had many good friends at the Hermitage Museum in St. Petersburg. You know Hermitage?"

Zek held his arms out as far as they could go. "Huge museum, many buildings. Paintings, sculpture, old Egyptian stuff, masterpieces. Makes your museums here look like shit. But the best part of the Hermitage is where no one goes—the basements! Locked rooms, vaults, caves, crates still sealed with stuff we took from the Nazis, from Napoleon. From everywhere. Only the chosen few get down to the basements, and they never leave with empty hands. Vanel has very big hands, and I'm told that he spent a lot of time in the basements. Who knows what the shithead took for himself before he fled Russia."

"Why did he leave France?"

"Peoples say he made enemies with local gangsters. Stole things from wrong people. So, he moved to England for short time and then he comes to United States, like me. Becomes American. Rich fucking American. Not easy be rich, Johnny O. Especially stay rich. I humble man, have good working boat, live in my building, nice kitchen, big bedroom."

Zek gave me a big lewd smile. "Lidiya, she clean bedroom, kitchen, Viktor, he help too. But Vanel, he has rich man's problems. Has big, big house. Needs maid, cook, gardener, bloodthirsty dogs for security, and bodyguard. Sure he has paintings, statues, worth lots of money, but he has to pay insurance for them. Very expensive insurance is. Has private jet plane. What fuck you think that costs? Then he has his boat. Too big a boat. He needs crew, cook, captain. Especially captain. Vanel would sink Titanic in Caribbean. All that adds up to much money. Money going out, not so much money coming in for Dimitri anymore. I thinking he have to sell something: some of his paintings. Maybe they get stolen. Insurance pays maybe."

My appetite was coming back. I coated a sausage with mustard and took a bite, while keeping a sharp eye on Zek.

"Would Vanel know Boris? Recognize him from the photo?"

"Could be he knew him back in Moscow. Recognize from picture? Maybe, maybe not."

"Is Vanel married, Alex?"

"Several times. Marries beautiful women, then dumps them when they start showing wrinkles. Latest one is very beautiful, and expensive to keep."

"What about children?"

"A son, Georgi, who died in Paris, from drugs. And a daughter, Nika, young, teenager."

"Tell me about Nika,"

"They say she hates father, blames him for what happened to brother and her mother. Mother killed herself after Vanel dumped her. Rumors say that Vanel mistreats daughter, maybe in bad ways. Why you so interested, Johnny O?"

"Because Boris is interested in Nika. And I'm definitely interested in Boris. He murdered the transvestite I told you about."

"Very bad for man like Boris to be associated with a *pèdik*, a homosexual. He would kill to keep people from knowing he was having sex that way."

"So why does Arkadi Kusmenko send Boris after Vanel? It must be something special for him to send him all the way to San Francisco."

"Could be anything; painting, statues, jewels." He wiped his mouth with the sleeve of his shirt. "Jewel, I think. There are rumors that Vanel has the Stalin Blue."

"What's the Stalin Blue?"

Zek's eyebrows rose toward his hairline. "You don't know? Is very large diamond. Is called the Stalin Blue in Russia. Was a present to Stalin from a Ukrainian businessman. He gives Stalin diamond, Stalin gives him a few more months to breathe fresh air. Many peoples would like to have it, including me."

"How valuable is the diamond?" I asked.

"Millions, but more than money in Russia. Is like owning England Queen's jewels, or Mona Lisa, first American flag. You be like rock star in Russia."

"Who actually owns the thing?"

"*Who* is right. Who knows? Who cares? Whoever has it in his hands owns it. Peoples have short memories. Stalin now very popular in Russia. All his sins have been forgiven. Dig up his bones, put a hat on his skull and he became top dog, Chairman of the Presidium. You tired of being policeman, Johnny? Tell me how I get my hands on the Stalin Blue and I make you very rich."

"What would you do with the diamond, Alex?"

"Give it to Arkadi Kusmenko."

"Give it?"

He gave me what for him was a shy smile. "Man like Kusmenko, you make more money and favors by giving him presents, not selling him things."

The boat's twin diesels rumbled into action.

I bounced a few more questions off Zek, and made sure I had all the names spelled correctly.

As I was leaving, Zek threw me a zinger. "I hear that there is a Chinaman not happy with you. Something to do with his father and your father. Is dangerous place, Chinatown. Be sure to bring gun if you go there, or a big dog."

I stopped as I walked back to the car and watched as the *Krùto's* propeller churned up a batch of oily, greenish-brown mud from the bottom of the bay as it took off on Alex's fishing trip. The poor, doomed goats started making loud baaaaahhhh noises, and one of the chum containers slid across the deck and crashed against a bulkhead.

As I climbed into the car I thought about how the Farralone Islands would make a perfect spot for someone like Zek to dispose of a human body—especially one drenched in chum.

\* \* \*

I used a phone booth by the Doggie Diner on 3<sup>rd</sup> Street to check in at the Hall. One call, from Myra Favre.

"Boris attacked another young girl, or transvestite I should say. She's with me now, a helpless child by the name of Aaron Walker who uses the name Wanda. I don't know how long I can keep her, so I suggest you come soon."

"I'm on my way."

In less than ten minutes I was back sitting in Favre's parlor again. She poured us both a glass of Port with a steady hand.

"Which name should I use?" I asked. "Aaron or Wanda?"

"Wanda would be best." She tapped her fingers lightly on my knee. "You will be gentle with her, won't you?"

Wanda, aka Aaron Walker, was a little over five feet tall. Her face was very pale. She had red-rimmed cornflower blue eyes and there was a small bulb at the end of her nose. Her hair was the color of peeled carrots.

She came into the room with slow, smooth movements, as if she was walking on water.

She was wearing a smoke-colored cotton robe which she held together with both of her hands. Her pasty ankles were wrapped with bruises. She looked like she was sixteen. An old sixteen.

"This is a friend, Wanda, Mr. O'Rourke." Myra Favre said. "He's here to help you. Don't be afraid."

That was a nice touch, "Mister" not Inspector. "Hello," I said, keeping my voice low and soft, as if I was talking to a small child, which, in a way I was.

"When did you meet the man who hurt you, Wanda?"

Favre stepped in. "On Tuesday, two nights ago, around midnight, isn't that what you told me, Wanda?"

"That's right, a little before midnight."

Favre and I stared at each other. If Wanda was telling the truth, than Boris had picked her up just hours after killing Vanessa.

"Can I show you a few photographs, Wanda?"

Her posture stiffened and she turned toward Favre.

"It's all right, dear. They're just pictures. Sit down and relax."

She sat, but didn't relax. She was in constant motion, fluffing her hair, scratching her nose, pulling at an earlobe, rubbing the scabbed needles marks on her arms.

Wanda flinched when she saw Boris's picture.

"That's him," she whispered.

"Did he tell you his name, Wanda?"

"Boris. He told me his name was Boris." There was a little stammer in her voice, and she bit down on her lower lip when she finished speaking.

"Did he have a gun?"

"Yes. It was in a holster and it made a noise when it hit the floor after he took his pants off."

"How about a knife?"

"I didn't see one. He...he just hit me."

"What about tattoos?"

"Oh, yes. Ugly ones on his arms and chest."

"Just where were you when you met him?"

"At the corner of Polk and Bush Streets, by the liquor store. It's just a block from my apartment."

That area of Polk Street was a prime location for restaurants and a slew of gay bars of all persuasions.

"Was Boris alone?" I asked.

"He was talking to a girl. At first I thought that she might have been working the streets, like me. But she was too well dressed for that; she was wearing one of those raincoats you see in the movies." Her hands moved to circle her waist. "With a belt."

"A trench coat."

"Yes. I think they were talking Russian."

"Why do you say that?"

"Oh, he ... he told me he was Russian. He told me to do things to him, in English, then he'd say it in Russian, and...like translate, 'That's what we tell whores to do in Moscow.'"

"And that's how he talked to this girl?"

"Yes. They talked loud. She seemed angry."

"What did she look like?"

"Just pretty, dark hair."

"Would you recognize her if I had her picture?"

Wanda shuddered and drew her robe tightly around her body. "I, I don't think so. I wasn't paying that much attention to her. I wasn't feeling very good." She turned to Favre. "Can I go now?"

"Yes, dear. Go to your room and finish packing."

The expensive trench coat. Polina had been wearing a Burberry when I'd seen her with Nika at the film site on the Embarcadero.

"Was that helpful?" Favre asked, sliding down onto the couch and reaching for her glass of Port.

"Yes. Thanks."

"I'm putting Wanda on a bus for Des Moines tonight."

"Do you think she'll get there?"

"I hope so. You can only do so much for these poor darlings. Imagine, being born a boy and wanting to be a girl. The things they go through. Some of them are so self-destructive."

She upended the port glass and smacked her lips. "I should talk. God, it's lucky she wasn't murdered, like Vanessa. He must be a cold-blooded son of a bitch."

Cold-blooded indeed. According to Garant, Vanessa was killed sometime between four and ten o'clock. Then Boris drives back to San Francisco and picks up Wanda and runs her through the wringer. Was he drunk? Or celebrating his kill? Why kill Vanessa and not Wanda? Because Vanessa was tough, a fighter? Wanda was weak, defenseless.

Myra Favre shoulders gave a quick little jerk, as if she'd gotten a chill. She reached out for the port bottle, and then quickly put it down.

"God, this can be an awful world at times. Would you care for a real drink, Inspector?"

# CHAPTER 19

There were three messages waiting for me on my desk at the Hall of Justice: the first, a call from Dr. Hester, aka FBI agent Charles Ledegue, asking for a meeting at noon. The place, the archery gallery in Golden Gate Park. "I'll bring sandwiches. If you can't make it, leave a message at my office."

The second note was regarding a call from Lieutenant Bogus Bob McCard of the Intelligence Detail. "How much more of the French cognac is available?" Meaning that he had some information for me, but that it would be costly.

The third message came from Alan Rickeby, Steve McQueen's production manager.

I called him first.

"Nothing important, Johnny," Rickeby said when we were connected. "Steve's got something for you. He appreciated what you did for Russ Cortig. Stop by, if I'm not here, my secretary can give it to you."

I thanked Rickeby, hung up and then leaned back in my chair and tried to imagine just how appreciative McQueen would be. For all of the Hollywood Superstar hoopla that surrounded him, he seemed to be a streetwise guy who knew how to play the game—you scratch my back, I'll scratch yours.

I checked my watch, a battle-scarred Timex. It was close to eleven o'clock, not leaving much time to see McCard before meeting with FBI agent Ledegue.

I made a quick call to the hospital. Pop was "asleep and doing well," according to the on duty nurse.

Like a kid who couldn't wait to open Santa's presents, I

stopped by Steve McQueen's place on Leavenworth Street. It was empty except for a woman with shoulder length dark hair who was busy pounding away on a typewriter. She had a pencil clamped between her teeth.

When I identified myself, she removed the pencil long enough to say, "The box on Mr. Rickeby's desk is for you," then returned the pencil and went back to work.

It was a small, neatly wrapped box, and I waited until I was back in the car to open it. A watch, made by a Swiss company I hadn't heard of—TAG Heuer.

It was a blue-faced Monaco chronograph. On the back was the inscription: For Johnny O—Steve McQueen.

The instructions in the box were slightly less complicated than those needed to construct an atomic bomb, but I finally got it set as to date and time, and then strapped the leather band to my wrist. A little gaudy, but nice.

I wore it for several years and thought of it as my "mistletoe watch." Shy, demurring young ladies would see the inscription and suddenly become quite kissable. Then somehow it just disappeared, which was a shame. They had recently auctioned off the tweed sport coat McQueen wore in *Bullitt* for seven hundred and twenty grand. What the hell would the watch be worth?


*Thwwwock* ! The arrow hit the center of the red bullseye target set in a bale of hay and burrowed into the wooden backing. The archer was a tall strapping man, dressed in saggy jeans and a leather vest that showed off his hairy chest and arms.

He took another arrow from the quiver hanging across his back, slotted it into a bow as long as he was tall, took aim, let it go and again hit the bullseye with tremendous force.

Saggy Jeans was one of the dozen or more archers taking advantage of the range, which was nothing more than a broad open meadow rimmed by wind-sculpted cypress trees at the far western edge of the park off of Fulton Avenue.

The other wannabe Robin Hoods were mostly young men dressed in casual clothes whose shots not only missed the bullseye, they didn't even reach the bale of hay.

FBI agent Charles Ledegue shook the paper bag he was holding in his right hand at me. "Egg salad on white bread and Cokes. There's a bench over there. Let's eat."

After spreading a paper napkin across his lap, Ledegue said, "I've put out a BOLO on Boris and checked with a number of brick agents who are working on the Russian problem, but so far nothing has turned up on him."

BOLO was slang for "be on the lookout for" and brick agents were the ones who worked the streets.

"That's too bad, Charlie." I pried the top piece of my sandwich up to find a lineup of sweet pickles covering a thin spread of egg salad. The sandwiches were as big a disappointment as the news he'd brought.

"Something may turn up, Johnny. You have to be patient. Russian agents can be quite devious."

"Deadly too. Boris murdered a man in Sausalito."

"Murdered? You're sure?"

"I'd bet a lot of money on it."

"Who? And why?"

"The transgendered person he beat up on a couple of days ago. Boris apparently followed the guy to his house in Sausalito, found him sitting alone in his hot tub and broke his neck. Someone told me that the comrades in the Kremlin don't think kindly of KGB agents who like to sodomize homosexuals."

Ledegue brushed some bread crumbs from his lap. "Why do you say Boris was KGB? Do you have any proof of that?"

I decided not to mention the last name Alex Zek had provided for Boris, Jakov. The more I thought about it, the phonier the name sounded—so close to "jack off." Zek would think that was a wonderful joke.

And if Ledegue and his FBI buddies hadn't already identified a KGB agent from the photograph I'd provided, they were in worse shape than I figured.

"An in-the-know source told me," I said.

That caught his interest. "Who is this source? Can he be trusted?"

The thought of trusting the Swine made me smile. "He definitely can't be trusted, Charlie, and he wouldn't want me passing his name to the FBI." I decided to throw him a curve. "What do you know about a Russian Mafia boss by the name of Arkadi Kusmenko?"

Ledegue coughed up some of his sandwich onto the napkin. "Kusmenko? How did you come up with that name?"

"My source, Charlie. He thinks that Boris was sent here by Kusmenko to pick up a piece of jewelry. The Stalin Blue."

"The Stalin Blue what?"

The trouble with dealing with Ledegue was that you never knew if he was playing dumb, or if he was just plain dumb.

"A large diamond that once belonged to Joseph Stalin."

"Who has it now?"

"Apparently that's what Boris is trying to find out. It could be a guy by the name of Dimitri Vanel, aka Vanelnikov. What can you tell me about him?"

Charlie chewed that over, literally, along with his sandwich. When his mouth was empty he said, "Vanel. A former colleague of Kusmenko. I know he is indeed very wealthy. Apparently the money came from dubious enterprises in Russia."

"Charlie, I hate it when you call me stupid."

Ledegue gave me a quick, probing look. "What do you mean?"

"Are you trying to tell me that the FBI knows next to nothing about a man like Vanel, a former heavy-duty Russian mobster, a rival to Arkadi Kusmenko? Apparently the two men hate each other."

"I've heard that Vanel had some dealings with the *unione corse*. You know of them, I suppose. French Mafia. Some say they're more vicious than the Sicilians. During World War II they helped the French Resistance, and they've acted as strikebreakers when there were problems on the waterfronts, which put them in good standing with many high ranking French politicians, who in turn have suggested that the police take it easy on the *unione*. They're a rough bunch—white collar crime, contract killings, money laundering, extortion, armed robberies, casinos, hotel nightclubs, political corrupttion, kidnapping young Russian girls for prostitution, and of course drugs. Their headquarters are in Marseilles. That's where they refine the drugs before shipping then to America. New York City is their favorite port of entry."

Charlie reeled all of that off calmly, emotionlessly, as if he was reading off someone's laundry list, but it still didn't tell me much about Vanel.

"What was Vanel's connection to them?" I asked.

"I can't say for sure. Could be anything, but I would imagine that fine-art theft and forgeries would be a possibility. There's no link between Vanel and any espionage efforts on behalf of Russia or anyone else that I'm aware of. I did hear that Vanel was in close contact with our State Department prior to his coming here. What he told them, or gave them, I don't know; though I certainly wish I did."

"His daughter, Nika, has a crush on Steve McQueen."

"What the hell has that got to do with anything?"

"I'm working with McQueen while he's filming a movie here in town." I rolled up the mostly untouched sandwich and tossed it into a park wastebasket. I stood up and stretched my arms over my head. "Thanks for lunch, Charlie. Was there anything else you wanted to talk about?"

"I suggest that you ask your contracts in the Intelligence

Unit about Boris. We know they keep an eye on the Russian Embassy. I've always been of the opinion that if the Unit and the FBI could work on a closer basis, we would be doing the country a great service."

I tried to keep the disgust from showing on my face. Charlie had tried to bribe me to get him access to the Unit's files by buying me a lousy egg salad sandwich. I'd been known to bribe easily, but not that easy.

"The Unit's a strange outfit, Charlie, but thanks for the suggestion."

Ledegue gave me a parting piece of advice. "I wouldn't waste a great deal of time on tying Boris to that murder. If he really is KGB, he'll go underground, and if you press the case the Embassy will cloak him in diplomatic immunity and hustle him out of the country."

"I don't want him out of the country, but I'd like to see him under ground."

Charlie looked puzzled, but I didn't bother to explain the difference between underground and under ground.

"This was taken Monday, at eleven-fifteen in the morning, Johnny. That's your man, isn't it?" Bogus Bob McCard asked, pointing to the flickering 16 mm images of two men sitting inside the Cinderella Russian Bakery on Balboa Street.

We were in McCard's rat trap of an office. One of the men in the film was indeed Boris. He was drinking coffee and eating a pastry. The other man was wearing a gray homburg hat.

"The guy on the right is my man Boris," I said. "Jakov is supposedly his last name. He's KGB, or ex-KGB, and he could be working for a Russian Mafia thug by the name of Arkadi Kusmenko."

"Kusmenko is a super heavyweight in the Russian Mafia. What's Boris Jakov doing for him in San Francisco?"

"That's what I'm trying to find out. Who's the guy with Boris?"

"Erik Gromov," McCard said, as if it was an important name I should recognize. "Officially he's the Assistant Consul General of the Russian Embassy in San Francisco. Unofficially he's the numero uno KGB officer in all of California. Here, I'll give you a better look."

McCard stepped over a box filled with camera lenses to get to the movie projector, clicked a few buttons and the screen fast forwarded to the two men finishing their coffee and walking out to Balboa Street.

McCard hit the freeze button as both men stood on the curb directly facing the camera.

"My guys were in a PG&E truck, Johnny. The Russians never suspected a thing."

Boris was dressed in a well-cut gray suit, a white spread collar shirt and a black knit tie. Even though the quality of the film wasn't the best, I could see that his shoes were buffed to a polished sheen.

Erik Gromov appeared to be in his mid-fifties. He had fleshy jowls and large bags under his eyes. His neck swelled over his shirt collar. He was dressed in an undertaker's style black suit.

Gromov was doing all of the talking, occasionally pushing an index finger into Boris's shoulder to get a point across.

For his part, Boris just stood there in a relaxed pose, his eyes wandering around the street.

McCard stopped the film. "We couldn't pick up the conversation, but Gromov doesn't wander off the Embassy reservation unless it's important. My guys got lucky; spotted his homburg hat getting into a limo and followed it. A lot of the Russians make stops at the Cinderella Bakery. They love the poppy seed rolls." McCard patted his stomach. "They're not bad."

He started the film again. The two Russians shook hands,

then Gromov waved his arm in the air and moments later a black Lincoln stretch limousine, the same model the Secret Service used to drive the president around, purred to the curb.

Boris opened the car's back door for Gromov and then slammed it shut. Then the screen went blank and McCard started to negotiate.

"Well, Johnny O, what did you think of all of that?"

"It was interesting, Bob, but it doesn't tell me much."

McCard rolled up the shades to unveil a view of the traffic on the freeway. "That was very good cognac, Johnny."

I knew that McCard was too good a cop to just let Boris slip away. Either there was more film of him, or he'd been followed after the meeting with Gromov.

"I've got more of the cognac and some choice Cuban cigars, but I have to know where Boris went after this meeting, Bob."

"He walked around the block and got into a white four-door Chevrolet Impala, license plate number JJZ108. He turned right on Geary Boulevard, heading toward downtown and pulled into the parking lot at the Jack Tar Hotel, Johnny."

The Jack Tar was a four-hundred-room hotel that was probably the most hated building in the city at the time. A badly flawed attempt at Mondrian-style modernism with pink and turquoise paneling, it looked more like a hospital than a hotel.

"Did your man see where Boris went once he was inside the hotel?"

McCard wagged his head from side to side. "No. He parked, and then disappeared. My guys were interested in him, but he wasn't a priority. They staked the Chevy out for a couple of hours, then made passing calls. It was still parked in the garage around midnight and at eight the following morning. Then we got busy with other stuff and forgot about him. I'll tell you one thing, Johnny, you won't find Boris living at the Russian Embassy. We keep a good watch on the place, and none of my guys had spotted him before or after his meeting with Gromov at the coffee shop."

I was tempted to ask McCard if the Unit knew of Dimitri Vanel, the wealthy Russian who lived in Hillsborough, but decided to hold off on that. With McCard, it was better to feed him information one bite at a time.

"How does six bottles of that cognac and a full box of Cuban cigars sound to you, Bob?"

"That sounds about just right, Johnny O." He rummaged around his desk and came up with a DMV printout. "I ran the JJZ108 plate. The car is registered to RTLK Holding, 1750 Vine Street, Los Angeles. I checked out the address—it's one of those private postal box things. There's no such business as RTLK Holding listed in directories, the L.A. Chamber of Commerce, or in state business filings. In other words, it's a dead end."

# CHAPTER 20

I parked in the underground garage of the Jack Tar Hotel and walked around, hoping that I'd get lucky and find the Chevrolet Boris had been driving. No such luck.

I headed for the lobby, which was only slightly less gaudy then the hotel's exterior.

There was a happy hour crowd of middle-aged conventioneers with plastic name tags hanging from cords around their necks and a mix of younger tourists enjoying themselves. Cocktail waitresses dressed in mini-skirt French maid outfits teetered on high heels as they delivered drinks. A half-dozen or more working girls made goo-goo eyes at the convention crowd.

I recognized one of the hookers from my days in the Burglary Detail. Her apartment had been broken into and trashed by a disgruntled client.

Sandy Marmalee was a sultry, well-spoken woman in the prime of her early-thirties with copper-colored hair who worked as a secretary, and, when the bills piled up, as an escort.

Marmalee caught my eye and frowned. She was wearing a tangerine-colored sleeveless sheath dress that showed off her figure.

I strolled over to say hi. "Don't worry, Sandy. I'm not here to interfere with your pursuit of free trade. Tell me, do you come here often?"

Her eyebrows cocked into a questioning arc. "What?"

"I'm serious." I steered her over to a bright blue lobby couch. "I'm looking for a man, Sandy. He's Russian. Boris is the name he uses. A car he was seen driving was parked in the hotel's garage yesterday." I took one of Boris's photos from my jacket pocket along with one of my business cards and handed them to her.

Her head swiveled back and forth before she accepted them.

"I'm waiting for a gentleman, Inspector. He should be here any minute."

"Boris is a bad dude, kid. He likes rough sex. Killed a transvestite who worked at Finocchio's."

She studied the photo closely, and then held it out to me.

"Never saw him before. I'm sure of it."

"Keep the photo," I said. "You might warn your friends about Boris, and if you do see him, call me right away, okay?"

Her back straightened and she rose to her feet. "Here comes my date. I've got to go."

"One more thing. Who's the house dick here?"

"A cowboy by the name of Joel Pardee. The jerk takes twenty percent, and then expects a freebee."

A balding man in his sixties in a pinstriped suit greeted Sandy with a discrete handshake and a nervous smile.

She slipped her hand under his arm and whispered something in his ear as they headed toward the exit.

A bellboy told me that Joel Pardee could be found in the hotel's security office, which was located in the basement.

The Jack Tar was one of the few hotels in town that I didn't know much about. I found Pardee's office next to the laundry room. The smell of strong detergent soap made me pinch my nostrils. I opened the door without knocking and caught a tall man crowding a young girl wearing a French maid's outfit against a wall.

He jerked his head around and shouted, "Get the fuck out of here."

"Are you Joel Pardee?" I asked calmly.

"Get out!"

The girl took the opportunity to duck out of harm's way and head for the door.

"I'll talk to you later, Nancy," Pardee threatened.

He had a slow juicy southern drawl. He turned his eyes on me. He was a slim guy wearing a tan western-style shirt with pearl snaps instead of buttons and a brown string tie. His face was lean and leathery. He had shaggy, mud-colored hair. He moved toward me as if he intended to throw me out the door.

Up close I could smell booze on his breath. He was maybe six-three and at least a couple of those inches came from the high-heeled cowboy boots he was wearing. He was wearing a belt with a silver horse-head buckle, and the butt end of a pearl-handled Derringer pistol peeked out from above his waist line.

"Listen, buddy. You ever come walking into my office without—"

"SFPD, Joel." I showed him my badge.

He sneered and tugged a seven-pointed metal shield from his pants pocket that was stamped Harris County Sheriff Deputy. "That's Texas, buddy. Twelve hundred square miles, including the city of Houston."

"Well you ain't in Texas now, you're in my town, so sit down and let's talk."

Pardee hitched up his zipper, made a clicking sound with his teeth, leaned his backside against the desk and folded his arms across his chest. Cowboy body language for don't fuck with me.

I decided to fuck with him. "Tell me about that pearl-handled Derringer sticking out of your pants."

"Those are real ivory handles, partner. Only an El Paso pimp would have pearl handles on his gun."

"Have you got a permit for it?"

"Permit? I did twenty-plus years in the department. That should be permit enough."

A concealed weapon permit was nearly impossible to obtain in San Francisco. Not even judges, senators, congressmen, newspaper owners or well-heeled businessmen were granted permits.

"Not here, Joel. Take it out and put in away in your desk. And if I see you with it again, I'll bust you."

He pulled the little gun from his waist, yanked open a desk drawer, dropped the gun inside, and then slammed the draw shut.

A Texas temper tantrum.

"Joel, a white Chevrolet Impala, license plate JJX108, parked in the hotel garage Monday around noon, and stayed in place overnight. It's not in the garage now. I want to know who it belongs to, and if he's a guest here, I want his room number."

Pardee gave the back of his chair a spin, and then straddled it, as if he was climbing into a saddle. "You want a lot, buddy."

"It's Inspector O'Rorke, not buddy. The man I'm interested in is Russian." I dropped a photo of Boris onto the desk. At the rate I was giving out Boris's pictures, I'd have to have some more made up.

Pardee gave it a quick glance, and then said, "Never saw him before."

"He uses the name Boris. His last name could be Jakov. Study the picture, and then we'll go out and check with the hotel's employees and see if he's staying here."

Pardee leaned back in his chair and took a few deep breaths. His face softened. He was getting his confidence back.

"I'd really like to help you, but I can't go giving out information on hotel guests, lessen you've got a warrant. That's how we do it in Texas."

I put my palms on the desk and leaned in close to him. "I know you're running a string of whores, Joel, and that you're squeezing the girls for a cut of their hard earned labor."

I decided to twist the knife in his back a little deeper. "And there have been a number of complaints that you've been abusing the hotel staff."

Pardee started to push himself to his feet, and then thought better of it.

"We've known about your running whores for months, but we let it slide. Professional courtesy for a fellow lawman. But sliding time is over. You find me Boris's room number. Right now."

Pardee, with me at his side, went through the motions: he spoke to the check-in clerks, flashed Boris's photograph around, but the results were negative. There was no one with an obvious Russian name registered with the hotel and none of the guests had listed the Impala when they'd signed in. We tried the parking attendants, bartenders, and cocktail waitresses next. Same story. Boris was unknown.

Which seemed fine with Pardee.

"I did my best for you, Inspector. Maybe your guy just parked in our garage and went out to dinner or a show."

"I want you to keep an eye out for the Impala. I want to know when it comes into the garage again, and I want the driver held for me. I don't care if you have to rope him, hogtie him and brand him, but shove him in the trunk of the Impala until I get here."

"Sheeit, man. I haven't got the manpower to—"

"Use some of your security staff, or do it yourself, Joel. If I find out that Boris has been here and you let him get away, I tell your bosses what you've been up to. And be careful, the man carries a gun."

"What's he wanted for?"

"Homicide and sexual assault."

Pardee pawed at the hotel lobby's carpeting with the heel of his boot. "I do all this, and you get off my back?"

"Absolutely. And one more thing." I reached into my shirt pocket and took out the hotel's parking ticket. "Validate this for me."

Before going back to the unmarked, I exited the Jack Tar by the front entrance and strolled out to Van Ness Avenue.

Where are you Boris? I whispered to myself. And why the hell are you here, in my town? How well do you know the city? Have you been here before? Have you been here for weeks? Months?

Somehow that didn't feel right to me. Bob McCard's crew had never seen him near the Russian Embassy, and Gromov, the Russian KGB chief, didn't look like he was happy with Boris, though Boris had acted cool and unperturbed during the filmed meeting. Then there was the silenced pistol, Boris getting sloppy drunk, allowing his picture to be taken at Finocchio's, the assault and then the murder of Vanessa the Undresser, followed up by the attack on little Wanda. Smart KGB agents don't let those kinds of things happen.

As much as I hated to admit it, Joel Pardee might have been right. Boris could have parked his car in the hotel's garage because it was convenient to the many restaurants and bars that lined Van Ness and the cross streets, not to mention the many apartments and rundown flophouses located in a four block perimeter from where I was standing.

The Jack Tar Hotel was one block from Polk Street, where Boris had picked up Wanda. It would take more time and manpower than I had access to have the area checked out properly—it would take something like the FBI to do that, so I'd have to trust to luck, and hope that Boris returned to the garage and that Pardee or one of his employees would spot the bastard and call me. It was a longshot, but as my bookie knew only too well, I was a sucker for longshots.

# CHAPTER 21

I trekked back into the hotel and used a lobby payphone to check for messages. There were two: one from Russ Cortig, which came in at 4:07 p.m. I caught him at the Sheraton, and he informed me that the mysterious Nika Vanel had invited him to a party tonight on her father's yacht, the *Dégager,* which was docked at the St. Francis Yacht Club.

"I won't be able to make the party. We'll be busy shooting all night again."

"You don't sound too disappointed," I told Cortig.

"Inspector, do you have any idea how many chicks are pestering me to set up a meeting with McQueen? Nika's hot, but she's getting to be a pain in the butt."

The other call had been from Francie Stevens, just fifteen minutes earlier.

"I'm hungry," she said, when she answered the phone.

"Francie, I'm working on this—"

"I've got some information on the investigation regarding your father's involvement in the death of Willie Mar. We should get together. Dinner?"

"How'd you like to go to a big yacht party? Can you be ready in an hour?"

"That's not much time. What should I wear?"

"Something sexy that will get us past the dock guards. We're sort of crashing the party."


Francie was wearing a brandy-colored, off the shoulder dress with a ruffled skirt when I picked her up. She gave me a peck on the cheek before delivering the bad news.

"Roy Creely has found what he believes are Willie Mar's remains in a grave site in the Chinese cemetery," she said, as she checked her lipstick in the rearview mirror. "The remains are now at the San Mateo Coroner's office. The cemetery is in their jurisdiction. Creely had the backing of Henry Mar. Apparently Mar pulled some strings with the cemetery. Creely expects a positive ID on the body by tomorrow, and he's in the process of obtaining a warrant for your father's house. According to his secretary 'It's in the bag.' Now tell me again just why we're crashing this party?"

"The yacht belongs to a Russian by the name of Dimitri Vanel. He's a former heavy duty Russian gangster who moved to France, then to America. He's currently living in Hillsborough.

"Vanel has a young daughter, Nika. I think that a Russian Mafia thug killed a transvestite in Sausalito and that now he's after Vanel's daughter."

Francie smiled and touched an earring. "You're making all of this up, aren't you? We are actually invited to the party?"

"No and no." I dug yet another photograph of Boris Jakov from my coat pocket and showed it to Francie. "This is the suspect. He's dangerous, so if you see him, don't let him know you're interested."

"I'm definitely not interested in this—"

"First name probably Boris, last name is possibly Jakov."

She shook her head, sending her glossy flaxen-colored hair spinning in front of her eyes. "This better be a damn good party with some damn good food."

The St. Francis Yacht Club was a private club located on the city's north shore, near the Marina Green. The main building was a sprawling, two-story white stucco Spanish-style structure with a red tile roof. There were dozens of well-maintained yachts of all sizes and shapes bobbing in their moorings. The sky was a dark, sapphire blue, the bay waters calm as a lake. Huge oil tankers, ferryboats, a rugged Coast

Guard Cutter, and wing-like sailboats crisscrossed the calm sea. A cooling tongue of fog was sliding in under the Golden Gate Bridge and the Alcatraz Island lighthouse beam made a lazy circle. Snowy-white egrets scissored the evening air and sea lions barked for food from the restaurants on Fisherman's Wharf.

I cruised past the ten-foot cast-iron Rolex street clock in front of the club's entrance and noticed a queue down the end of the pier waiting to board a sharp-hulled ship with the name *Dégager* painted on its side. It was the biggest yacht I'd ever seen.

"There it is," I told Francie.

"Clever name for a boat, isn't it?"

I wasn't sure about that, but she was.

"It translates to free, or clear route. But you know the French; if you slur or growl a vowel, it could be something else."

The hull was painted dark brown, the two streamlined upper decks were a creamy white, which gave the ship a racy, elegant look—it seemed to be moving even when tied up to the dock. It suddenly dawned on me that Dimitri Vanel's yacht was painted the same colors as his Rolls Royce.

A rail-thin young man of medium height and trim build wearing a navy-style uniform was checking names on the guest list attached to a clipboard as he questioned a lanky, sandy-haired woman with a hard face and harder attitude.

I parked, killed the engine, and then scooted out in order to open the door for Francie.

I was trying to figure the best way to get past the security guard. Flashing the badge didn't seem like a good option. I thumbed through my wallet and found Alan Rickeby's business card. When we reached the front of the line I showed the guard the card. "I'm with Solar Productions. We're filming the new Steve McQueen movie. We may be using Mr. Vanel's yacht in several scenes."

The guard had a nameplate pinned to his chest. Misha. I was expecting a garbled Russia response, but Misha spoke perfect English.

His face lit up. "Steve McQueen. Cool. Welcome aboard."

There had to be at least a hundred guests crammed into the main cabin, as well as others who were outside leaning against the railings. They all seemed to be having a good time. The women were wearing elegant dresses, the men either dark suits or tuxedos. My brown wool sport coat and tan turtleneck sweater were a little out of place.

A pale-faced, red-haired man in a white dinner jacket was playing Gershwin tunes on a standup piano—ivory hands on ivory keys.

Francie nodded her head toward a buffet table groaning under the weight of racks of prime rib, stacks of lobsters, two large turkeys, and stainless steel trays filled with things that I couldn't identify.

"That's for me," she said.

"I'm going to mingle a bit. Save some lobster for me."

I nodded hellos to people I'd never met, and rubbed shoulders with a couple that I did know, or at least recognized—rock star impresario Bill Graham and billionaire patron of the arts Gordon Getty. There was a bevy of attractive, up-chinned women who were used to getting their pictures in the newspapers on opening night at the opera.

The walls were of smooth molded honey-maple. The low ceiling was covered in gold-colored mirror tiles.

Someone bumped into my shoulder and said, "Johnny O. I did not expect the Fixer to be here tonight."

It was Alex Zek, cocooned in a maroon-colored tuxedo. His black leather bow tie looked as if it could break off and fly away if he sneezed or coughed.

"Alex, you didn't tell me you and Dimitri Vanel were buddies."

"We're not," Zek said, backing away to allow a waiter

with a tray filled with hors d'oeuvres to pass by.

"Vanel and I have mutual business interests on occasion." His eyes wandered around the room. "And we both enjoy owning boats."

"This one is a little fancier than yours, Alex."

"My *Krùto* is a rough water boat, a working boat, Johnny. This is to show off and hold parties. He only take it out when water is smooth like glass."

The Swine had a point—the *Krùto* was used to pick up illegal cargo shipments of narcotics, liquor, and God knows what from freighters anchored out at sea. Vanel's was a floating palace.

Zek held up his wineglass, took a sip, swirled it around in his mouth, and then made a face that made me think he was going to spit the wine out on the floor.

"Domestic. Not even Napa Valley. I have some French Bordeaux that is fantastic. I send you a case."

"Don't bother, Alex. Tell me, is there a specific reason for this party?"

Zek pointed his glass to a woman talking to a stocky bald man wearing a black suit. "Beautiful, no?"

Actually, no. The woman was plump, had a wide, plain featured face and was wearing an egg-shell colored dress with a deep V cut in the front. She appeared to be in her mid-forties.

"I wouldn't call the lady beautiful, Alex."

"Not *her.*" Zek put the tips of the fingers on his right hand against his lips and made kissing sounds. "The jewel dangling from chain between her boobies is the Stalin Blue! Svetlana Allilyueva, in the flesh. Too much flesh, don't you think?"

The diamond didn't seem all that impressive from where we were standing, and it took me a few seconds to place the name. "Stalin's daughter?"

"Yes, the bloody bastard's daughter. She has defected to the United States, with the help of Vanel. He very smart—uses

Svetlana to show off the Stalin Blue. Most peoples here don't even notice it, but the right ones do."

"Who are the right ones, Alex?"

Zek thumbed his chest. "Me, Henry Mar. Ones who know the history between Vanel and Arkadi.

"Why Mar?"

"Mar's bosses in New York City, they want diamond too." He chuckled loudly. "They want the Blue, but they don't want to pay for it."

The man talking to Svetlana turned around and I got a good look at his face. He was bald, save for a horseshoe of short dark hair from ear to ear.

"Who's the guy talking to Svetlana, Alex?"

"Is honorable Erik Gromov, of Russian Embassy. Big joke. He KGB still."

I hadn't recognized Gromov without his hat. I'd been paying too much attention to Boris while watching Bob McCard's surveillance film. Gromov's suit jacket was weighted down by a cluster of ribbons and medals, those gaudy brass and silver types that communist nations pin on the chests of their military heroes.

"He and Boris were dunking poppy seed rolls in their coffee at a bakery on Balboa Street recently."

That got Zek's attention. "You sure? Was Gromov?"

"Positive. What did he get all the medals for?"

"Kissing Kremlin ass," Zek said. "Erik always a kiss ass when I know him in Moscow. See big man standing behind to Svetlana?"

I did indeed. The man with the Zapata mustache who picked up Nika in the Rolls Royce. His thick shoulders were stuffed into a leather bomber-style jacket which made him stand out from the pack.

"Name is Trower," Zek said. "Vanel's bodyguard. He here to keep close eye on diamond. Former British Commando who supposed to be very tough." Zek giggled like a teenager.

"Would be good to see him in fight with my Viktor, no? See who toughest. He can't speak Russian! Or French. So Vanel can say whatever he wants and dumb ex-solider doesn't know what he's talking about. I call him bad names in Russian and he just smile at me. Someone here you should talk to, Johnny. The Chinaman over by the piano."

It was Henry Mar, Willie Mar's son. He was bantamweight size. His hair was brushed very flat against the sides of his head. He was wearing a black Mandarin collar jacket and green-tinted aviator-style sunglasses.

Mar was talking to a lovely Asian woman wrapped in a form-fitting red sleeveless dress. Her skin was the color of weak tea, her inky-black hair was worn in a chignon style. She was wearing red velvet shoes with stiletto heels that were as thin as chopsticks.

Zek noticed my interest. "Woman is Kim Lee. Supposed to be Mar's personal secretary, but some say she's the one in charge of Mar."

Henry Mar turned in my direction briefly, but because of the sunglasses, I couldn't tell if he'd noticed me or not.

"Where is Dimitri Vanel?"

"He's the one by the bar, in the white suit." Zek patted me lightly on the shoulder. "Be careful, Johnny. There are sharks onboard tonight. More dangerous than the great whites."

Zek laughed at his own joke, laughed so loud that he went into a coughing fit. Viktor, his bodyguard, hurried over and patted Zek on the back.

Dimitri Vanel was the centerpiece in a cluster of fawning middle-aged men and women.

He was a brawny, big-waisted man with carefully groomed silver-colored hair. His weathered face was scored with frown lines down his cheeks and between his eyes. He had one arm draped around the shoulders of Stalin's daughter, the other around a stunning lady in a bright yellow strapless dress. Her hair was several shades of carefully blended blonde. She had a smooth forehead, crayon-blue eyes, and a nose that had the look of a Beverly Hills surgeon's best efforts.

As I backed away searching for a glass of wine, I spotted another gorgeous girl—Nika Vanel. She was wearing a see-through white blouse over a see-through bra and tight black slacks. Her face was flushed, her eyes were blinking as if the lights were bothering her and she was humming to herself. Cocaine or speed, I guessed—or maybe both.

"Hi, Nika," I said. "Nice to see you."

She stopped and peered myopically at me. "Who are you?"

"Johnny O'Rorke. I'm a friend of Russ Cortig."

"Russ," she said, hissing out the last two letters. "Why is he so mean to me? He's makes a date, and never shows up. Do you work with him? And Steve McQueen?"

"Yes. I'm McQueen's bodyguard while they're here shooting the movie."

"Really?" She tilted her head to one side and studied me. "I don't believe you. People tell me they know him, and they lie."

Her accent was intriguing, a little rough, a little soft—a mixture of Russian and French? "It's true," I said, as I unbuckled my wrist watch. "Steve gave me this for helping him out."

She took the TAG Heuer, brought it up close to her eyes and squinted as her lips silently read the inscription.

She rubbed the watch between her two fingers before handing it back. "I want to meet him. My father said he would fix it, but he hasn't. Can you bring me to McQueen? I want to be in his movie."

"Steve is always anxious to meet beautiful young actresses. I'll do my best."

There was a loud round of applause from behind us and I turned to see Dimitri Vanel holding his wine glass up in some sort of a toast. The beautiful blended-blonde at his side seemed bored with it all.

"Who's the lady standing next to your father, Nika?"

"That is no lady, that is his wife," she said, not realizing that she was repeating an old joke. "His third wife, Gaby. She's a slut. Call me when you can fix me to see Steve."

I dug out a notebook and pencil. "Write your number down for me."

She did just that, in a barely legible scrawl.

"Nika, there's a man who has been following you. Let me show you his picture."

I was reaching for Boris's photo when we were interrupted by the pretty brunette I'd seen with Nika at the Embarcadero photo shoot. Her face was also flushed and there was a trace of white powder under her right nostril. Her flame-colored dress had zippers from the wrist all the way up to her neck. She was holding hands with a man in his mid-thirties. He was of medium height and had reddish-brown hair that was styled in calculated disarray to cover the top half of his ears. He had dark eyes, with droopy lids. He was wearing a yellow button-down collar shirt and Levi's and was rattling away in French while he focused on Nika's see-through blouse and bra.

The brunette rattled back, calling him "Maurice" and he called her "Polina" as he touched her arm.

"Hello, Polina," I said.

She gave me a onceover from toes to hairline. Apparently I didn't pass inspection, because she put her mouth close to Nika's ear and whispered something while she tugged at Nika's elbow.

"I have to go," Nika said, "Call me."

The three of them hustled off towards a stairway that I assumed led to an upper deck.

Dimitri Vanel was still surrounded by his adoring fans, so I didn't have a chance to get close to him.

It seemed to be my night for bumping into attractive women. Kim Lee, Henry Mar's personal secretary stepped right in front of me.

She stuck her chin out, stretching her elegant neck. Everything about Kim Lee was elegant.

"You are Inspector John O'Rorke?" she asked.

"That's right."

"Mr. Mar suggests that you meet with him tomorrow. At seven o'clock, at the Red Dragon, in Chinatown. You are familiar with it?"

Indeed I was. It was a crummy bar situated over one of Mar's gambling dens. His office was located in the penthouse of a twenty-story building on Stockton Street, a block or so from the Red Dragon.

"I'll be there. Should I come alone? Or bring a few extra cops for protection? Someone told me Henry is upset with me."

Lee gave a twitch of a smile. "I'm sure you'll be safe." She took a few backwards steps and said, "For the time being."

That was cheerful news. I was suddenly thirsty and hungry, and it dawned on me that I'd been ignoring Francie Stevens.

I spotted her over by the buffet table. She was nodding her head sideways and mouthing something I couldn't hear.

I hurried over.

"Where have you been, Johnny?" She did that thing with her head again. "That's Boris standing by the salad bar, isn't it?"

Damned if it wasn't Boris. Dressed to blend in with the crowd in a tuxedo that could have been worn by a guest or a waiter.

As far as I knew, Boris had never seen me. Or maybe he had, because when our eyes met for just a fraction of a second, he slipped behind the buffet table and walked toward the same stairway that I'd seen Nika and Polina use. His pace picked up with each step. I started after him, feeling a sudden surge of heat in my heart and thinking that Vanel's guests were going to have quite a bit to talk about tomorrow, because I was going to drag Boris off the boat in handcuffs.

Boris snuck a quick peek over his shoulder as he started up the stairs. He didn't like what he saw—me.

A man with his eyeglasses perched precariously on the edge of his nose while doing a balancing act with small plates of hors d'oeuvres in each hand bumped into me, giving Boris a few precious seconds head start.

I took the steps two at a time, pausing as I stepped onto the *Dégager's* top deck.

The music was loud, speakers were blaring out Mick Jagger complaining "I Can't Get No Satisfaction."

The ship's handrails had been garlanded with dozens of tiny red bulbs, like electric blossoms. The smell of marijuana hung heavy in the night air. I crept slowly across the butternut-colored decking, my right hand resting on the butt of the holstered .38 revolver under my arm. There was no reason not to believe that Boris had his silenced pistol tucked under his tuxedo jacket.

The deck chairs and lounges were filled with young men and women in various stages of undress. A molded fiberglass hot tub at the stern was shoulder-to-shoulder with writhing bodies.

I waited in the shadows for several minutes, but there was no sign of Boris. He could have double-backed to the stairs, used another exit, or simply climbed over the railing and dropped down to the deck below.

As I headed back for the stairs, I spotted Polina, down on her knees, her head nestled between the legs of Maurice, the Frenchman I'd seen her with earlier.

I hustled over to the ship's gangplank. Misha, the dock guard, had abandoned his post. Boris could be hiding somewhere on the yacht, but I doubted that. He'd want to get away—fast.

What really bothered me was that Boris *had* recognized me. That brief meeting of our eyes—and then he took off.

Where had he seen me? Or had someone on the boat—Zek, or Henry Mar, pointed me out to him?

I moved down the gangplank. It was dark in the parking lot. I kept crouched over, moving slowly, trying to suppress the sound of my nervous breathing, my eyes swiveling back and forth.

Suddenly there was movement, a man darting between lines of parked cars.

I gave chase. Then there was a sound, like a small balloon popping, and something whizzed past my head. Another pop. I dropped flat on the ground, my gun in hand, cocked and ready, but there was no target. I lay still for several moments, then got to my feet, and edged my head up over the roof of a Buick sedan.

A car started up. A roaring motor, a screech of brakes. I followed the cars headlights as it sped away toward Marina Boulevard. It was a white sedan, but I couldn't make out the license plates or the driver.

Winston Churchill had a great quote during his soldiering years: "There is nothing more exhilarating than to be shot at without result."

I didn't feel exhilarated—I was scared, and mad.

Francie Stevens was waiting for me, not patiently, on the *Dégager*.

Vanel's party was going full blast. The noise level had increased, drowning out the piano player. Kim Lee was toe-to-toe with Trower, the bodyguard. Gaby, Vanel's wife, was whispering something into the ear of a leering Alex Zek, and Svetlana had one hand firmly clamped around the blue diamond, the other around a highball glass as she chatted with Henry Mar and Erik Gromov.

"Johnny," Francie said. "Did you find Boris?"

"No, he got away."

"Let's go. I've had my share of champagne, and I'm tired of being hit on by geezers in tuxedoes."

"Give me one minute," I told Francie. I went over to Zek and pulled him away from Gaby.

"You know a lot about guns, Alex. Tell me, do silencers sound like they do in the movies?"

"No. Sound nothing like in movies."

"Like small balloons popping?"

"Yes. Is good description."

I moved in close, so close our noses were almost touching. "I just chased Boris off the yacht and into the parking lot. I heard two of those balloons popping. If an ex-Russian KGB agent, who you've known since he was a kid shoots a San Francisco cop, the department will come down hard on you, Alex. So find Boris for me, and find him damn fast."

# CHAPTER 22

I wanted to know a lot more about the Stalin Blue diamond that had been hanging from a gold chain around Stalin's daughter's plump neck last night.

Alex Zek knew quite a bit about the diamond, but he might never tell me the full story. And I wanted the full story before I went up against Dimitri Vanel.

This left me with Marty Rothman.

Rothman was a jeweler and diamond cutter who was used by police departments around the Bay Area to value gems involved in thefts. He was a Holocaust survivor and had a reputation as a man who could keep his lips tightly sealed, so he also dealt with some shady characters—those in that gray area between thieves and people who had to sell family jewels without benefit of the government knowing of it, and, on occasion, out and out crooks. He was in his early-fifties, with smooth skin, a full head of snow-white hair and a matching guardsman's mustache. He wore thick, round-lens eyeglasses that gave him a slightly owlish appearance.

His office was located on Union Street, a block from where he lived, so I wasn't surprised to find him hard at work early the next morning. There was a glass display case filled with jeweled pins, broaches, necklaces, and expensive watches. Two of the walls were covered with oak cabinets that had long, narrow drawers. That's where Rothman kept his stock of semiprecious stones. The good stuff was kept in a safe built into the floor.

Rothman ran the Cuban under his nose several times. "So what do you want from me that is worth this very nice cigar?"

"I'm interested in information on a diamond."

"Any particular diamond?"

"The Stalin Blue."

Rothman removed his glasses, exhaled on each lens and wiped them with a silk handkerchief. "Do you know the stone's history, Johnny?"

"Just that Joseph Stalin took possession of it during his reign of terror."

"That is an unfortunate stigma. Stalin only had possession of the diamond for a year or so, but his name is now the only one associated with it. He used it as a paperweight on his desk, and he would put it in one eye like a monocle when he was drunk and pantomime being a British diplomat."

Rothman leaned back in his chair. "The legend is that a seventeenth century French adventurer by the name of Julian Chenot was traveling near the Golconda mine fields in central India when he came across a statue of a golden snake-goddess with one bright blue diamond eye. Chenot pried it out, and somehow got back to France with the stone. At first it was called the *Diamant Bleu de Chenot*. The Blue Chenot."

Rothman brought his hands together in a soft clap. "Then it disappeared. It was thought to have been lost. But one day it turned up in Paris. A Ukrainian by the name of Alferov, whose family were wealthy sugar beet farmers in pre-communist Russia, had a large blue diamond examined by Cartier's in Paris. It had some scratches and had too high a crown and a shallow pavilion. So Cartier recut it. They did a marvelous job. The stone was now pear-shaped and weighed forty-two carats. It was simply called *Le Bleu*—The Blue, which is the name I still prefer.

"Alferov brought it back to Russia. Then came the Revolution. Stalin was confiscating everything to pay for his armies. He was crafty though—he didn't just take the stone, he paid Alferov a ridiculously low price, which included keeping his head on his shoulders. A year or so later Stalin sold it to an unnamed American arms merchant, who supposedly became an enemy of the Kremlin and was shot in the back of the head while kneeling in a cell in the notorious Lubyanka prison in Moscow. And again the stone went into hiding."

"Educate me, Marty. What's the difference between a blue diamond, and a sapphire?"

"Basically, their atomic makeup. Diamonds are made of carbon and sapphires of aluminum oxide."

"What's the Blue worth?"

"Millions. Its size, its color, its rarity. For some the attachment of Stalin's name to the stone would be a detriment, for others that would make it even more valuable. Tremendously valuable."

He opened a desk drawer, took out two shot glasses and a bottle of Tomintoul twenty-one-year-old single-malt scotch.

He poured the whisky, and downed his in a single gulp. "It's Kosher. *L'chaim.* Johnny. Do you know who has the stone now?"

It was a little early for a shot of whiskey, even for me, but I tossed it back.

"I do know who has it. What I don't know is if it's legally his. I mean, what do you do with a stone with a history like this? You don't just show a receipt signed by Stalin, do you?"

Rothman dry-washed his hands and smiled. "You're right. Ownership dates all the way to the diamond mine in India, when it was stolen from the snake-goddess statue. Then there's the Chenot connection. Is there anyone left of his family that knows about the diamond? Did they sell it to the Russian Alferov? Or was it stolen from him? And Stalin, it would be hard to prove he was the legal owner. Like all dictators, he took what he wanted. There may be a document somewhere that shows he sold it to the American arms merchant, but I doubt it. Who else had possession after that? There's been a lot of interest in the Stalin Blue, Johnny. Its disappearance has had fortune hunters and every jeweler worth his salt searching for it for a long time."

"What would you do with it if I suddenly dropped it into your hand, Marty?"

"Drop to my knees and kiss your hand. Listen, the man with the stone, he wants to deal, I can handle it for him. He wants to keep it private, I can do that. No one will know. He goes to Christie's or Sotheby's and *everybody* knows. And, if he wants to alter it a bit, a tiny bit, some shavings—nothing drastic. I could transform it into another stone, and with very little loss of quality. Of course, there would be a very large commission for you. If you get your hands on the Blue, bring it to me, Johnny. Even if just for a few minutes. A diamond like that you see and hold once in a lifetime."

Sausalito police detective Duane Garant saved me the trouble of phoning him. He was sitting in my chair, behind my desk, when I walked into the Fraud Detail. He was wearing his brass button blazer and looked more like a college kid than a cop.

Garant bolted to his feet and said, "Sorry, Inspector. I was told I could sit here while waiting for you."

The morning is the busiest time for all the details at the Hall: cops signing in for the shift, meeting with witnesses or suspects, prepping for a court appearance, or just showing up to let everyone know that they are still among the living. There was the clatter of typewriters, the ringing of phones, the smell of cigarettes, overdone coffee, and yesterday's donuts. Copland.

"I'm glad you stopped by," I said, as I reclaimed my seat. "Anything new on your investigation?"

Garant's fingers fiddled with his tie clip. "Well, yes. Something I wanted to talk to you about before I took action. The crime lab ran the fingerprints from Mr. Alverson's residence. There were dozens that haven't been identified yet. We've sent them to the FBI. Ronald Tremaine, Trixie, his fingerprints were found everywhere, including all over the hot tub. And we found some prints belonging to a policeman. A San Francisco policeman." He held up his hand as if to stop traffic. "Not yours, they belong to—"

"Inspector Ed Cornell. Why were Tremaine's prints on file with the ID bureau?"

"He was busted six years ago on a petty theft charge. He'd stolen some clothing from a department store." Garant coughed into his hand, and then added, "Women's clothing."

"I was about to call you. Inspector Cornell handled the original investigation when Alverson was assaulted. I showed him the photographs of the suspect that Alverson had given me, and Cornell decided it was worth interviewing him again. He was at the house the afternoon of the killing. You can talk to him if you want to, his office is right down the hall. He's probably got a dozen witnesses that will put him on this side of the bay when the killing took place."

"You've personally spoken to Cornell?"

"Absolutely."

Garant glanced down at his shoes. "I think I should interview him for my report."

"That's your prerogative." I picked up the phone and punched in the extension for the Sexual Assault Detail. When I was connected to Cornell, I said, "Ed, Detective Duane Garant from Sausalito PD is here in my office. He's coming down to see you. Your prints were found at Alverson's cottage."

"You backed me up didn't you?" Cornell asked.

"I told him you were following up the original assault, doing your job."

"I owe you one, Johnny O."

I broke the connection, paused for a beat or two, and then said, "I saw Boris, the Russian, last night."

That snapped his head up. "You what?"

I gave Garant a condensed version of the party on Dimitri Vanel's yacht, including Boris's interest in Dimitri Vanel's daughter and the blue diamond, but left out the part about the shooting in the parking lot. I couldn't prove it was Boris who'd shot at me, or if in fact anyone had.

I put my elbows on my desk and lowered my voice. "Detective, I can't give you my source on this; it involves a federal government agent. Boris's last name may be Jakov. He's a Russian gangster, and he's on the Fed's BOLO list. He was filmed in a local coffee shop having a conversation with the top KGB agent in the Russian Embassy. His car was then followed to the parking garage at the Jack Tar Hotel."

I rustled through the papers on my desk, found the Chevrolet's license plate number and gave it to Garant. "The car was in the hotel's lot last night, but it was gone this morning. I've got the hotel security staff watching out for it."

Garant let out a whistle of the type used to hail taxicabs.

Gina Abbott, the detail's receptionist waved a hand at me. "Call on line one. You'll want to take it, Johnny."

It was Francie Stevens.

"Johnny," she said softly, "Creely has positive ID on the body from the Chinese cemetery. It's Willie Mar. He was buried right over a coffin. Mar had something called Paget's disease, deformed bones in his hips and lower back. So does the body they dug up. Creely found two bullets in the grave. He's picking up a warrant right now to search your father's house."

"Thanks," I said, "I appreciate your letting me know."

Garant had ants in his pants. "I want to check on the hotel."

"Be my guest. What about Inspector Cornell?"

He hitched up his antsy pants. "I'll talk to him later."

"The head security man at the Jack Tar is Joel Pardee. He's supposed to call if they spot Boris or the car. Pardee's a jerk.

Treat him like one. Let me know how it goes."

Garant almost ran out of the room. I called out to him, but he didn't hear me. I'd wanted to tell him about Boris's attack on little Wanda.

I wondered about those "dozens" of unidentified fingerprints found in Vanessa's cottage. Outside of the ransacked bedroom, the cottage was neat, orderly, well-cared for—something that couldn't be said for the room at the Rendezvous Hotel, where Boris had assaulted Vanessa. Those rooms weren't cleaned on a daily basis, not even a monthly basis. There would be hundreds of overlapping prints everywhere, and I didn't think Wanda's apartment would be much better.

There was no DNA evidence, no digital cameras, and no forensic latent print scanners in 1968. The technicians weren't skilled, highly trained specialists—most of them were cops who had to use the brush-and-powder technique to pull a print, and there was not a single international criminal finger-print database back then.

The FBI lab was the best of the bunch, but they wouldn't have prints of every Moscow hoodlum.

So the only way to get Boris's prints for sure was to catch the son of a bitch.

And he wasn't making that easy.

# CHAPTER 23

I was anxious to get over to my father's house, but first I made two phone calls—one to the Laguna Honda Hospital. There had been no change in his condition.

The second call was to Fiona O'Day, his housekeeper.

"Can you meet met at the house, Fiona? The District Attorney's Office is on their way to search the place."

"Whatever for?"

"They're trying to pin an old crime on Rory. Something that happened years and years ago."

"Fucking *gobdaws*! I'm on my way."

I had never heard Fiona mutter a single swear word before. *Gobdaw* was a nice Irish word for an idiot or moron. Bless Fiona, though it was a too charitable a description of Roy Creely.

Creely had come dressed for digging into dusty corners: coveralls, sneakers, and a San Francisco Giants baseball cap worn backwards. His hands were stuffed into black rubber gloves, the kind that reached half-way up the forearm.

"You can't stop me, O'Rorke. I've got a warrant."

"I wouldn't think of it."

Creely eyed Mrs. O'Day. "Who's this?"

"Fiona O'Day, our housekeeper. What are you searching for? Maybe I can save you some time."

He stuffed the warrant into the coverall's breast pocket. "You know damn well what this is all about. Your father's service revolver."

"Well, you're wasting your time," I said calmly. "It's gone."

Creely planted his right hand between his knees and tugged

it free of the glove. "You took it, didn't you, asshole? You fucking—"

"Watch your language, Officer," Fiona said in a loud clear voice.

"I didn't take the gun, Roy. My mother did."

Creely was seething; his face was turning redder by the second.

"Your *mother*? And where is she?"

"In heaven," Fiona said.

"She passed away a couple of years ago," I told Creely. "She always hated guns. She got rid of his revolver when my father retired from the department."

"Rid of it? How? Who'd she give it to?"

"I don't know. She probably threw it down the sewer or into the ocean."

Creely turned to Mrs. O'Day and said, "Did you happen to come across any gold coins or Chinese gambling chips while you were working around here?"

Fiona was confused by the question. "Gold coins? Gambling chips? Indeed not."

"Do you think your dear mother would have gotten rid of them, O'Rorke?" Creely said, biting off the words one at a time.

"They were never in the house, Roy. I'm telling you, you're wasting your time."

Creely slapped the glove against his knee while he glared at me. He knew that I was the one who got rid of the gun, the coins and the chips. I never said he was stupid—just a jerk.

"I'm going to get you, O'Rorke. The Fixer. Well I'm going to fix it so that you spend time in jail and lose your job. And I'm still going to tear this place apart."

"Tear it neatly then, because if there are any damages, I'm going to sue you and the District Attorney's office. Mrs. O'Day will be right here with you, putting things back in their proper place."

Creely stormed up the steps to the second floor, with Mrs. O'Day right at his heels. I used the phone in the kitchen to call my sister Peggy at her home in Southern California. Peg and her husband, a prosperous real estate agent, were off on a long-planned tour of Europe, and I wasn't sure when they'd be back. We'd talked, and she'd thought of cancelling the tour because of Pop's health, but we both decided there was no sense in that. There was no answer.

I hung around for about an hour, listening to Creely and his two man crew slam drawers and move furniture around. He obviously intended to make a day of it, so I left him under the watchful eyes of Fiona.

# CHAPTER 24

I stopped by the Laguna Honda Hospital to see my father. Out of habit, I'd picked up a sandwich, a pint of bourbon, two beers, and more Old Spice.

Pop was in no condition to sample any of them. When I first walked into his room, I thought that he'd passed—his complexion was a waxy gray color. I put my ear to his chest and heard what I hoped to be was a heartbeat. Up close I could tell that he was still breathing, a shallow, hollow sound—weak and unsteady.

It was time to drive down to Hillsborough and talk to Dimitri Vanel. I found his house hiding behind a lacework of ivy that covered the outer brick wall. I parked in front of a high iron fence with gilt spears. A black steel post held an entry control system with a Push-to-Call button. I stretched an arm out the car's window and pushed. Two minutes later a garbled voice asked: "What do you want?"

"Inspector O'Rorke of the San Francisco Police Department to see Mr. Vanel."

"Do you have an appointment?"

"No. But he'll want to see me."

"Hold on," the garbled voice said.

There were loud grinding sounds coming from hidden mechanical devices, and the gates slowly swung open. I drove along a gravel road boarded by walls of flowering oleanders, past an open area with an emerald lawn the size of a small airport runway. The road funneled into a flower-rimmed courtyard where two beautiful cars were parked alongside each other: the stately, but somehow sexy dark chocolate-and-cream Rolls Royce sedan, and a sleek, racy, low to the ground

Jaguar E-type convertible painted the luscious red color that always reminded me of Marilyn Monroe's lipstick.

I nosed the unmarked to the curb, making sure it was far enough away so as not to contaminate the others.

The sound of two leaf blowers in combat competed with the barking of several dogs. The noise didn't seem to bother a pair of blue birds chasing each other around the silver gleam of rustling poplar leaves.

The house was Georgian style, four floors of red brick with a white portico and gabled dormers. I kept a wary eye out for the dogs as I walked up a set of wide granite stairs. The oversized brass hardware on the front door was bright and shiny and the black paint so glossy I could see my reflection in the lacquer.

I used the brass doorknocker and waited. And waited. It was three minutes before the door swung open to reveal Trower, Vanel's commando bodyguard.

He was wearing a sweat-drenched T-shirt, the sleeves cut off at the shoulders to show off his bulging biceps, dark khaki cotton shorts and ankle-high boxing shoes. His dark hair was matted to his head—even his mustache was damp.

"If you're a cop, prove it," he said between deep breaths.

I showed him my badge, and when he didn't budge, my photo ID card.

He didn't seem impressed. "What do you want?"

Trower had a clipped, crisp, speech pattern, like those of a soldier used to barking out orders.

"I'd like to see Mr. Vanel. I have information relating to his daughter, Nika."

Trower grunted. "You'll have to do better than that, copper. O'Rorke. You're a Mick. I saw a lot of you guys in Belfast. Too damn many. They didn't take much to us soldiers over there."

Mick. A derogatory—especially when used by a Brit—slang word for an Irish Catholic. "You spent a lot of time in Northern Ireland?"

"Six months of ducking rocks, dodging booby traps and dismantling roadside bombs."

"Well, you're in my town now, and I'm a police inspector here to help Vanel's family." I moved a foot closer to the door. "Tell the man I'm here."

Trower's shoulders hunched, and his left hand turned into a fist and moved up to chest height. "Vanel's not home."

"Then you and I better have a long talk, or when I do meet with Vanel I'm going to tell him that you put his daughter's life in danger."

After we played stare-down for a few seconds, he said, "Okay. Come on in."

I kept a wary eye on Trower—he reminded me of Roy Creely, a man ready to hit you with a sucker punch at the first opportunity.

I followed him into the house. The floors were white marble for the first thirty yards or so, then gave way to an aubergine fleur-de-lis carpet. Trower kept glancing over his shoulder to make sure I didn't get lost.

When he came to a stop, he said, "This is Vanel's office. We can talk here."

A half-circle bay window framed the view of a figure-eight shaped swimming pool. A woman in a chartreuse bikini was stretched out on a chaise lounge, a towel draped over her face. The room was dominated by an elaborate Swedish Empire desk with gilded winged sphinxes. Paintings of all types and styles were hanging frame-to-frame along the walls: modern abstracts, impressionists, religious-themed icons, portraits, seascapes, still life, and pop art. I recognized what could have been, and probably were, works by Picasso, Monet, and Paul Klee.

"Why do you want to see Vanel?" Trower asked, as he slid into a green, high-back Windsor leather chair behind the desk.

No *Mr.* in front of Vanel, and Trower seemed at home in the chair. I pulled out one of my dwindling supply of photographs of Boris from my coat pocket and flicked it over to him.

"This man has been following Nika."

Trowel took his time with the photo, twisting it from one angle to another.

"This joker hasn't been anywhere near Nika when I was with her."

"A couple of days ago he was at a party in the Haight-Ashbury, harassing a man who had talked to Nika. The cops showed up, and Nika and Polina were lucky they weren't among those who ended up in a paddy wagon. And he was there on Vanel's yacht last night."

Trower pursed his lips and flicked the edge of the photo with his thumbnail. "Who is he?"

"A former Russian KGB agent, now in the employ of a Moscow Mafia leader, Arkadi Kusmenko."

Trower acted as if he'd never heard the name before.

"Kusmenko and Vanel used to be partners," I told him.

"What does he want with Nika?"

"You tell me, soldier. Has anyone made any threats against Vanel lately?"

"Not that he told me about. A KGB agent, huh?"

"He's killed a transvestite in Sausalito and beat up another one here in the city."

"You mean he's a poof? A queer?"

"Who's a queer?" a languid female voice asked.

I turned around to see Gaby, Vanel's wife. Her hardened nipples were visible through the thin material of her bikini. Her face was a shade lighter than the long, lovely rest of her. There was a beauty mark on her left cheek and she had the slight, sexy overbite that appealed to many men—this one included. She wasn't wearing makeup and tiny wrinkles were starting to show up around her eyes and between her brows.

"This guy," Trower said, standing up and handing her the photograph.

She barely glanced at the picture. "Who cares?"

"I think he's out to do harm to your daughter, Mrs. Vanel," I said.

"And who are you?"

"Inspector O'Rorke of the San Francisco Police Department."

"Well Inspector, I do not have a daughter. If you're talking about Nika, then you should tell her father, because she pays me no attention. Nika has some unusual friends, and I'm sure that many of them are queer, though I think that they prefer to be called gay."

With that she pirouetted like one of those Victoria Secret models do on a runway and strode away. She paused at a doorway, doing a half-turned in order to show off her busty profile. "The gym in ten minutes, Raleigh."

"Raleigh?"

He sank back into the chair. "It's an old British name. But you can stick with Trower."

"Tell me about this girl Polina that's always around Nika."

"They're cousins. Polina helps Vanel with his art collecting."

"What's Polina's last name?"

"Hey, I'm not doing your work for you—ask her."

"I'm asking you, Raleigh."

"Well, Mick, keep asking."

"Is she Nika's bodyguard?"

"No," he said quickly. "I'm the bodyguard."

"Do you speak French?"

"Enough to order a cup of coffee."

"And you don't speak Russian."

"Who told you that, copper?"

"A Russian. Tell me, since you can't speak Russian, why would Vanel hire you as a bodyguard?"

"Because I'm damn good at what I do."

"Where's Mr. Vanel?"

"Out of town."

"Where?"

"Wherever he wants."

"When will he be back?"

Trower stretched and yawned without bothering to cover his mouth. "Whenever he wants."

"What does he do for protection when you're not around, Trower?"

"I have a network of people I know, and trust. Vanel never goes anywhere unless I cover him with top-notch guys."

"What about Svetlana, Stalin's daughter? Is she still here?"

"Left this morning. I dropped her off at the airport."

"Where was she going?"

"Raleigh," Gaby cooed from the doorway. "I'm ready for you."

Trower pushed himself to his feet. "I'll see you to the door, O'Rorke."

"I can find my own way out."

"I'm responsible for security here; the people and the silverware. I'll see you out."

# CHAPTER 25

I mulled over my visit to Vanel's house as I drove back to my father's place.

There was something bothering me about former commando Raleigh Trower. I could understand why he didn't want to tell me where Vanel was, or when he was coming back home. And I could understand his macho attitude about not volunteering more information on Polina, other than that she and Nika were cousins.

But he was acting much too casual about the threat to Nika. Trower had to be close to forty, and to survive that long in a first-rate military unit you had to have some smarts. I'd have to find out more about Trower, and that meant cozying up to FBI agent Charles Ledegue and doing some trading—a background check on Trower for the news. Knowing Charlie, it would be news that Stalin's daughter had been at Vanel's party, and that she was wearing a large blue diamond around her neck that had once been owned by her father and was worth a fortune.

The crime lab van and Roy Creely's car were nowhere in sight when I parked in my father's driveway. Mrs. O'Day was back to being her cheerful old self.

"I kept a good eye on them, Johnny," she said as she ran a vacuum around the living room rug. "They made a mess in the basement. I'll get to it tomorrow."

I asked Mrs. O'Day to shut down the vacuum and we went to the kitchen and toasted the day with a shot of bourbon, and then finished off the sandwich I'd bought for my father's lunch.

\* \* \*

I swung by the Jack Tar Hotel. There was no sign of Boris's car in the garage, and no sign of Joel Pardee.

I found Pardee's evening shift supervisor, Gabriel Holt, sitting in Pardee's chair, his feet up on the desk.

Holt was pigeon-chested and had jug ears that helped hold up the snap-brim hat resting on top of his head.

I showed him my badge. "Where's Pardee? He's supposed to be keeping an eye out for a certain white Chevrolet in the garage."

"He left a little early. I know the car you're talking about. I sat on it for a while last night. It came in around ten o'clock. I called Pardee at his house and he told me to stay on it. Some Sausalito cop came by and I told him all about it."

I tried to keep my temper under control. "What happened to the car and the man who was driving it?"

"Dark-haired guy in a suit? I saw him walking toward Van Ness Avenue. When Pardee got here, the Chevy was still in place, so Pardee told me to take off."

"Where is Pardee now?"

"Damned if I know. The last time I saw him, he was sitting in his big Caddie convertible, sipping tequila and keeping an eye on the Chevy."

"I was to be contacted as soon as the car was sighted. Where does Pardee live?"

"In Pacifica. He's got a small horse ranch. Loves horses, that man."

Pacifica was a sprawling coastal town with beaches that were popular with surfers and fisherman. Clusters of single-family homes mixed in nicely with small farms and ranches.

"Get me his address"

Holt picked up a Rolodex with fumbling fingers and copied down Pardee's address and phone number.

"Is Pardee married?" I asked.

"No. Who would want to marry him?"

"Tell me about his Cadillac. Year, color, license plate."

"It's a kind of gold color, and instead of the Caddie hood ornament, Pardee stuck on a golden palomino horse statue. You can't miss the thing. It's got Texas license plates, but I'm not sure about the numbers."

I opened the drawers to Pardee's desk. The ivory-handled Derringer was gone. I used the desk phone to call Pardee's home number. No answer.

"Let's go talk to the garage attendant."

The attendant, who bore a strong facial resemblance to The Beatles drummer Ringo Starr, didn't know anything about the Chevy, but he remembered Pardee driving out in his Cadillac at about eleven a.m.

I reached out and patted Holt on the shoulder. "This is a very important investigation, Gabriel. Just between the two of us, I don't think Joel Pardee will be around much longer, and they'll be searching for a good man to replace him. I think you're that man. I need someone here at the hotel that I can trust. If you hear from Pardee or he comes back to the hotel, call me. Don't say anything to him, call me".

Holt seemed surprised, both at my attitude, and the news on Pardee.

"I'll do that, Inspector, I really will."

We shook hands and I left the hotel and crossed the street to Tommy Harris's Joint, a cozy hofbrau renowned for its buffalo meat and a beer list of more than a hundred domestic and imported brews.

I tried Pardee's place again—still no answer. I was furious with Pardee. What was he thinking? Not calling me, playing cowboy games, following a dangerous character like Boris in a gold convertible complete with a horse hood ornament.

I called the Sausalito Police Department. Detective Garant was "out in the field." Garant was someone else I wasn't happy with. He should have notified me with the information regarding Pardee.

I then called Gina Abbott at the office and asked her to run Joel Pardee through Texas DMV, get the license number for his Cadillac and have it placed on the department's hot sheet for stolen cars and to have the Pacifica Police Department check out his home address.

My next call was to Charlie Ledegue, who went into that cautious, low-tone voice he always used when at his desk. He lived in fear that his every call was recorded and monitored, and knowing the FBI mentality, he was probably right.

I gave him the payphone number and nursed a second beer while waiting for it to ring.

"I hope this is important," he said when he called ten minutes later.

"Would it interest you to know that Svetlana, Joseph Stalin's daughter, is in town, Charlie? Along with a huge blue diamond that her father once used as a desk paperweight. And that she may be staying at Dimitri Vanel's house."

"That...is interesting."

"A person who interests me is Raleigh Trower, Vanel's bodyguard. A former British commando. He's about forty, claims he spent some time in Belfast. I'd like to know about his military record and anything else you can dig up. Have you come up with anything on Boris, the Russian I'm after?"

"Not yet."

"I need the information in a hurry."

"Meet me tomorrow at Sam's for lunch and I'll have the information for you," he promised, and, for all of his other faults, Charlie kept his promises.

# CHAPTER 26

The night had turned cold. Fog slipped over Alcatraz like a crawling cat and the wind was brisk enough to make me wish I'd worn a heavier coat.

The weather never puts a damper on Chinatown. Grant Avenue was shoulder-to-shoulder with a mixture of tourists and locals—the tourists smiling as they gazed into storefront windows featuring cheap kimonos, decorative fans, Buddha statues, and shelves crammed with an endless array of colorful knickknacks—the locals scowling, a look of distaste on their faces, their sharp elbows clearing a path along the sidewalk. The tourists were a necessary evil—they spent a great deal of money in Chinatown, but that was no reason to have to be polite to the *gweilos.*

Henry Mar's Red Dragon Club was sandwiched in between an herb shop and a newsstand that sold Chinese papers, magazines, and tickets for *puck-apu, a* numbers game similar to keno.

I pushed the entrance door to the club open and slipped inside. There were groups of older Chinese men sitting around wood-topped tables, talking in staccato Cantonese and playing cards with gambling chips the color of smooth bones. Their voices dropped to a whisper when they spotted me. A white man in a sport jacket meant just one thing to them—a cop.

The man behind the bar had a beach ball-size head and an off-kilter nose.

"Is Henry around?" I asked. "He's expecting me. Johnny O'Rorke."

He pointed to a door at the far end of the room.

The door was nothing special, yellowish paint covered with grimy fingerprints. Eight time-worn stone steps led to a rusty grilled door that swung open with a loud, creaking noise.

I stepped inside a narrow hallway and blinked my eyes a few times.

Naked electric light bulbs spotted with fly droppings threw an ugly glare over the slick concrete flooring.

Kim Lee was waiting for me. She was wearing a pale blue sheath dress, her neck laced with pearls, her long dark hair in a ponytail as thick as a python.

"You're late, Inspector O'Rorke."

"Sorry about that. Police business."

Kim Lee opened yet another door, and waved me through.

Black-on-white Chinese calligraphy scrolls were mounted on the brick walls. The floors were covered in overlapping Oriental rugs. A black iron safe of the size that Butch Cassidy and the Sundance Kid were always blowing up squatted in the corner of the room. Henry Mar was sitting behind a massive, elaborately carved rosewood desk featuring fire eating dragons and long-winged birds.

There was a dank, musty smell about the room, as if it hadn't been put to use in a long time and I could hear voices and shouting from the adjoining room. I realized I'd been lured to the very room where my father had shot and killed Willie Mar.

All of Chinatown's gambling dens were located in basements or subterranean cellars. There a Chinese superstition about luck being better below ground. The Chinatown underground was honeycombed with tunnels, some high enough to stand up in, as long as you were careful not to trip over a rat; others of the height and width of those crawlways that soldiers dug to escape concentration camps.

Henry Mar snubbed out his cigarette in a jade ashtray in the shape of an upturned turtle, got out of his chair and walked over to greet me. He was wearing a black silk robe that reached down to his shoes, and, although the room was dimly lit, green-tinted sunglasses.

There was a low growling sound, and a big, white, muscular dog trotted out from behind the desk, its lips peeled back revealing twin rows of sharp, meat-eating teeth. Drool rolled off his jaw and puddled around his paws.

Mar said something in Chinese and the dog slumped to the floor. His pale brown eyes seemed to be focused on my groin area.

"Claw is a Dogo Argentino, a Mastiff breed developed in Argentina primarily for the purpose of big game hunting."

"Does Claw get much hunting time around here?"

"You'd be surprised," Kim Lee said. She'd been standing directly alongside me.

Mar said something in Chinese and Lee reluctantly backed away and slipped out the door.

I decided to lay a few false cards on the table.

"Henry, I'm happy to meet with you, but as a courtesy I must tell you that Inspectors Cutter, MacChesney, and Ballentine know the exact time I came into your club, and if I don't leave in thirty minutes, there will be a raid on your gambling den."

Mar waved a hand, as if dismissing a waiter. "That was unnecessary, Inspector. Have you heard the news of my father's remains?"

"My condolences. I never met your father."

"Nor I yours. But the two of them did meet." He let his eyes wander around the room. "Right here. My father may have been standing exactly where I am now when your father shot and killed him."

"It never happened, Henry. The story that Jumbo Flagg told about the killing was just that. A story. Flagg was an acute alcoholic. After too many drinks he'd brag about shooting Mafia bosses when he was a kid living in Chicago. That never happened either."

Mar stroked his jaw for a few seconds. "Mr. Flagg's death bed confession was quite convincing to the district attorney. He certainly didn't make up the part about where my father was buried."

He pointed his finger to the floor. The rug was faded browns and blacks in a geometric grid design. "What was left of my father had been wrapped in a rug, very much like the one you're standing on now. A Nighsia, made in the eighteenth century by Buddhist monks in western China. Beautiful, is it not? The rug used to carry my father to his pitiful grave was dumped over the coffin of a man called Wu, a fucking janitor—and then covered with dirt!"

Mar's tone had gotten Claw excited. He scrambled to his feet, only to drop back to the floor when Mar snapped his fingers.

Mar said, "When my father disappeared, I was a young man. I had no idea what had happened to him. There was no trace, and believe me, I looked for him—all of Chinatown looked for him. After a short time, I realized he was dead, and I would never see him again. I vowed that one day I would find out who had killed my father, and that that person would be punished severely. You are Irish, a Catholic no doubt, Inspector. Do you believe in the afterlife? A heaven?"

"That's what I was taught in school."

"We Chinese also believe in an afterlife, and that the soul of the deceased must be carefully prepared for the journey. For a man of my father's stature, an expert in *feng-shu* is needed to determine the time, place and orientation of the grave site. We believe that if the corpse is not buried in the right way he will turn into a ghost, and his *hun*, his soul, is doomed to wander in space. We also believe that sometimes the son must pay for the sins of the father."

I was getting tired of Mar's preaching. "You're lucky your

father wasn't Catholic—he'd have gone straight to hell. Whoever put him in that grave knew about all of these traditions, so if I were you I'd start checking out his old Chinese enemies. Anyone with any smarts who wanted to get rid of a body would never bury it. They'd dump it in the bay."

"Is that what you did with your father's revolver?"

I had to give Mar credit for coming up with that guess, but before I could respond, he said, "Mr. Creely of the District Attorney's office is of the opinion that Rory O'Rorke did indeed shoot my father, and that you, his faithful son, disposed of the weapon."

"I'd agree with Creely, but then we'd both be wrong."

Mar skirted the dog and slid into his chair. He plucked a cigarette from his robe pocket, lit it with a rolled-gold lighter, pulling the smoke slowly through his lips and letting it escape just as slowly through his nostrils.

"I understand that your father's health is deteriorating."

"He's hanging in there," I said.

"As you will no doubt find out very soon, losing one's father is a traumatic event. I was surprised to see you at Mr. Vanel's yacht party. Is he a friend of yours?"

"I've never met him."

"But surely Alex Zek is a friend. The two of you seemed to be having a stimulating conversation."

"Zek was telling me about Stalin's daughter, Svetlana. Did you notice the big blue diamond she was wearing?"

"It was hard not to notice the diamond. Do the police have an interest in the stone?"

Interesting question, interesting as to why he asked it. "Not that I know of. How about you and Dimitri Vanel, Henry? Friends? Or business associates?"

"We both have a passion for fine art. The attractive woman you were with, Miss Stevens. She works for the district attorney. That must be helpful to you."

I wondered who'd pointed out Francie to Mar. Alex Zek was the obvious suspect. I was getting tired of standing up, but there wasn't another chair in the room.

"Henry, I think we're through here, don't you?"

Mar wasn't going to let me go without dropping another surprise.

"Have you had any luck in running down the man you seek? The Russian. Boris is his name, isn't it?"

"I haven't found him yet."

Mar rotated the cigarette nervously between his thumb and index finger. "Good night, Inspector. Kim Lee will show you the way out."

# CHAPTER 27

"You look like a man who could use a drink," Kim Lee said.

"Some people are born looking that way. What did you have in mind?"

She raised a languid hand in the air and said, "This way."

This way took us down the darkened hallway to a small elevator. Very small. There was just room for the two of us. Lee edged into me, molding her body against mine. She had an intriguing aroma mixture of perfume and sweat. The golden skin on her face had a slick sheen to it.

The elevator pinged to a halt and the doors slapped open to reveal a small lobby with mirrored walls and a carpet the color of swimming pool water.

Kim Lee hooked her arm under mine and steered us through a revolving glass door out to Stockton Street—the real Chinatown, with shops selling live turtles, snakes, rabbits, and fish of all kinds that were scooped out of a tank and then wrapped in newspapers while they thrashed around.

It was cold, but all Lee had around her shoulders was a lace shawl.

The sidewalks were mobbed, but the oncoming pedestrians parted like small boats making way for an ocean liner when they saw Kim Lee. Some bowed their heads as if greeting royalty.

I glanced over my shoulder in a hopeless attempt to spot a tail, friend or foe. At that time of the night, for every hundred people on the streets of Chinatown two or three are federal or state drug enforcement agents, and there may be a couple of CIA or FBI undercover men thrown into the mix, maybe even one of Bogus Bob McCard's Unit cops. At least five or six of that hundred will be members of local Chinese gangs. Then there are the run of the mill crooks: purse snatchers, con artists, car thieves. That leaves the rest of us. I hope I haven't spoiled your next walk.

We crossed a wide thoroughfare that at the time separated Chinatown from North Beach the way that the Rio Grande River separated Texas from Mexico.

Lee surprised me by stopping at Capp's Corner, a cozy Italian restaurant with a busy bar. The greeter was an exotic red-haired woman who used the name Magnolia Thunder-pussy—I kid you not.

"I thought you'd feel more comfortable here than in Chinatown," Lee said as she settled her tightly-wound bottom on a stool at the end corner of the bar.

I knew Marco, the hawk-nosed bartender well. He gave me a quick smile as he placed a napkin in front of Kim Lee.

"What can I fix you, ma'am?"

"I'll have what he's having," Lee said, while she flung her ponytail from shoulder to shoulder.

"Two double Jacks, Marco." I slipped a ten spot onto the bar and frowned at Lee. "What are we doing here?"

"Getting drunk, I think. Every once in a while I like to get drunk." She picked up her Jack Daniel's and took a healthy, or, depending on your point of view, unhealthy swallow.

Ah, every man's fantasy—ply a gorgeous woman with liquor and she'll tell you all her secrets and reveal all of her charms. I winked at Marco, a signal to keep the booze flowing.

"Did Henry Mar suggest this little get-together?"

"Definitely not," Lee said. She removed her shawl and crossed her legs. Her dress was the kind with slits up both sides that went all the way up to her thighs.

She began chatting aimlessly about the city, the restau-rants. "I like the veal cutlets here," and then she veered off to the weather and how she loved to sail and drive fast cars.

All of this discourse took us through two more double Jack Daniel's. I was starting to feel them, but she seemed as sober as a judge, which, thinking back isn't that much of a recommendation. I've known many a drunken judge, both on and off the bench.

I ordered a plate of the veal cutlets and cannelloni and we ate right at the bar. Or at least I ate. Kim Lee nibbled and sipped at her drink.

She finally got down to business after Marco brought over a complimentary bottle of red wine.

"Did Henry try to intimidate you, Johnny?"

"He said something about the son paying for the sins of the father."

She re-crossed those lovely legs again and bumped her knee into mine. "Henry's father's death was regrettable, but it happened a long time ago. It is ancient history." Her right hand dropped to my lap. "There is no reason to create unrest. Everything is going smoothly, and we do not want to do anything foolish. Life, and business, goes on."

"What is it with Mar and those green sunglasses?"

"His eyes are very sensitive to light. He gets migraine headaches if he doesn't wear the glasses."

She tested the wine, decided she didn't like it and ordered a brandy.

She ran her index finger over my nose. "You're an attractive man, but your nose is broken. Why don't you get it fixed?"

"Someone would probably just break it again."

"Do you like being a policeman, Johnny?"

"It has its moments."

Her hand was on my lap again. "What do you like best about being a cop?"

"I get to meet a lot of interesting people."

She laughed, and her hand began making circles. "You

mean like Dimitri Vanel? And his daughter? I saw you talking to her."

"She wants to meet Steve McQueen."

"Who doesn't?" Lee said cheerfully. "I know a lot about you, Johnny. How much money you make, at least the money from being an Inspector. Then there's your other job—taking care of all of those celebrities. 'The Fixer'—you must make a little money doing that. You think you're a tough guy, like your father. And you like colored girls. Your ex-wife was colored, wasn't she?"

"She still is." I didn't have to scratch too deep to figure out where she'd gotten all of this information. Roy Creely must have told Henry Mar everything he knew about me, and what he didn't know he'd made up.

"And I know you're friendly with Alex Zek," Kim said.

She was making bigger circles with her hand.

"No one is friendly with Zek. He and Henry are in the same type of business. I've heard that Zek uses his boat to pick up things for Henry."

She drew her hand back. "Who told you that?"

"Just a rumor." A rumor I'd just made up, but thinking about it made sense.

"We would never do business with Zek," Kim Lee assured me.

"The two of you seemed to be pretty friendly at Dimitri Vanel's party. How about doing business with Vanel? He was a top Russian gangster before he moved to France, and they tell me he ran with the French Mafia when he was in Paris."

"That's news to me. Did you have a good time at Vanel's party?"

"The food was terrific."

"The man on the boat, the big one, Trower—Vanel's man. What do you think of him? Is he competent? "

"To do what, Kim? Protect Vanel? I guess so. He's an ex-British commando. What's your interest in Trower?"

She did that thing with her legs again. "He doesn't seem all that bright, yet Vanel hired him for protection: for himself, his wife, and his daughter. And now Vanel has a diamond, the Stalin Blue, which is worth millions of dollars. I wouldn't trust Mr. Trower with that responsibility. No, I would hire someone like you."

This time her hand went right for my crotch. "If you should happen to...find it somewhere, I would pay you a great deal of money, more than you'd make in your entire life as a policeman."

With that she stood up and tossed what was left of the brandy down with a quick flick of her wrist.

"I have to go. Keep in touch. And don't forget about my offer."

"I'll walk you back to Mar's place."

"Not necessary." She pointed to the exit door. "I have friends waiting for me."

I watched her stroll out of the place. Every man in the restaurant watched her.

Marco came over and picked up the dinner plates. "Johnny, why you let her get away? That is one beautiful woman."

A beautiful woman who talked as if she had Henry Mar under her control, and who wanted me to steal a priceless diamond for her.

What was it about me that made people think I was a jewel thief? Alex Zek hinted I should go after the Stalin Blue, and now Kim Lee wanted me "to find it somewhere. " Even the jeweler, Marty Rothman, had told me I'd be in for a very large commission if I happened to bring the diamond to him.

On top of that, I had a Russian assassin taking pot shots at me, a district attorney's investigator who threatened to put me in jail, and a Chinese ganglord who wanted me out of the way.

"Can I get you something?" Dino asked.

"Coffee. Lots of coffee."

Being busted for drunk driving was not the way I wanted to end the night.

# CHAPTER 28

My doorbell rang at a little after seven in the morning. By the time I struggled out of bed and got to the door the bell-ringer was gone, but he'd left a package—a wooden wine box stamped with a fancy label and the words 1966 Chateau Mouton Rothschild Bordeaux.

I hurried down the steps and saw Alex Zek's hearse driving away. The Swine had mentioned something at Vanel's yacht party about delivering some wine to me.

I felt a little uneasy about accepting all of the cognac, wine, and cigars from Zek, but I soothed my conscience by telling myself that if I turned the goodies down, he'd think that I was too honest to deal with. As long as Zek thought I was in his pocket, I could pick that pocket clean.

I lugged the case of Bordeaux into the flat, stared longingly at the warm, inviting bed, and then headed for the shower.

"Was Johnny a bad boy last night?" Gina Abbott asked when I wandered into the office.

"Do I look as bad as I feel?"

"I've seen you better. Here's the Texas DMV printout on Joel Pardee's car. He has a California driver's license that shows the Pacifica address. The local cops checked it out; no sign of Mr. Pardee."

"Were there any calls from a Sausalito cop named Garant?"

She thumbed through some notes on her desk. "Yes. One from late last night. He just says that 'Pardee is missing.' Then ten minutes ago you received a call from a Russ Cortig. He said that the *Bullitt* crew is working at Enrico's on Broadway this morning." She squinted at her note. "And someone named Nika was going to be there."

Nika, who always seemed to travel with the mysterious Polina. This was my chance to get some ID on Polina. I picked up the phone and called for a Yellow Cab.

The streets were blocked off for the film crews: motorcycle cops working overtime hours at double pay were smiling behind their helmet shields while the uniforms were manning the barricades and chatting up the excited onlookers.

Danny Higgins parked his Yellow Cab alongside my unmarked and nervously approached me, tugging at the brim of his tweed hat.

"Hey, Inspector. I didn't mean nothing with that fly rod, I mean I bought and paid for it, I haven't got the receipt, but I—"

"Forget about the rod, Danny. I need a favor. I want you to help me return a lady's purse."

"What purse?"

"I'll show it to you."

I used my badge to get us through the barricades. Steve McQueen was standing in front of Enrico's, talking to Peter Yates, the film's director. I spotted Russ Cortig sitting on the back bumper of a film van, drinking coffee.

"Thanks for the call, Russ. Is Nika here?"

He jerked a thumb over his shoulder. "She and her pal are over by the barricades. She called me last night. I think I can get her to McQueen in an hour or so." He shook his head. "All he has to do is say 'Hi' and grin, and women go crazy. What a life, huh?"

I scanned the area and spotted Fred Breen, Sergeant Sunshine himself, sitting at an indoor table at Enrico's, every hair in place, his suntan standing out against his white shirt.

I steered Danny through the cops, crew, and crowd until we had a view of Nika and Polina. It was a nice morning, not warm, but not cold. Nika was dressed for warm—a tight red tank-top and a faded denim mini skirt. Polina wore frayed bell bottoms, a tie-dyed shirt and a headband. A black leather purse was looped over her shoulder. Maurice, the Frenchman I'd seen Polina with on Vanel's yacht, was standing next to her. I was afraid that would complicate things, but after a couple of minutes he kissed her on her cheek and took off.

"See the brunette with the headband standing next to the cute blonde, Danny? That's the purse I want to return."

"She's still got it."

"I know. That's why I called you."

It took a few seconds, but then he got the picture. "Let me get this straight. You *want* me to steal? I get caught doing something like this and I'm back in San Quentin, I mean I could—"

"Nothing will happen to you, Danny. You're not going to steal anything, just borrow it for a few minutes. If you can't get the purse, try and get her wallet, something that would have her ID."

"Jesus, I...you cover me on this, right?"

"Right. You're covered."

If Danny did get caught I would take the hit, but, knowing his skills, the odds on that were small.

He slipped on a pair of thin leather gloves, rubbed his palms together and melted into the crowd.

Director Peter Yates used a bullhorn to ask for quiet and the camera followed Steve McQueen as he trotted across Broadway, entered Enrico's, chatted with a tall man at a table, right next to where Fred Breen was sitting.

They shot this scene three times. I kept my eye on Danny, who was standing behind Polina and Nika. When he came back he had a sad expression on his face.

"Couldn't get the purse, Inspector. She had it clamped down good. But I did get these."

He handed me a black alligator leather wallet and a red

velvet box, of the size that could hold a single ring or a broach.

"I couldn't resist the box. She's got a gun in the purse. I left it there."

I carried the wallet and box over to the shelter of the shuttered entrance to a topless nightclub, turned my back to Danny and examined the wallet's contents. Money, crisp new bills, a few hundred dollars' worth. A credit card under the name Polina Morel. A temporary California driver's license issued last month under the Morel name, and a much-creased pinkish document entitled *Permits de conducive*, with Polina's photograph, the last name Morel. A French driver's license, issued two years ago. She was twenty-six years of age, born on May 29th.

I scribbled down the info in my notebook, and then opened the box. How can I describe my reaction? Eyes popped? Sweat broke out on my forehead? Zing went the strings of my heart? All of that and more. Nestled in the box was a large blue diamond.

"Everything okay?" Danny asked.

"I hope so."

I dropped the diamond into my jacket pocket, snapped the box closed, and then handed it and the wallet to Danny.

"One more favor. Can you put these back in the lady's purse?"

Always the professional, Danny wiped the box and wallet on the sleeve of his coat to get rid of my fingerprints. "Tell you the truth, Inspector, I ain't never done that before. Put something back, I mean."

# CHAPTER 29

Marty Rothman pulled his head back from a double-lens microscope and made clicking noises with his tongue.

"Well?" I asked anxiously.

"It's not the Blue. It's paste, Johnny."

The zing went out of the strings of my heart. "A fake?"

"Yes. But an excellent one. The facets were cut and polished. The paste is colorless to begin with. To get this shade of blue the jeweler had to add cobalt to the mix. See for yourself. There are two minute air bubbles. A real diamond never has that."

I used the microscope. I saw the bubbles. I swore several times.

"Smell it," Rothman said. "It's been polished recently. The jeweler used coconut oil to smooth out any scratches."

I sniffed. I couldn't pick up a scent, but I took his word for it.

Rothman stooped down, opened a drawer and came out with three small stones.

"These are real diamonds. All of them are a little over two carats. Nothing special, but very nice. Here, put them in your hand."

I picked up the stones, rubbed them between my palms, they felt cool.

"Put them to your lips," Rothman said. "Hold them there for a few seconds. You'll notice they are cold, not because of the lower temperature in the diamonds, but because the diamonds take the heat from your lips. That's why diamonds are called *ice*, Johnny."

I followed instructions. The diamonds did indeed start to feel cold.

Rothman took his diamonds back and gave me a sad smile. "It's not unusual in the least for owners of a precious stone to have a duplicate made, sometimes more than one duplicate. That way they can wear it to dinners and parties while the real thing is locked in a bank vault. In 1929 a Paris thief thought he'd pulled off the perfect crime; stealing a two hundred and twenty carat, cushion-shaped ruby from a safe in the home of a French banker. He was greatly disappointed—it was a duplicate. The banker kept the real ruby in a hollowed out section of his mattress, so that he could sleep with it every night."

"Is this an exact copy of the Stalin Blue, Marty?"

"I couldn't tell you. I'd have to compare it to the actual Blue. There are no exact diagrams of the Blue that I know of. Maybe Cartier's in Paris would have the original cutter's diagrams and charts."

"If you were at a party and saw a woman is wearing this blue stone around her neck, could you tell it was a fake?"

"No, not until I got it in my hands. Would you mind if I took some photographs of this one, Johnny?"

"Not at all, as long as you give me a couple of them."

Marty poured me a glass of his kosher Scotch and then placed the copy of the Stalin Blue on a small silk pillow and clicked away with a Polaroid Instant camera.

I was so pumped up about Danny Higgins purse snatch, that when I got back to the Hall, I rode the elevator down to the basement and ordered the cafeteria's version of eggs Benedict. My first mistake of the day.

Charlie Ledegue must have run out of meeting places in Golden Gate Park. This time he'd picked Sam's Grill, one of the city's best fish joints. It was located in the middle of the financial district and had a time-has-stopped aura about it. Crusty waiters and wooden booths with curtains that made you think you were back in the 1930s during prohibition.

Nestor, the waiter, was a skinny, fast-talking man in his sixties. Charlie ordered grilled Petrale Sole, fried zucchini sticks and a bottle of white wine.

My stomach was still recovering from eggs at the Hall, so I just asked for a bowl of clam chowder.

"What did you find out about Raleigh Trower, Charlie?"

He tucked a napkin into his shirt collar and spread the cloth across his chest. "An interesting man, Mr. Trower. He served his Queen and County as a Royal Marine commando for sixteen years. He worked his way up to be a warrant officer, only to get busted down to sergeant, the result of a drunken brawl where he nearly killed one of his fellow commandos. He was stationed in the British Crown Colony of Hong Kong for two years.

"He was transferred back to England and shortly found himself in real trouble. Trower was accused of the viscous assault of a bartender in an alley behind a pub in London. Trower was allowed to resign from the service. He had one stint as a mercenary—a bungled attempt at a coup in North Africa, then he went private, started his own security firm in London. Apparently that's where he met Dimitri Vanel."

"Of all the security operators in the world, why would Vanel hire this bozo?"

Nestor dropped our orders on the table and poured some wine.

"Mr. Trower has some skills that may have attracted Vanel's attention, Johnny. He was a sniper in the Royal Marines, and he's also an expert in small arm weapons. My source on all of this, a British MI6 chap, hinted that Trower was borrowed by government agencies for delicate missions, and he was very good at completing those missions."

"You mean he was an assassin," I said.

"That would seem to be a logical conclusion. And he also is very good with languages—one of those lucky ones who picks them up easily. He speaks Russian, French, and Cantonese."

"You're sure of that, Charlie?"

"My source was positive."

While Charlie dug into the fish, I ran the information about Trower around in my brain. Dimitri Vanel had the money to hire anyone as a family bodyguard, but he picks a British military trained killer who moonlighted for the British Secret Service. Guys like Trower can't hide in the dark. Their reputations, or qualifications, become known to those who want to know. The same information Charlie had dug up could be accessed by Vanel's enemies.

So Vanel was sending those enemies a message—my bodyguard is badder than your bodyguard. Not only that, but people like the Swine thought Trower couldn't understand Russian, so they spouted off in front of him. Trower was getting more interesting by the moment.

"You should have ordered the fish, Johnny," Ledegue said. "It's delicious."

He was one of those slow, methodical eaters, chewing each bite a dozen or more times, dabbing at his lips with the napkin.

"I guess you guys keep a pretty good eye on Erik Gromov, Charlie."

He swallowed some zucchini and coughed. "Gromov. What do you know about him?"

"That he's the head KGB man at the Russian Embassy and that he and Boris had coffee and poppy seed rolls at a bakery on Balboa Street." I gave him the date and time of the meeting.

"You're certain of this?"

"Saw it with my own eyes. At least I saw the Unit's surveillance film. They seemed chummy."

"What would Gromov be doing with someone like Boris?" Ledegue asked. I had the feeling he was directing the question to himself as well as to me. "Who else was there?"

"Just the two of them. Unfortunately, the Unit couldn't pick up their conversation. I saw both of them two nights ago at a party on Dimitri Vanel's yacht. Svetlana Allilyueva, Stalin's daughter, was there, wearing the Stalin Blue diamond. She and Gromov were chatting like old friends. Trower was close by, keeping an eye on the diamond."

"Why the hell didn't you tell me about this before?"

"I've been busy looking for Boris and waiting for you to provide me with information on him."

That didn't sit too well with Charlie. His lips extended in a thoughtful pout.

"Who else did Gromov talk to?"

"Everybody. It was that kind of a party, Charlie. The in-crowd: Gordon Getty, Bill Graham, and a lot of beautiful women. Henry Mar was there, too."

I left Alex Zek's name off the list.

"Gromov spoke to Mar?"

"I saw them having a drink together. When Boris showed up I chased after him, but he got away—after firing two shots at me."

"He shot at you?"

"Yes," I said, though I'd been thinking about the incident. I was an easy target in the parking lot. Boris could have missed on purpose. Warning shots to let me know I should stay out of his way.

"Well, here's some information for you. Boris's last name is Rurov."

"Spell it."

Charlie did just that. "He's also been known as Sikorov, Egorov, and Mihailov."

"What about the last name Jakov?"

"I couldn't find any record of him using that name. Where did you pick that up?"

"A source told me it was a possibility."

Charlie wasn't happy about that. "How long have you had that information?"

"Just picked it up this morning."

"Rurov is a former KGB agent. The fact that he met with Erik Gromov may mean that he's back in the fold. We know that Rurov's heavily involved with the Russian Mafia. I'd like to see that film of the meeting between the two of them."

"I'll talk to the Unit about that, Charlie."

He screwed up his napkin, picked up a spoon and used its tip to draw a pattern on the tablecloth. "If you happen to find Boris before we do, I want to know about it. I want the opportunity to interview him."

FBI interviews of that type were usually carried out on a ship, at sea, in international waters, and though the term "enhanced interrogations" hadn't become popular yet, they could get really rough.

"What if you find Boris before I do?" I asked.

"After we're finished with him, he's all yours."

I had to give Charlie credit—he lied with an absolute straight face. After the FBI was finished with the interview, Boris would either be a double agent or he'd be dead.

"That's fine with me, Charlie. Oh, I've got some more news for you. Svetlana Stalin has left town. Trower drove her to the airport—"

"I know all about that. She flew out on Vanel's private jet. Her destination was Princeton, New Jersey. A limo took her to a house on Cherry Drive." He gave me a sly smile. "She had a lot of luggage with her."

"Why Princeton?"

"I don't know. Maybe she wants to go to college. The house is located in a prestigious neighborhood, and, as of two days ago, she is the listed owner of the property. She paid cash for the house."

Vanel's cash? There was one thing that I was pretty sure wasn't in her luggage—the Stalin Blue Diamond.

I was tempted to give Charlie Polina's full name and date of birth, to see what he could pick up on her, but decided not to. Polina was going to be all mine for a while.

Nestor came over and handed me the check. I didn't try to go double or nothing with him—he played for keeps.

# CHAPTER 30

I spent most of the next day working with Steve McQueen and the *Bullitt* crew at the Thunderbird Hotel near the airport. Not exactly hard work, chatting with Jacqueline Bisset and Pat Renella, who played the villain in the picture.

My biggest contribution was coaching McQueen when he approached the hotel's check-in desk. Originally he'd flashed his badge at the clerk's face. I showed him how it should be done, with the badge discretely palmed and out of sight of any onlookers. If you watch the movie again, check out that scene—Steve did it perfectly.

When I got back to my office it was close to five o'clock and Sausalito Detective Duane Garant was sitting in my chair again, one foot up on the desk, the phone cradled against his ear while he wrote something down on a notepad.

"Getting comfortable, Detective?"

"I'll get back to you," he said into the phone receiver before dropping it into its cradle. He rolled the chair back, got to his feet and pulled down the hem of his sport coat. The blue blazer again. Either Garant had a limited wardrobe or the blazer was a uniform. requirement for Sausalito PD detectives.

"I didn't think you'd mind me using the phone while I waited for you. Inspector Lucca said it was okay to use your desk."

The Fraud Detail was nearly deserted—just one cop, Inspector Jack Lucca, a curly haired Italian who was the detail's expert on bank fraud, clicked away with two fingers on a typewriter while the cigarette between his lips dribbled ashes onto his lap.

"Where've you been, Duane? I haven't talked to you since you went over to check on the Impala at the Jack Tar Hotel."

"The car was gone. According to DMV records it belongs to—"

"RTLK Holding on Vine Street in Los Angeles. It's a dead end, a private postal box."

"You're sure of that?"

"Our Intelligence Unit checked it out," I said, as I slid into my chair.

He added that information to his notepad, and then said, "Joel Pardee, the hotel security chief you told me to talk to, was gone, according to his assistant, Gabriel Holt, who told me—"

"He had seen Boris come into the garage in the Impala, had called Pardee and that Pardee had taken it upon himself to follow the car in his cowboy Cadillac. I know all about that, but why the hell didn't you call me?"

"I did call. You were out and I had to return to Sausalito. This isn't the only case I'm working on."

"You should have kept calling."

"Later, I checked out Pardee's place in Pacifica. There was no sign of either him or his car."

"So the Pacifica cops informed us. Yesterday."

"Look," Garant said. "Maybe I screwed up. I did drop by the hotel before I came here, and Mr. Pardee is still missing."

"He'll probably be missing forever."

"You mean, you think that Boris might have—"

Garant was getting on my nerves. I pounded my hand on the desk hard enough to make the phone jingle.

"Do I think that a trained KGB agent, a professional killer who enjoys his work, could have spotted that idiot Pardee trailing him and then did something about it? You're damned right I do. He probably led Pardee into a trap and then finished him off."

"I checked the bars and restaurants near the Jack Tar,"

Garant said. "No one recognized Boris's picture."

"Did you happen to hit any of the gay bars on Polk Street?"

Garant coughed and cleared his throat. "A couple, again with negative results."

"The feds have come up with a last name for Boris. Rurov." I spelled it out. "He picked up a transvestite on the corner of Polk and Bush Streets, around midnight, just a few hours after Robert Alverson had been murdered. The victim was a young kid by the name of Aaron Walker, who uses the name Wanda. Boris took Wanda to her apartment on Larkin Street and he beat the hell out of her. Do you feel like going back to Polk Street late tonight and checking around? "

The question hung in the air for a few seconds.

"This took place *hours* after Alverson was killed?"

"That's right, Duane."

"And you interviewed this transvestite, Inspector?"

"Yes. Walker recognized Boris from the photo. No doubt about it."

"I'd like to interview this second victim."

"It's too late for that. He packed his bag and headed for home. Some place in Iowa."

Garant was getting as fed up with me as I was with him.

"I'd like to see your report, Inspector."

"I haven't made one, Duane. A confidential source brought me the information."

"I'd like to meet with Mr. Walker, and check out the scene of the crime."

I leaned back in the chair. "You're not getting the picture. Walker never officially reported the incident to the police. He's a heroin addict, a nervous wreck—he'd fall apart under any kind of interrogation."

There was the sound of a drawer slamming, and then Inspector Lucca walked over, tying his tie. "Johnny O, I'm heading over to Cookie's. Are you stopping by?"

"Yeah, Jack. See you in a bit."

When Lucca closed the door, Garant and I were all alone, and his voice became more assertive.

"You're not going to allow me to interview Aaron Walker?"

"Interview him all you want, if you can find him."

Garant moved his head in a quick negative gesture. "I can't talk to Walker, and Ronald Tremaine, Trixie, the last person we know to have seen the murder victim in Sausalito while he was alive, has gone missing. You wouldn't happen to know anything about that, would you, Inspector?"

"Tremaine is frightened, and with good reason. He took off for parts unknown."

"You spoke to him, didn't you? After you left the murder scene. After I gave you his address."

"I did. He's going to call me when he gets settled, and when he does, I'll pass along his new address."

"That would be swell," he said sarcastically.

I could understand why Garant was upset. I'd been playing fast and loose with the investigation.

"Listen, Duane. I think your best bet would be to hit those gay clubs on Polk Street. After dark. Boris could be on the prowl for another victim."

"I would think that would be your job, Inspector. It's your territory."

"But it's your case," I reminded him.

Garant narrowed his eyes and gave me a hard stare that might have intimidated a jaywalker. He thumbed through the pages of his notebook. "I'm still trying to verify Inspector Cornell's whereabouts at the time of Robert Alverson's death. He claims to have spent several hours at a place called Cookie's Star Buffet on Kearny Street. Is this the same place Inspector Lucca was heading for?"

"It is indeed. Go check it out. I'm sure you'll find someone there who will verify Cornell's alibi."

I found out later that Garant did stop at Cookie's, and had Cornell's alibi backed up by a longshoreman, a bread driver, and an insurance salesman.

I called Francie Stevens to see if she was in the mood for a quiet dinner.

"Wish I could, Johnny, but my sister has made plans for us."

"I met with Henry Mar last night."

"That must have been interesting."

"It was. Mar saw you at Vanel's yacht party and made a crack that you're working for the D.A. must be helpful to me."

"Henry Mar couldn't know me, or what I look like. Who told him I worked for the District Attorney?"

"Roy Creely would be my best bet."

"Creely wasn't at the party," Francie pointed out.

"Right. But my guess is that Mar has contacted him, so be ready for a little heat when you go to work tomorrow."

After we hung up, I ran the yacht party guests through my mind again, and the only one that I was certain knew about Francie and me was Alex Zek. Francie and I had been having dinner at the Iron Horse some months ago, and Zek had spotted me and came over. I'd introduced Francie to him and foolishly mentioned her position at the District Attorney's Office.

But why would he dump on Francie to Henry Mar?

I was in no mood to join Garant and Lucca at Cookie's, so I walked over to the detail's mini-kitchenette, rescued the office bottle of Jack Daniel's from under the sink, poured myself a stiff one and went back to my desk.

Marty Rothman said that diamonds were cold; maybe so, but the fake Stalin Blue seemed to be burning a hole in my pocket.

Mr. Daniel's magic potent finally pointed me in a direction. I wasn't sure if was the *right* direction. I dug the phone number Nika Vanel had given me from my wallet and dialed the number.

Nika answered on the first ring with a dull "Hello."

I clenched my jaws and tried to put a little British accent into my voice.

"Is Polina Morel available?"

"Huh?"

"Polina Morel."

"You want to talk to her?"

"Yes."

There was the sound of the phone being dropped on something hard, then a forty-six second wait, as clocked by the second hand on my new watch, before Polina came on the line.

"Who is this?" she asked.

"Did you lose something from your purse, Miss Morel?"

"Who is this?" she repeated angrily.

"A man holding a large blue diamond in his hand."

"What do you want?"

"The same thing you do, Polina."

"Listen, you really don't know what you have. It's not real. It's just costume jewelry."

"How much is it worth to you?"

"You already have the three hundred and sixty dollars you took from my purse."

The money. Danny Higgins couldn't just leave it in her wallet. "I'm thinking a little more than that. Five thousand dollars."

"That's crazy. I don't have that much money."

"Why don't you get it from Boris?"

"Boris? I don't know who you're talking about," she said with a little stammer in her voice.

"Sure you do. He's Russian. Sharp dresser. Has a lot of tattoos. You were seen strolling along Polk Street with him a few days ago."

"Who are you?"

"The man with the replica of the Stalin Blue, Polina. Talk to Boris. I'll get back to you."

I clicked the receiver gently into its cradle. The call to Polina had gone well. She hadn't denied she'd been on Polk Street with Boris.

The question bothering me was why she was walking around with the phony diamond in her purse? Was she going to deliver it to someone? Boris? Someone else? Or was she ready to make a switch for the real diamond herself?

Interesting questions, and ones I was coming close to getting the answers to.

You should celebrate, I told myself. Unfortunately, I took my own advice and reached for the Jack Daniel's bottle.

# CHAPTER 31

The Irish have a saying: Starve a cold, but feed a hangover. Bright and early the next morning I nursed my hangover with a breakfast of steak, eggs, toast, and several cups of coffee at the Golden Eagle, a waterfront dive that catered to hungry longshoremen.

I wanted to surprise Alex Zek and throw another scare into him.

I rang the doorbell at his warehouse on Vermont Street, and after a minute or two the peephole slid back, and the booming voice of Viktor, his bodyguard, asked me, "Why you here?"

"To see Zek."

The peephole was slammed shut, and then swung open. Viktor was dressed just as he had been at my last visit: jeans, a sweatshirt and an AK-47 hanging from his shoulder.

He came with me in the elevator, his index finger tapping on the assault weapon's trigger the entire time.

Zek greeted me with a hearty handshake.

"Johnny O. Listen, I have all my peoples try find Boris. Even call Moscow. They very mad. Believe me, Boris will not try to harm you or other policeman. What you want? Whiskey? Vodka?"

"I want to know why you told Henry Mar that Francie Stevens worked for the District Attorneys' office."

"Me? What you talk about?"

"At Dimitri Vanel's yacht party. You told Mar that Francie was with me and that she worked for the D.A."

Zek dragged a chair away from a table and sat down. The tabletop was cluttered with bottles of wine and a short-barreled pump-action shotgun.

"I tell Mar shit. And lady, what's her name? Francie? She your girlfriend, right? I didn't even see her that night. I met her what...once? Very pretty, very nice, but kind of skinny." He used his hands to outline a busty woman. "I like them *zoftig*, with meat on their bones." His eyes narrowed. "Did Henry Mar say I told him this?"

"I saw you talking to Mar on the yacht. You looked like old friends."

"I talk to everyone. I'm a businessman, Johnny O. I have to make myself friendly to people, even people like Henry Mar."

"Do you do much business with Mar, Alex?"

"I sell him rugs. He loves rugs, buys maybe six or ten from me already."

I could hear movement behind me. Viktor was trying to be quiet, but having a pair of size sixteen shoes made that hard to do.

"Send him away, Alex. I want to show you something."

Zek pointed two fingers to the door and Viktor clomped his way out of the room.

I took the Polaroid of the fake Stalin Blue from my coat pocket and handed it to Zek.

"Recognize it?"

"Sure. Is picture of Stalin Blue diamond."

"Is it? There's a rumor going around that Vanel doesn't have the real diamond—that a fake was made of the Blue in Paris. Maybe all he has is a fake."

"I saw Svetlana at party on yacht. It look like real diamond to me."

"Svetlana is gone, Alex. Vanel had her flown to New Jersey yesterday in his private jet."

"Who fuck want go to New Jersey?"

"Svetlana. Vanel bought a big house for her there."

Zek's lips molded into a half-smile. "Vanel gets her to

America, buys her a big house, she gives him diamond?"

"That makes sense to me."

"Is bullshit," he said sharply. "Svetlana, she had some respect in Russia because of her father, but not enough respect that many someones wouldn't cut her throat for Stalin Blue. No, she window dressing—make Vanel respectable, peoples think he got diamond from her."

"If that's true, then how did Vanel come into possession of the diamond?"

"He kill someone, probably. Who? I don't know. Maybe recently, maybe years ago, or maybe he has diamond for long time. Maybe he had it when he left Russia, maybe he hiding it until now. Where do you think he keeps it, Johnny?"

"Somewhere safe."

"Safe! You bet. He has big safe in his house. Keeps paintings, little statues, many valuable things there. That's where he keeps Stalin Blue."

"Why not in a bank vault?"

"Because Vanel not like that. He keeps treasures close, he likes be near them, feel them, show them off to people."

"How do you know about the safe in his house?"

"He show me. A few weeks ago I try to sell him a painting by Frenchman, Jean Corot. You know him? Very famous, very what you say...prolific? Died a hundred years ago. Big joke about him. Corot painted two thousand canvases, and four thousand of them are in America."

"Did you sell Vanel a fake?"

Zek shrugged and tucked in the corners of his mouth. "Would I do such a thing? No. Dimitri Vanel very smart when it comes to paintings. He and his niece, Polina—they examine it closely, say no good."

"What do you know about Polina?"

"Her mother is Vanel's sister, so she is cousin to Nika. Her father is big French crook. She smart about paintings, not so smart about mens. Screws lots of them—maybe Uncle Dimitri, maybe Trower. Once she tried make nice with me. I turn bitch down."

That was hard for me to believe—first that Polina would go after Zek, and second that he'd turn her down if she was that foolish.

"Tell me about his safe, Alex."

"Very big, like a big closet. Is behind a wall in room he calls his office. Behind a big fancy desk. Why you want to know, Johnny? You thinking of getting into safe? Replace real diamond with fake?"

"Not me, Alex."

"Who then? Me? No." The sound of Zek snapping his fingers sounded like a gunshot. "Who has the fake? Who makes switch? Trower? Big stupid bodyguard?"

"Don't take Trower lightly. He had a specialty when he was in the British commandos."

"What specialty?"

I decided not to let Zek in on the fact that Trower was fluent in Russian, so I just said, "Killing people. I'm told he is very good at it."

Zek wasn't impressed. "Okay, but that's different than switching diamond." He snapped his fingers again. "Gaby, the wife? Could be, huh? She still very pretty but is getting wrinkles and her boobies are drooping. That's when Vanel gets rid of his wives. And they sign a legal paper, nuptial agreement. When divorced, no money."

Zek leaned forward in his chair and lowered his voice into a conspiratorial whisper. "I hear Vanel having troubles with wife. He's serving boneless pork—you understand? Can't get his cock up anymore."

"Why doesn't your badass Moscow buddy Arkadi Kusmenko just send Boris or some other flunky to Vanel's house, make him open the safe and then kill him?"

"You don't understand man like Arkadi. Killing Vanel would be easy, but people like Arkadi, they like to kill an enemy slowly, by taking away what he loves most. His family, huh? Maybe turn son into a drug addict. The daughter? Make her a whore. Then take the Stalin Blue and some of his paintings. "

"I know someone who could shave the Stalin Blue, make some minor alterations and turn it into a different stone. It would still be worth a fortune."

We stared deadpan at each other for several seconds, and then Zek said, "You think Vanel makes switch himself? Keeps fake, sells real diamond."

"The diamond must be insured for a lot of money, Alex."

"Some peoples say Vanel having money troubles. He selling some of his paintings. Even say his boat is for sale. This fake diamond. Who told you about it?"

"An agent from Interpol. And he gave me the photograph."

Zek swallowed hard, and then ran his fingers over the shotgun lying on the table.

Interpol is one of the oldest, largest, and most misunderstood police agencies in the world. Its headquarters were located in St. Cloud, on the outskirts of Paris, and while the TV and movie boys had given their agents a distinct whiff of James Bond, in fact Interpol agents didn't carry a gun, couldn't make an arrest, and seldom left their comfortable offices. I'd met two of their agents, both good, hardworking, intelligent guys—but they weren't cops. They handed the information over to us and stepped back out of harm's way.

What Interpol did have was a huge budget and contacts with police departments worldwide. Illicit traffic in works of art and drugs were a specialty. Things like that worried people like Alex Zek. Worried him a lot. Which is why I made up the whole story.

"Did this Interpol agent tell you who has this fake?"

"He thinks it's someone here in San Francisco."

I put the photo back into my pocket, and then said, "You've been lying to me, Alex."

He did that "who me?" shrug again. "What you mean? You don't trust me?"

"No, I don't. No one does. Even *you* don't trust you. Boris's last name isn't Jakov, it's Rurov."

"Bullshit. Who told you this?"

"Someone who should know."

"Well, *he* lies to you. Last name is Jakov. I knew his mother, Anya. This is when I was in Moscow, when he was just a little boy. She was nice lady—not a whore. What you Americans call a good sport. Husband was solider, always away somewhere. I brought her food—a ham, sausage, fresh eggs, stuff like that."

"And where was little Boris while you were being the Good Samaritan?"

"On streets, getting in troubles. He never there when I was with Anya."

"He's here. In my town, Alex. I want him."

"I find him for you, Johnny. I have Viktor turn him into pretzel then drop him on your front door."

Zek offered me a case of Dom Perignon champagne, but I told him I was in a hurry. A worry-hurry. If Zek wasn't lying, and Boris's real name was Jakov, then FBI agent Charlie Ledegue had lied to me.

# CHAPTER 32

I stopped at the Chevron station across from the Hall of Justice and used the payphone to call Lou Papas, my source at the phone company. I didn't like calling Lou from my desk at the Hall—he was too good a source to risk exposing to a neighboring nosy cop. When we were connected I asked him for the number for every phone in Dimitri Vanel's house in Hillsborough.

"Give me a few minutes, Johnny," Lou said.

I spent the time watching Chevron customers filling up their tanks at thirty-eight cents a gallon and trying to figure out my next move. I'd put the heat on Boris, both through Polina and Zek. What would be his reaction? If Zek was in this with Boris, the two of them would be worrying about the Interpol agent that I'd made up. Just the mere mention of Interpol had caused Zek to sweat.

When Papas came back on the line he read off seven different numbers listed for Vanel's house—one of which his daughter Nika had provided me. The one I'd called to talk to Polina.

I tried the phone number again, connecting to Nika's drowsy voice on an answering machine. "I'm not here. Call again, please."

The next call got me connected me to the grumpy voice of Raleigh Trower on his machine. "Trower. Leave a message."

Two more calls went unanswered, and then I hooked up with the soft seductive voice of Vanel's wife, Gaby.

She said "Hello" as if the word had six syllables, and "Leave your number and I will try and get back to you."

On the next call I hit pay dirt. A man's voice, irritable, impatient.

"Who is this?"

"Mr. Vanel? This is Inspector John O'Rorke of the San Francisco Police Department."

"How'd you get this number?"

"It's important that I talk to you, Mr. Vanel."

"Who did you say you were?"

"Inspector O'Rorke, San Francisco Police Department. I was by your house yesterday and spoke to Raleigh Trower."

"Good for you."

"He didn't tell you I was there?"

"He might have mentioned it."

"Someone is stalking your daughter. A Russian thug who works for Arkadi Kusmenko."

"Stalking Nika? Why would Arkadi do that?"

"I think it has something to do with that big blue diamond you have stored in the safe in your office. I can be at your house in thirty minutes."

"That is not convenient, Officer—"

"Inspector O'Rorke."

"I can see you at four o'clock."

"All right. Will your daughter be there?"

"I imagine so," Vanel said, and then broke the connection.

It wasn't yet noon, but Vanel was too busy to see a policeman who told him his daughter was being stalked by a killer until four in the afternoon.

I called Francie Stevens, caught her at her desk in the D.A.'s office and invited her to dinner at my place. "The *Bullitt* crew is all finished, and they left a refrigerator full of goodies. Can I pick you up around six-thirty?"

"I've got some errands to do, Johnny. I'll meet you there at seven, okay?"

Okay indeed.

I had time to kill, so I called Alan Rickeby to see how

*Bullitt* was going, and to find out where they were filming that day.

"How'd you like the wristwatch?" Rickeby asked.

"Terrific. Thank Mr. McQueen for me."

"You can thank him yourself. He's got an idea that he can use you in a scene when we start filming at the Hall of Justice."

"A scene?"

"Nothing big, just a line or two. We'll give you a screen test. You'll be playing a cop, so it won't be much of a stretch."

"Where are you shooting today?"

"Out at 2700 Vallejo Street; should be there all day. Take care, Johnny."

*Just a line or two.* Here I'd been laughing over how my fellow cops were dying to get in the movie, and now a part was dropped into my lap. My stomach actually started feeling queasy. *A line or two.*

I headed out to the Vallejo Street film site, hoping to spot Nika Vanel and Polina. They weren't around, but Russ Cortig was. He was all smiles.

"Nika was really happy about meeting McQueen yesterday. We went to dinner last night." The smile got wider. "She was great."

"Was her buddy Polina, the brunette, with her?"

"No. Just the two of us." Cortig adjusted a few knobs on some kind of transformer. "She wants to be in the movies, Inspector. Like all of them."

"Russ, that night you first met Nika at the party on Clayton Street. The Russian who came up to you and started asking questions. Could he have been asking about Polina, rather than Nika?"

Cortig brushed his lower lip with a thumbnail. "I don't know. I just figured he was bugging me about Nika, because she was the only one I was interested in."

"But he could have been bugging you about Polina?"

"Yeah, I guess so."

Steve McQueen was dressed in a suit, tie and raincoat, while he filmed a scene with Robert Vaughn on the terrace of the Beau Arts mansion.

They went at it for more than an hour. Between one of the takes McQueen came over, bummed a cigarette from Cortig and gave me one of those cool, squinty grins of his.

I tapped the crystal on my new watch with a finger and said, "Thanks."

*Just a line or two.*


I arrived at Dimitri Vanel's house promptly at four o'clock. The iron gates were open, so I drove right through. The chocolate-and-cream Rolls Royce was parked in front of the house, along with the red Jaguar convertible I'd seen on my last visit.

Raleigh Trower was leaning on the open front door, his arms crossed against his chest. He was wearing chinos and a black knit polo shirt.

"You're back," he said in a way of greeting. "What took you so long?"

"I've been working on a case. Some commando beat up a bartender in the back of a pub. You ever run into anything like that?"

Trower straightened up and his hands curled into fists. "You been checking up on me, Mick?"

"Why would I do that? Have you got something to hide?"

I brushed past him and walked into the house. "You never did tell me why you left the commandos, Raleigh."

He put his hand on my shoulder and said, "Hold it right there, Mick. I don't know who you've been talking to, but you better keep your mouth shut around here."

Cops' rule number one—you never allow a bad guy to put

his hands on you. Never. I swiveled around, my left elbow knocking his hand away. The punch didn't travel more than eighteen inches, but I put all of my two hundred pounds behind it and I hit that magic little button spot on side of his jaw. A straight right hand. You might think a big tough guy like Trower could handle a punch like that, but he collapsed to the marble flooring in a slow motion move, like a puppet whose strings had been cut.

When the jaw is struck that hard, the head accelerates sideways and then the muscles, tendons and bones work to keep the head from spinning around. By this time the brain is a floating bowl of mush that crashes into the inside of the skull. Lights out.

I rubbed my knuckles and waited for Trower to come back to life. After a count of ten he started to move, shaking his head, and slowly, awkwardly getting to one knee.

"Raleigh, you told me you had a network of bodyguards in place to take care of Mr. Vanel, wherever he goes; well I've got my own network, fellow cops, so if something happens to me—a bullet, or a car accident, they'll know you were the one behind it, and your ass will be grass." I held out a hand to Trower. "So let's you and I forget that this ever happened."

He took hold of my right hand and I hoisted him to his feet. He wobbled a bit then rubbed his jaw.

"Vanel's expecting you."

# CHAPTER 33

I followed Trower down that long hallway to Dimitri Vanel's office. The shutters were closed, cutting off the view of the swimming pool.

Vanel was leaning on the corner of the elaborate desk with the gilded winged sphinxes. He was wearing a smoking jacket of burgundy silk, pinstriped slacks and black velvet slippers embroidered with a ships' anchor. He was smoking a long narrow cigar. His silver colored hair was carefully sprayed in place and he had a predatory look in his dark eyes.

"So you're the cop," he said.

"I'm Inspector O'Rorke."

"Trower, bring us a drink," Vanel said, before walking around the desk and sliding into his chair. "All right, Inspector, tell me all about this man who's supposedly stalking Nika."

I did just that, telling him that Boris had murdered one crossdresser, assaulted another, had been seen asking questions about Nika at a shindig in the Haight, and had been on board the *Dégager* the night of the party.

Trower came back with a silver tray holding two long stemmed martini glasses, complete with olives.

He handed one to Vanel, the other to me. Mine was room temperature. I could see the frost on Vanel's glass. Trower's small way of getting even with me.

When Trower left, I showed Vanel two photographs of Boris. "Recognize the man?"

Vanel put on a pair of reading glasses, and then leaned back in his chair, puffed until the cigar tip turned red and blew a perfect smoke ring.

"No. You told me he's working for Arkadi Kusmenko. What's your proof of that?"

"A federal intelligent agency. Boris uses several last names: Rurov, Jakov, Sikorov, Egorov and Milailov."

Vanel worked on his drink and studied the photos again. "I've never seen this man, and I haven't seen Arkadi in years. Arkadi would have a dozen like him. We've had our differences, but they've never involved anything like attacking each other's families."

"But now you have something he wants, the Stalin Blue, and he may use Nika in order to get it."

"You mean kidnap her, hold her for ransom?"

"That's exactly what I mean."

"Do you have children, Inspector?"

"No."

Vanel sucked the olive off of the martini toothpick and chewed it slowly. "Wise decision. They can make your life miserable. My son became a drug addict. I sent him to the best clinics in Switzerland in hopes of a cure, however, despite a great deal of time, money and effort from me, he could not stop taking drugs. He was young, handsome, and talented, but in the end all of that meant nothing."

"What kind of drugs was he into?"

"Heroin," Vanel said.

"We're having a lot of trouble with heroin here on the West Coast, especially China White."

"Are you trying to make some kind of a point, Inspector?"

"No. I'm sorry about your son, but you still have Nika."

"Not for long. We're not on the best of terms. She wants to be an actress, in Hollywood, and she expects me to get into the film business so that I can arrange for her to attain roles in movies. Two years ago she wanted to be a ballerina, after that a singer."

"In addition to Arkadi Kusmenko, there are some local villains who would do just about anything to get the diamond. May I see it?"

The question surprised Vanel. "The Blue? You want to see it?"

"Yes. There are rumors out that Kusmenko had a duplicate made, and that he intends to make a switch."

Vanel blew another smoke ring. "That would not be possible. The Blue is in a safe place."

"It wasn't all that safe at the party on your yacht the other night. Boris was there."

We were interrupted by Gaby, Vanel's wife. She was dressed for a party—a low cut aqua-colored dress and gold earrings the size of curtain rings.

"Dimitri, I have to leave. Is it all right if Trower drives me?"

"This is Inspector O'Rorke," Vanel said. "He thinks someone is out to harm Nika."

Gaby flicked her eyes in my direction. "Then he should catch him."

For some reason Vanel chuckled. "Yes. Let's hope he does. He also wants to see the Blue. He says someone has made a duplicate."

Vanel inspected his fingernails. "We're having a birthday party Wednesday evening to celebrate Gaby's...what is it, dear? Your thirty-fourth or—"

"Thirty-first," she shot back quickly. "And you did promise I could wear the diamond. You also promised to invite Steve McQueen."

I put an oar in the water. "I'm working with McQueen on his movie. I'll pass along the invitation if you want."

Vanel's feathers were a little ruffled. "Both my wife and daughter seem to be fascinated by this actor."

Gaby touched one of her earrings. "Dimitri, I must run or I'll be late for cocktails at the Getty's house."

"We wouldn't want that, would we, dear? Take Trower. I'm sure I'll be safe with the Inspector."

After Gaby had high-heeled her way out of the room, I said, "Aren't you worried about a robbery, Mr. Vanel? Anyone could kick in a window and take off with some of your artwork."

Vanel took a pistol from the pocket of his smoking jacket. It was a slim Colt .32 semi-automatic—the kind that Bogart had in his trench coat pocket when he shot the Nazi major in *Casablanca*. The kind that often jams after the first shot in real life.

"I can handle myself, and I have the best alarm system in the world. The fences, the windows, and the doors are electrified. Every one of my paintings is alarmed—just touch one and all hell breaks loose. And at night we let the dogs loose. Dobermans—six of them, so you needn't be concerned. Do you know much about diamonds, Inspector?"

"Next to nothing."

He put the gun away, placed the cigar in a cut glass ashtray, then heaved himself to his feet, turned his back to me and did something to the wall that caused it to slide open like an elevator door, revealing a small room with a concrete floor.

Vanel walked over to a wall safe that stretched from knee-high to the ceiling and spun the safe's combination dial. The safe was stamped with the manufacture's name—Mosler. I was ten feet away, but I could hear the oily metal sound of the tumblers twirling as Vanel twisted the dial right, left, right, and a final left.

The safe door swung open and he turned to face me, a vulture-like smile on his face, a large blue diamond dangling from a chain pinched between the index finger and thumb of his right hand.

"Say hello to the Stalin Blue, Inspector."

Vanel carefully removed the diamond from the clasp on

the chain, and then handed it to me.

"Sit down," Vanel suggested. "Pull the lamp close." He opened a desk drawer, took out a jeweler's loupe and handed it to me.

I screwed the loupe into my right eye and examined the Blue. It was, for lack of a better word, breathtaking, because I unconsciously held my breath as I rotated it slowly. It was a beautiful shade of blue, flawless as far as I could determine, brilliant, the cuts crisp, sharp, and it seemed to get colder the longer I held it.

"It's magnificent," I said as I passed the diamond back to Vanel.

"Yes, it is. And neither Boris nor anyone else is going to take it from me."

Vanel might not be frightened of Boris, but his daughter should be. "Is Nika here?" I asked.

"No. She's out, with Polina."

"Can you trust her?"

"My daughter?"

"Polina Morel."

Vanel sat back in his chair and interlaced the fingers of his hands across his chest. "She is my niece. I've known her all of her life."

"What was her Russian name?"

Vanel seemed annoyed by the question. "Popov."

"She may be your niece, but she wouldn't offer much protection if someone goes after Nika."

"You're incorrect, Inspector. Polina would give Trower a good run for his money. She's an expert in martial arts and a crack shot, so Nika's in good hands."

I picked up my untouched martini. Warm gin was better than no gin. "A young woman with a strong resemblance to Polina was seen speaking Russian with Boris on Polk Street a few nights ago, just before Boris picked up a transvestite and nearly killed her."

Vanel got to his feet, put the blue diamond back into the safe and did his trick that slid the wall shut.

"So Boris has a young Russian girlfriend. I assure you it was not Polina. I appreciate your stopping by, Inspector, but I have things under control. Trower will handle Boris, and when he finds him I'll make sure you're notified. I did send Steve McQueen an invitation, but he hasn't had the courtesy to respond. Do you have any influence with him?"

"A little."

"If you could persuade him to drop by for Gaby's party, I'd appreciate it."

"Is it going to be here, or on your yacht?"

"On the *Dégager*. That's about all I use it for now, parties. This is a charming city, Inspector, but the cool weather is really not the best for sailing."

Vanel used his little finger to scratch his eyebrow. "Are you thinking that Boris would have the nerve to try to crash the party and steal my diamond?"

"It's a possibility. He did it once. I'd like to be around just in case."

He eyed my sport coat. "All right. I imagine it would be a good idea to have a police presence there. But it's black tie. Gaby insisted. Cocktails at seven. Come, I'll show you out. The dogs are loose by now."

When I was safely behind the wheel of the unmarked, I took the fake Stalin Blue from my pocket and pressed it against my lips. It felt...not warm, just dull, lifeless, nothing like the stone that Dimitri Vanel had placed in my hand.

He hadn't seem bothered by the fact that a Russian killer could be after his daughter, and he treated the possibility of Polina being seen with Boris on Polk Street with outright disdain.

One thing was certain, Gaby wouldn't want to be seen wearing a fake diamond at her birthday party.

Vanel was acting awfully casual about putting the Blue on display again. Too casual?

It was going to be quite a party, one that I felt I owed to Francie Stevens.

I had one small problem—the tuxedo.

# CHAPTER 34

When I arrived back at my flat, I found that I had a visitor. Parked in front of my favorite fire hydrant was Alex Zek's gleaming black Cadillac hearse. The Beatles "Hey Jude" lyrics and cigar smoke were streaming out the rear window on the passenger side.

I parked the unmarked behind the hearse and climbed out cautiously.

Zek opened the Caddie's door and shouted out, "Johnny O. Come. Have drink."

The interior of the hearse had been converted into a mini disco lounge, with purple leather seats and neon tube light bars rimming the ceiling. Zek was in full disco mode himself—tight denim pants and a crimson raw silk jacket with threads of gold running through it. An ornate silver ice bucket with large circular handles was nestled between his black snakeskin boots.

"Sit, sit," he shouted in order to be heard over the Beatles.

"I'll sit if you turn the off the music."

He reached over to the car's stereo and dimmed the volume down so that at least it was bearable.

"Tell me, Alex," I said as I slid into one of the seats. "How long do you have to wear that outfit to win the bet?"

That one sailed right over his pompadour.

"Bet? What bet?"

"Never mind. What have you got for me?"

"Champagne." He pulled a bottle from the ice bucket and poured me a glass.

"The best. Dom Perignon. The French, they can't fight for shit, but they make great wines, huh? Viktor put a case on your steps."

"What about Boris?"

He hunched his shoulders and leaned forward. "People from Moscow tell me Boris on way back to Russia. They very upset with him."

"When? How?"

"Could already be gone. Slow boat to Vladivostok." Zek paused and grinned. "Where Bolsheviks shop."

Coming from Zek, that was a pretty clever line. Vladivostok is a Russian city not far from the borders of China and Korea, and home port to the Russian Pacific Fleet.

"That man from Interpol, Johnny. What was his name? You never tell me."

"Louis."

"He's here? In San Francisco?"

"He was yesterday."

"What does he look like?"

My made up Interpol agent had gotten under his skin. "Like a Frenchman, Alex."

I sipped the icy cold champagne. Zek was quick with a refill. He augered the bottle back into the ice bucket and said, "If you can find fake diamond, you give to me and I give you a thousand dollars, Johnny. Good money. Cash. You can buy something nice."

"A thousand dollars for a piece of paste, Alex? Why do you want it so bad?"

"For sentimental value, Johnny O. We Russians very sentimental."

"I just came from a very unsentimental Russian—Dimitri Vanel. He showed me the real Stalin Blue. I had it right in my hand, and then he put it back into his safe. A Mosler safe, Alex. Burglars and safecrackers hate Moslers. What would happen if Vanel died while the Stalin Blue was locked up in the safe? Who would inherit his fortune?"

Zek drained his champagne and dropped the glass into the ice bucket.

"That good question. Wife? Daughter? Sister? You tell me when you find out."

The case of Dom Perignon champagne was sitting on the steps leading to my flat. I lugged it up the stairs and through the door and onto the kitchen table.

I checked my new watch. Ten minutes to seven. Francie Stevens was seldom on time, so I figured I had time to run across the street to the Mom and Pop grocery store, pick up a loaf of French bread and use their payphone.

I cradled the loaf of bread under my arms as I dialed the number for Nika Vanel. She answered on the first ring, sounding slightly wasted.

"Let me talk to Polina," I said in my terrible British accent.

"Okay," she said, and a few moments later Polina said, "Who is it?"

"The man with your fake blue diamond."

"You're asking for too much money. I'll give you five hundred dollars."

"I want the five thousand, and I want to deal directly with Boris."

"Why? I can tell you—"

"Boris or no deal."

Polina said something in Russian that sounded impolite. "All right. Call me tomorrow, at five o'clock. That will give me time to set up a meeting. Don't do anything with the diamond, understand. Call me here at five o'clock. Not before."

"Tell Boris to have the money when I meet with him."

\* \* \*

Francie Stevens had never been overly impressed with my furniture or decorations before, but this time she went from room to room, running her hands across the backs of chairs, and the kitchen counter. As I pulled a cooked chicken, a platter of cheese, and a bottle of champagne from the refrigerator, she patted the case of Dom Perignon on the kitchen table, and then pointed to the box of French Bordeaux on the floor.

"Did Steve McQueen leave all of this for you?"

"Most of it."

"Mike Rhodes and Roy Creely have given up on going after your father on the Willie Mar murder, but they're both still really mad at you, Johnny. Creely was swearing, calling you the 'Fucking Fixer' and promising Rhodes that he was going to put you away. If Creely ever got in here and saw all of this expensive wine, he might try to make some sort of a case against you."

Francie had a point, but I didn't want to ruin our evening. We devoured most of the chicken, the cheese, the French bread, a bottle of the Bordeaux and half of a bottle of champagne.

When we moved to my bedroom she paused for a moment, then smiled with her eyes and said, "Did they film in here? In the bed?"

I had no idea, but I learned early in life that it's not polite to disappoint a lady. "Several scenes with McQueen and Jacqueline Bisset making love. Right here."

Francie made a sort of mewing sound, then reared back and kicked out one long leg, sending her shoe up toward the ceiling. The second shoe soon followed.

She reached for the bedcover. "I don't have to be to work until one o'clock tomorrow, Johnny."

Sometime later, at the premiere of *Bullitt*, I saw that McQueen and the lovely Miss Bisset did have a romantic romp in my bed. A movie romp—the room filled with cameramen, directors, makeup artists, and guys like Russ Cortig hovering around.

It was much better with just me and Francie.

# CHAPTER 35

There was a big commotion at the Hall of Justice the next day, with TV and radio station vehicles taking up most of the parking spots, all caused by the fact that J. Edgar Hoover was there to meet with Chief Cahill.

Security was tight, every entrance and exit manned by uniformed cops.

The elevators were roped off, so I had to climb the stairs up to the fourth floor. The Fraud Detail seemed unaffected by Hoover's visit; there was the usual mixture of cops and crooks, victims and witnesses, and a fog of cigarette smoke.

Francie and I had stopped off for lunch at Original Joe's on Taylor Street, so my stomach was rumbling from the cheeseburger, the fries and pure nerves. I kept a close watch on the office clock as I worked on upcoming security events.

After six cups of coffee and several aimless walks around the Hall of Justice, the clock finally struck five.

I dialed the number for Polina.

"We're all set," she said. "Give me a call at eleven o'clock at 362-9053."

I wrote the number down on a calendar page. "Boris will be there, right?"

"Yes, yes, yes," she said, irritably. "What's your name? What do I call you?"

"James," I said, trying to put a little of Sean Connery's Scottish burr into the word.

"All right then, James. Just make sure you're alone and you have the diamond."

"Where will the meet take place?"

"I'll tell you at eleven o'clock. And don't call that number before then, or the whole deal is off."

I broke the connection and called Lou Papas at the phone company. Lou usually got off work at five o'clock. His phone was answered by a harsh-voiced woman. "Lou? You just missed him. He'll be back at nine in the morning."

I dialed the number for telephone information and was connected to an operator who listened to my plea for an address for 362-9053.

"Come on, Inspector. You know I can't do that if the number's unlisted."

"I know, but this is an emergency. Check for me, please? "

"Okay, okay." I could hear clicking sounds and the voices of other operators in the background.

"Well, it's not unlisted, Inspector, but it's not really listed either, so I guess I can give it to you. It belongs to a payphone located at a place called the Bullpen on Polk Street."

I thanked her, hung up, wiped the sweat off my forehead with my shirtsleeve and swiveled my chair around to take in the city's jagged skyline.

The Bullpen had nothing to do with baseball—it was an S&M bar just a block or so from where Wanda had met with Boris. It catered to a rough clientele that liked whips, chains and kinky, painful sex, including insertion of fists or large hard objects into body orifices. No one had heard of HIV/AIDS in 1968, so there were no taboos. I recalled my ex-wife telling me that a patient had come into the emergency ward from the Bullpen with an eggbeater up his butt. I kid you not. It seemed like a place where Boris would feel right at home.

I'd been there once, a couple of years earlier, investigating an aggravated assault on a sailor off of the USS Ranger aircraft carrier, which had been undergoing repairs at the Naval Station in Alameda.

From what I remembered, the Bullpen was a dark, rank-smelling dump with an in-house disk jockey that played heavy rock at ear-splitting volume.

There had been a couple of payphones near the entrance to the restrooms, and a string of gloryhole rooms, where the furniture consisted of a single stool. Bagel-sized holes had been cut into the walls at crotch height to facilitate anonymous blowjobs from the guy in the adjoining room.

I had to know who would answer the phone when I called, but Polina or Boris would recognize me if I was anywhere close by. I needed a partner, someone unknown to Polina. A boyishly handsome young man would do nicely.

I called Detective Duane Garant in Sausalito and explained the situation to him. He was game, even eager to get into the action. We arranged to meet at the Jack Tar Hotel at ten o'clock. The Bullpen was just a few blocks from the hotel.

I was putting a plan together when my phone rang. It was from Laguna Honda Hospital.

"Inspector O'Rorke. This is Alisi. I think you should get over here as soon as possible."

"Is my father all right?"

"Yes, he is. But something has happened, and I don't wish to talk about it on the phone."


When I got to the hospital, my father wasn't in his room. I weaved my way between caravans of wheelchairs and gurneys until I came upon Alisi. She was positioned behind a counter-top loaded with patient charts.

"Your father is fine," she assured me. "We've moved him to another room. Right over there."

I followed her finger and saw Pop lying comfortably on his bed.

"There's been no change to his condition, Inspector, for better or worse, but there was an incident here last night."

She glanced up at the wall clock. "Early this morning, actually. A little before one o'clock."

"What kind of an incident?"

"A man wearing a doctor's lab coat, complete with a stethoscope around his neck, was examining your father. The ward's senior nurse was concerned. The man was Chinese. We do not have any Chinese doctors on the midnight shift. When she approached the man, he became agitated. She said that he was slurring his speech, but she didn't smell alcohol. His pupils were very tiny, and the color of his irises was very pronounced."

"Which means he was on heroin."

"It has that effect on people, Inspector. When she tried to question him, he pushed her to the floor and ran away."

"Why wasn't I called about this?" I shouted angrily.

Alisi raised her hands to her shoulders and then let them fall to her hips. "It was reported right away to the night supervisor, but she didn't think it was worth reporting to the police since your father wasn't harmed. She put it off until this morning when the head administrator arrived. I came on duty an hour ago, Inspector. He's checking to see if it could have been a doctor from S.F. General. They have several Chinese doctors on night duty."

Bureaucrats. They were the same everywhere—in government, the police department, and hospitals. I apologized to Alisi for shouting at her. "They were certain that he was Chinese?"

She picked up a clipboard and paged through it. "Yes. He was short, medium build, somewhere around forty years of age, dark hair, and was wearing green colored sunglasses."


"Henry Mar is gone, Johnny," Kim Lee said. "And he won't be back."

"Where the hell is he?"

We were toe-to-toe in Mar's penthouse office. I had bulled my way past several guards and startled secretaries to gain entrance to his office.

Claw, the big muscular white dog, trotted out from somewhere and growled at me.

"Silence," Kim Lee said softly. She knelt down and whispered something to the dog.

When Lee stood up, she said, "Come, pet Claw, Johnny. Do so now and he will be your friend and protector forever."

She gently guided my left hand toward the dog. Claw sniffed my fingers, and then sat on his haunches while I scratched his head.

"See. I told you, Johnny. You don't have to worry about Claw, and..." she paused for dramatic effect. "You no longer have to worry about Henry."

"He tried to kill my father this morning, and I'm going to find him if I have to bring in half of the department and tear this place apart."

"That won't be necessary. Henry Mar is no longer associated with our businesses in San Francisco. If you don't believe me, then by all means tear this place apart. Close a few gambling dens, the whorehouses, arrest some of our business associates. It will be painful and embarrassing, for us, and for several of your fellow policemen who provide us with help from time to time, as do many local politicians. But in three weeks, a month, it will be as if it had never happened. I give you my word that Henry is gone. I'm aware of what took place at the hospital. When I reported this latest episode to my superiors, it was immediately decided that it was time to replace him. "

"Replace him with you?"

"Oh, no. There are no women in charge of a triad, Johnny. We are not permitted such a position."

"Where is he, Kim?"

"He has been recalled to New York City. That is all I know."

Her voice was husky, saturated with sympathy. "I...we do feel some responsibility for what took place, and I've been granted permission to offer you something in a form of compensation."

I'd never heard a bribe described in quite that way.

"What did you have in mind?"

"The question is what do you have in mind, Johnny?"

"How about the Stalin Blue?"

Her arched eyebrows drew together. "I'm afraid that is a little more than I can provide."

She did that soft, gentle hand on my hand thing again and led me over to an alcove that featured a sofa done entirely in leopard skin. There were two chairs, the wood carved in a woven pattern that resembled snakeskin; the seats were covered with more of the leopard skin.

"Sit, relax. I'll get us a drink."

Kim Lee glided out of the room and Claw came over and rubbed his head against my leg, then dropped to the floor and rolled over on his back. His pink stomach was dotted with black spots the size of pennies.

Lee came back carrying a silver tray that held two glasses and a ceramic bottle shaped like a ukulele.

"Have you tried this before, Johnny? It's Bai Joi, called White Liquor in China."

She placed the tray on one of the chairs, poured me a glass and watched as I sampled it. The taste was somewhere between vodka and smoky kerosene.

She poured herself one and knocked it back before settling down next to me on the couch.

"You asked for the Stalin Blue diamond, Johnny. It is in the possession of Dimitri Vanel. Why do you think I could provide it to you? "

"Quite a few people want to take it away from Vanel,

including a Russian assassin who uses the name Boris. I want to find him."

I two-fingered a photo out of my coat pocket and handed it to her. "This is Boris. He was at the yacht party."

She took her time with the photo, trailing a long lavender enameled fingernail across Boris's face. "I don't like Russian men. They're terrible lovers. All take and no give. I don't remember seeing him at the party."

"I saw you talking to a couple of Russians at the party. Erik Gromov and Alex Zek."

"Zek." She spat the name out. "He wants everything he can get his hands on, including me. He has the manners of a pig."

"This compensation you have been permitted to offer me, how about you help me find Boris? You have dozens of foot soldiers and gang members throughout the city. Find him for me."

Claw nuzzled my leg again. "I thought that loyalty was a dog's best trait. He doesn't seem to be missing Henry very much."

"No one will miss Henry Mar," Lee said.

She tilted her head to one side and removed an earring. "I'll do what I can to help you find this Boris."

The other earring came off. She arched her back, reached behind her, unzipped the dress and wriggled her shoulders. The upper part of the dress fell to her lap, revealing her sharp pointed breasts. "Is there anything else I can do for you?"

I checked my wrist watch. I had plenty of time to check out the Bullpen and then meet with Garant at the hotel.

"Get rid of the dog," I said.

# CHAPTER 36

I went home and changed into an old brown leather bomber jacket, a black cashmere scarf and a dark blue fishing cap, similar to a baseball cap, but with a longer bill.

I parked the unmarked in a red zone on California Street, around the corner from the Bullpen.

It was cold, windy, and foggy. Hell, it was San Francisco. Street lights hung in the fog like yellow balloons. That area of Polk Street consisted of four- and five-story apartment houses with small business located at street level.

The Royal Theatre sat majestically in the middle of the block, an old fashioned motion picture palace that dated back to the days when it had an organ to highlight the silent movies. Its large red-and-white neon sign brightened up the street. *The Graduate*, with Dustin Hoffman, was playing, a film I was anxious to see.

Across the street from the Royal was a gay bar that went by the name the Cubbyhole, and featured exotic dance shows similar to Finocchio's.

Next door to the Royal was Swann's Oyster Depot, an always crowded little place with just nineteen stools that served great seafood, if you had the patience to wait for a seat.

And next to Swann's was the Bullpen.

I pulled the scarf up high around my neck, tugged down the brim of my cap and put one of the Swine's cigars between my teeth. Stick one in your mouth and people focus on it, not your face.

I edged the door open and stepped inside. Pinpoint light-fixtures flickered on and off, changing colors from red to yellow to blue.

There was a one-man bandstand for the in-house disk jockey, who didn't come on until ten o'clock. A mural, depicting handsome, bare-chested men in cowboy hats and chaps—nothing else, their erections proudly on display, ringed the walls.

The bartender was a sleepy-eyed man with bristly gray eyebrows that turned up at the end. He wasn't anyone I'd talked to when I had investigated that aggravated assault two years ago.

The bar was U-shaped, and most of the stools were occupied by men in leather and jeans, or men in slinky dresses and towering synthetic wigs.

I ordered a Rainier's Ale, in a bottle—the glasses in my fellow drinker's hands didn't look to clean—and then strolled past the dance floor, which was circular and half-ringed by a white, corral-style wooden fence.

Two payphones were positioned under an arrow-shaped red ceiling light fixture that pointed the way to the restrooms and the gloryhole rooms.

The phones were rotary dial, with the number printed in the center of the dialer. The number Polina had given me matched the phone nearest the hall.

I walked quickly past the restrooms and the six brass numbered doors that opened to the gloryhole rooms. There was a dented and scratched metal door marked Fire Exit at the back. The door was propped open by an empty wooden box that had once held bottles of J&B Scotch.

A bright red cast iron fire alarm box, the pull down handle type, was hanging alongside the door.

I stepped outside. A ribbon of an alleyway, barely shoulders width, ran alongside the south side of the building and out to Polk Street.

My concern now was to find a phone within sight of the Bullpen for my call to Polina, or, hopefully Boris.

There wasn't a telephone booth in the line of sight, but there was a place called Bepo's—a coffee shop-ice cream parlor on the opposite side of the street some fifty yards away. It had red vinyl booths, an open grill, and pictures of Elvis and James Dean on the walls. In the front, by the window, positioned between two pinball machines, was a payphone.

The baby-faced waitress handling the cash register assured me that they stayed open until midnight. Mission accomplished.

I was sitting in the Jack Tar Hotel's grill sipping iced tea and working at drawing a sketch of Polina's face when Detective Duane Garant strolled up to my table. He wasn't wearing his blazer outfit, but he was preppy as ever. Creased Levi's, an up-collared, coral-colored polo shirt under a beige suede jacket and moccasin style deck shoes. His hair was neatly combed and he reeked of English Leather cologne.

I had a genuine fear that he'd never get out of the Bullpen alive.

Garant kept up his preppy image by ordering a Cherry Herring, a sickly sweet Danish liqueur, over ice, with a lemon twist.

I showed him the drawing. "This is a pretty good likeness of Polina, the young woman who gave me a telephone number to contact her. I traced it to a payphone in the Bullpen. She will probably be the one who answers my call. She's slim, pretty, and carries a gun in her purse. She's seen me once, at a yacht party. When I talked her into this meeting, I disguised my voice, so she's not sure who she's dealing with. She may want to meet with me at the Bullpen, or she may send me on some wild goose chase. And remember, Boris should be sticking close to Polina, and he's a stone cold killer."

Garant stirred his drink with a plastic toothpick. "What about backup?"

"It's just you and me. Right now we don't have anything solid to charge Boris with—no witnesses to the murder or the assault, and your lab didn't turn up anything at the crime scene. If we find him and he's carrying a weapon, we can bust him and then sweat the hell out of him."

"You never told me why you think Boris may be at this bar."

"Polina is working with him. I have something that they want."

"What?"

"A fake diamond, worth no more than fifty bucks."

Garant titled his head to one side and rubbed the back of his index finger along his chin line. "Why do they want this fake diamond if it's not worth anything?"

"To swap if for the real thing. It's complicated, but I'll explain it all to you later." I gave him the number for the payphone at Bepo's.

"Are you all set?" I asked Garant when he'd finished his drink.

"As ready as I'll ever be," he said confidently.

"One final piece of advice. The Bullpen's a rough joint—the customers are the type that think rape is foreplay. If you catch sight of Boris, call me, or come and get me right away."

# CHAPTER 37

A pimply-faced teenager with fuzz on his lip that one day hoped to be a mustache was hanging onto the payphone at Bepo's. He gave me the finger when I said I needed the phone. I waved a dollar bill in front of his bumpy nose and he quickly plucked it from my hand and hung up.

It was five minutes to eleven. I'd been watching the entrance to the Bullpen and the adjoining alleyway for fifteen minutes, and there'd been no sign of Polina, or Boris, or any of the other characters who were possible contenders for the fake blue diamond resting in my right pants pocket.

I waited until a couple of minutes past the hour, and then made the call. It was picked up on the first ring.

"Who is this?" Polina asked

"James."

"Have you got it?"

The sound from the loud, raunchy music coming from the Bullpen caused Polina to shout out the question.

"I have it. Where's my money?"

"In my purse."

"Where's Boris?"

"What is it with you? I've got the money, that's all you need."

"Boris pays me or no deal."

"Fuck," she shouted eloquently. "Where are you now?"

"In the city," I said vaguely.

"How soon could you get to the fifteen hundred block of Polk Street?"

"Oh, twenty minutes."

"Good. Go to a place called the Bullpen. Across the hall

221

from the men's room are a row of doors leading to some gloryhole rooms."

Her voice took on a mocking tone. "Do you know what they are, James?"

"I've heard of them."

"I bet you have. Go into the room marked number two. Boris will pass your money through the hole in the wall, you give him the diamond. It's that simple, James. Satisfied?"

She broke the connection, and I hung up quickly, waiting for Garant's call. It never came. He erupted out of the Bullpen's door and started jogging toward Bepo's. I met him in the street. His hair was messed up and his suede jacket was buttoned tight.

"Damn, that place is a hellhole." He shook his head and went on. "Two guys and an old woman grabbed my ass."

"The phone, Duane. What happened?"

"Polina, the one in your drawing, she answered your call. She was alone, I didn't see anyone who looked like Boris."

"Okay. We go back in. I'm supposed to meet Boris in one of the gloryhole rooms in about fifteen minutes."

"Gloryhole rooms? You mean where they—"

"Exactly. They're in the back, across from the restrooms. I'm supposed to go into room number two and wait for Boris to pass the money to me. I want you to be sitting in room number one, or, if it's occupied, in number three. That way we'll only have one room to worry about."

"Then what?" Garant said between clenched teeth.

"We grab Boris, or whoever is there for the switch."

"I think we should call for backup."

"This is the big leagues, Duane. If you want to wait out in the street, that's fine. I'm going in."

"Fuck," he said, even more eloquently than Polina had.

Garant was right about one thing, the Bullpen was a hellhole. The disc jockey was a tall, skinny guy, his puny bare arms brocaded with tattoos. He had the volume cranked up high and was dancing to, I kid you not, Gene Autry's version of "Back in the Saddle Again." He was waving his hands around as if he was conducting the orchestra.

The thick-pressed crowd was in various stages of sobriety, everything from having a light buzz on to knee-walking drunk. Smoke hung in the air like Los Angeles smog on an August day. I lit up a cigar in self-defense with the lighter Zek had given me.

Garant was sticking close, his elbow touching mine. Old Gene had had enough time in the saddle—the music switched to heavy metal, electric guitars powering out an onslaught of sound that made talking, even thinking, practically impossible.

"What was Polina wearing?" I asked Garant.

"Black leather jacket and pants."

The dance floor was jammed with same-sex couples stomping boots, bumping butts, and a few twirling their partners like 1940's jitterbuggers.

The two payphones were in use, one by a waif of a transvestite with skin the color of flour. The other caller was a guy in his thirties wearing a leather motorcycle jacket with the slogan WHY RUN? YOU'LL JUST DIE SOONER printed on the back.

I checked the gloryhole rooms. A handwritten tag on room number one said it was out of order. I couldn't remember the tag being there on my earlier visit. Boris could be in there, waiting.

I grabbed Garant by his bicep. "Showtime. Room three."

I watched as he tugged the door open wide, checked out the room and then slipped inside.

There was no sign of Polina or Boris. Garant stuck his head out of the door and looked around.

A man in his thirties with a belly the size of a watermelon, wearing a plaid shirt and hiking boots headed for the restrooms, spotted Garant and must have liked what he saw, because he grabbed the knob for room two and slammed it behind him.

Then two things happened at the same time—the music cut off and a man with reddish-brown hair wearing a navy style pea coat burst out of the men's room, jerked open the door to number one and squeezed himself inside. It was Maurice, the Frenchman Polina had been romancing on the upper deck of the Vanel's yacht the night of the party, the man who'd been standing right next to Polina before Danny Higgins plucked the fake Stalin Blue from her purse.

Moments later Garant popped out of his room.

"I heard someone go into the room next to me," he said. "Was it Boris?"

Before I could answer there was a shrill scream and the door to room two burst open and the man in the plaid shirt stumbled out, hunched over, moaning, his hands cupped around his crotch.

Maurice came out into the hallway. He was holding a short length of pipe wrapped in black tape in his right hand. He grabbed Plaid Shirt by the collar and jabbed the pipe into the guy's butt.

I shot a right hand into Maurice's left kidney. There was no response. I followed with another punch. He grunted and dropped the pipe. The third kidney shot dropped him to his knees. I slammed an elbow into his temple and he flopped to the floor—his head making a cracked-ice sound as it hit the cement.

Garant said, "Who the hell is he?"

Plaid Shirt was screaming in pain. I patted Maurice down—no gun, no packages thick enough to hold five thousand dollars. I was going for his wallet when someone screamed, "Someone should call the cops!"

"Good idea," I screamed back. The Fire Exit door was closed. I pulled down the fire alarm handle, then shouldered my way through the door and out to the alleyway.

# CHAPTER 38

Bedlam was one word you could use to describe Polk Street. The people who had enjoyed *The Graduate* were filing out of the Royal Theatre, only to run into the boisterous Bullpen crowd, most of whom were carrying their beer bottles or drink glasses while they bitched about the loud beep-beep-beep of the fire alarm. The curious and colorful patrons of the Cubbyhole came out to join the party.

When you pull a fire box in San Francisco you get a quick response of four fire engines, at least one hook-and-ladder truck, all with their sirens on full blast, along with two or three police department black-and-whites making use of their sirens.

There were drunken cheers when the fire engines pulled up, and some nasty name-calling for the police. Everyone loves a fireman; only the scared and the lonely like cops.

I finally found Duane Garant huddled in the storefront entrance of a closed hardware store.

"Have you seen Boris or Polina?"

"No," he said, his voice hard and belligerent. "I did see that guy in the pea coat that you beat the hell out of. His face was all busted up."

"His name is Maurice; he's a friend of Polina's. Where'd he go?"

Garant jerked a thumb toward California Street. "That way, he was all hunched over. He could hardly walk."

That wasn't a surprise. Even with his thick jacket for protection, those blows to Maurice's kidney were the kind that could put him into the hospital.

"Find him, Duane."

Garant shoved his hands into his pants pocket and stalked off, bobbing along in the middle of the crowd like a fishing float.

I was feeling a little guilty about dragging the firemen from their beds and pinochle games. Hoses were hooked up to hydrants, the fire truck's aerial aluminum ladder stretched up to the roof of the building housing the Bullpen, and the firemen, axes drawn, struggled through the crowd to get into the building.

All of this frantic action took no more than five minutes.

An ambulance showed up, bumping over fire hoses and scattering drunks. Two emergency attendants pushed a gurney into the Bullpen. I followed right behind them, flashing my badge to the jut-jawed fireman guarding the front door.

Someone had turned the lights on. It wasn't a pretty sight: bottles and cans strewn around the floor, overturned chairs, a few drunks draped over the bar.

The ambulance crew stopped to give aid to the guy in the plaid shirt. He whimpered and sniveled as they laid him gently on the gurney.

"I didn't do nothin'," he said. "The guy told me to give it to him, and I just showed him my junk, man."

I had a hunch his "junk" was going to be sore for a long time.

I went back out to the street. The partying was breaking up, the firemen were picking up their hoses.

Garant approached me. "Your pal Maurice has disappeared. This was a disaster, O'Rorke."

"It didn't go quite like I planned, but it could have been worse."

Garant mumbled something I couldn't make out, and then pushed his way past me as he headed for his car.

I mingled with what was left of the crowd for a bit, then decided to call it a night. A long, tough, disappointing night.

# CHAPTER 39

Very early the following morning, just a little after seven o'clock, Francie Stevens and I entered the District Attorney's office, me lugging two cardboard boxes that had once contained oranges grown in Visalia, California.

Francie wanted to move out most of her belongings before the D.A. staff arrived for work. While she filled up the boxes, I strolled down to the half-glass door leading to the office of Mike Rhodes, the special prosecutor. I tested the knob. Locked. A few feet away was a desk with a brass desk plaque the size of an envelope with Roy Creely's name engraved on it. The files sitting on the top of the desk were awfully tempting.

Francie coughed loudly and when I turned to look at her she told me *no* with her eyes.

I picked up Creely's telephone and with the help of the operator was connected to the Harris County Sheriff's Office in Houston, Texas.

I was transferred around a few times, and finally ended up talking to Sergeant Boswell, a gruff-voiced guy, who, after verifying my credentials said, "How can I help you, Inspector?"

"Joel Pardee."

"Oh, shit," he groaned. "Pardee's in San Francisco? What the hell did he do now?"

"He's disappeared. I think he stuck his nose in the wrong place."

"That sounds like him."

"What kind of a cop was Pardee?"

"He wasn't," Boswell said bluntly. "He was a volunteer deputy."

"The badge he showed me didn't say volunteer, Sergeant."

"Yeah, Pardee probably swiped some guys badge before he moved out of town. He wasn't a bad guy, just not very bright. Wanted to be a real cop in the worse way, but he couldn't pass the entrance test. I used him for parades, guard duty, riding out in the desert hunting for missing kids. You guys got horses up there?"

"Sure. They patrol Golden Gate Park and are used to break up demonstrations."

"Well, about the only good thing I can tell you about Pardee is that he rides real good. His saddle was all gussied up with silver doodads. Our standard issue firearm is a Smith & Wesson three-inch barrel revolver. It wasn't good enough for Pardee. He had ivory grips put on his gun."

"He had an ivory handled derringer when I last saw him."

"Got one myself, but with the stock grips. I carry it in my right boot. They're made in Mexico. You drive over to Puebla, and you can pick them up for a few bucks. Just what kind of work is Pardee doing in your town?"

"Security guard at a hotel."

"That's about his speed, Inspector."

"Does he have family in Texas, Sergeant?"

"He was married a couple of times, but the wives got smart, got rid of him quick and took off for parts unknown. Never had kids, thank God. I know his father died in the war. His mother could still be around, I guess. You figure something bad happened to him?"

"I'm afraid so."

"Well, let me know how it turns out. I can probably find his mother. She used to run a coffee shop downtown. But do me a favor; if Pardee's still alive and kicking, when you see him, please don't mention my name."

I promised to do that, then pressed the disconnect bar,

turned my back to Francie and dialed the telephone number at Dimitri Vanel's house that I was using to make contact with Polina.

All I got was a recorded message from Nika, her statutory-rape voice cooing, "Hi, I'm busy. Please call back."

In my lousy British accent I whispered, "This is for Polina. You messed up last night. Where were you? Where was Boris? The price has gone up. I'll be in touch."

After I'd driven Francie home and lugged the two filled-to-the-brim boxes up to her apartment, I went back to my place for a kip, an Irish nap, that helped clear away the cobwebs from last night's adventures at the Bullpen.

I woke up feeling almost human, and went to visit with my father.

He was lying flat on his bed, his face pale, his breathing shallow.

Alisi came in and pulled up the bed sheet so that it covered his neck. She gave me a sad smile, and then said, "Did you take care of that Chinese gentleman, Inspector?"

"All taken care of," I assured her.

# CHAPTER 40

My heart was pounding and I could feel sweat running down my chest and across my ribs. I grabbed Steve McQueen by the leather elbow patch on his sport coat and said, "You had a call from the San Mateo Sherriff's Office, Lieutenant."

"What do they want?" he answered, in slow, deliberate voice.

"The suitcases you took from the hotel in Millbrae."

"Tell them you couldn't find me."

"Cut," Peter Yates, the director yelled.

"How was it?" McQueen asked.

"Good, it was good," Yates said with little enthusiasm.

McQueen shook my hand. "Johnny O. One take. You're a natural."

He moved over to Yates and they discussed the next scene to be filmed. The *Bullitt* crew had half of the fifth floor of the Hall of Justice blocked off for a full day of filming.

Alan Rickeby had called in the morning and gave me the two lines I was to speak. I had studied them for at least an hour in front of a mirror.

After a quick screen test that seemed to go well, I'd told Rickeby about Dimitri Vanel's yacht party invitation.

"Steve's not much for parties, Johnny."

"Understood. But Vanel is loaded, and thinking about investing in the movie business. Half of the guests will be bankers and money managers, the other half will be beautiful women. Vanel's wife will be wearing a priceless blue diamond. I think there may be an attempt to steal it."

Interest crept into Rickeby's voice. "Is just Steve invited?"

"No," I said, since it wasn't my money. "He can bring anyone he wants, including you."

Madge, a middle-aged makeup artist with hair the color of cotton candy, grabbed my hand and said, "Come on and sit down and I'll take off your war paint."

"You were good," Madge said, as she wiped my face down with cold cream. "Did you ever think of getting that nose fixed? You might get some bigger parts."

I went back to my desk and called Alex Zek's office. No answer.

I drove over to where Zek docked his tug. There was no sign of the *Krùto*, but his shiny hearse was parked nearby, as was a sporty red Jaguar convertible, the same type car I'd seen parked in front of Dimitri Vanel's house on my first visit.

I checked the Jag out. There was a gold scarf with Louis Vuitton printed in large bold letters on its edge draped across the passenger seat, the kind of expensive scarf that Gaby Vanel would enjoy putting on display.

I parked a half a block away, in a spot where the warm sun poured in the unmarked's side window and decided to wait. I'd dozed off, and was awakened by the rumbling of the *Krùto's* big engines as Zek maneuvered the tug to the dock.

Viktor made a stork-like leap from the bow of the tug to the dock and secured the lines to the dock cleats.

The engines coughed, sputtered and finally went quiet.

Viktor stayed on the dock, stretching his big arms above his head and rolling his shoulders.

Alex Zek came out of the cabin door, his hand on the lower back of Gaby Vanel, steering her to the bow. She was dressed for a cruise: a wide blue-and-white striped top that drooped low in front, tight, white designer jeans and sandals with cork soles.

Zek was in full slob mode, his shirtfront open revealing a hairy chest, his pants hanging under his protruding stomach.

Viktor reached out for Gaby's hands and hoisted her

effortlessly over the gunwale and onto the deck, and then she strolled over to the Jaguar.

I ducked down low and Gaby didn't give the unmarked a glance as she cruised by, one hand on the Jag's steering wheel, the other running a brush through her hair.

I waited ten minutes so Zek wouldn't think I'd seen Gaby's departure, and then walked down to the tug.

"Permission to come aboard," I yelled loudly.

Viktor poked his head out of a window. "What you want?"

"What you got?" I shouted back.

Zek's head popped out from under Viktor's. He forced a smile.

"Johnny O. Come. Good to see you."

The galley was in shambles, as usual: pots and pans on the stove, magazines strewn around, newspapers on the floor, fishing gear and guns on the table, and bottles and glasses on the counter next to the sink. One of the glasses was flush with red lipstick on the rim.

"Johnny. You hungry? I cook some sausage."

"No, just a beer, Alex." I made sniffing noises with my nose. "Have you changed your aftershave lotion or switched to expensive women's perfume?"

Zek laughed, one of those "that's not funny" laughs.

He plucked two Spaten beer bottles from the refrigerator, popped the tops with a church key and handed me one.

He said something in Russian, and then translated it. "To your health, my friend. What can I do for you?"

"I came close to getting my hands on the fake Stalin Blue last night, Alex. Someone phoned and said that he wanted to sell it to me."

"To you? Why you? Why to cop?"

"He said he was an ex-cop, and thought he could trust me."

"Who this man?"

"I don't know. He had a British accent. Said his name was James."

"What he want for fake diamond? How much money?"

"Five thousand dollars. I said I'd have to see it first. He set up a meeting at a gay bar called the Bullpen on Polk Street. Do you know it?"

"No."

"It's the kind of place Boris Jakov would like. Rough gay guys and transvestites."

Zek put his untouched beer on the table, and then moved over to a galley cabinet, took out a glass, filled it with ice from the refrigerator and then poured Johnny Walker Black scotch until the cubes floated. He took a deep sip, his eyes narrowed, his lips sucked in.

"So did this James show you diamond?"

"No. I was supposed to meet him at the Bullpen, in one of their gloryholes."

Zek feigned ignorance of gloryholes, and when I explained them to him, he laughed so hard he nearly went into convulsions.

When he finally settled down, he said, "So, Johnny O. You waiting on stool for British man to shove diamond through hole in wall to you?"

I decided to keep Maurice's name out of the conversation for now, because I didn't know what Zek knew about him, and the less he knew of what I knew, the better.

"Before I could get there, some guy took my place, and then a man in a pea coat, like sailors wear, beat the hell out of him with a pipe. I hammered the man pretty good. He was out cold. No ID, and no fake diamond on him. Then someone pulled a fire alarm and everyone took off, including me."

Zek worked on his drink for a minute or so.

"So, what you tell me? British man named James set you up. Was waiting there to beat you with pipe. Why?"

"Maybe I'm making someone nervous, someone who

wants the real Stalin Blue and wants me out of the way. I was thinking that description could fit you."

"Me? You crazy. We friends. I never do that to friend; especially policeman friend."

"That's what I thought, too, Alex. Maybe Boris never got on that boat to Russia. Maybe he's still here. He'd know all about the Bullpen, he'd picked up a tranny near there once—it's his kind of place."

Zek scratched the top of his head with his drink glass. "Could be, I guess. You think this British asshole will call you again?"

"Anything's possible. Or maybe I can find him."

Zek drained his glass and tossed the ice cubes into the sink. "I have to go bathroom."

I sipped at the beer and wandered over to the sink. I could see Viktor through the galley window. He had a chisel in his hand was scraping at rust spots on the decking. To the left of the sink was a stained wooden cutting board. There was a black plastic handled chef's knife lying next to the board, and next to it was an ivory handled Derringer pistol.

I could hear Zek's footsteps getting closer. I pocketed the Derringer and turned to see him come into the galley

I started to sit down, only to jump up when my butt made contact with a gun. It was the big pistol I'd seen in Viktor's hands a few days earlier.

Zek grabbed it and rubbed his hands down the long barrel as if he was caressing a work of art.

"Is Thompson Contender, fourteen-inch barrel single shot pistol. Considered to be most accurate gun in world." He wheeled around and sighted the weapon in the vicinity of Viktor. "Shoot shark's eye out from fifty yards."

"Someone told me that Polina Morel, Vanel's niece, might have connections to Boris."

Zek carefully placed the gun on the table. "Who told you this?"

"The Interpol agent. He thinks Polina is involved somehow. She'd be one of my picks if I wanted help stealing the Stalin Blue."

Zek worked on his drink. "Who else your picks?"

"Trower."

"Could be good pick, Johnny."

I picked up the big pistol. It reminded me of those guns you see hanging from a pirate's belt in the movies. I broke the barrel. There was a single cartridge in place, waiting to be fired.

"Or how about Nika, Vanel's daughter? He must show off the diamond to his little girl now and then."

"Nika? She baby. Pretty baby. Likes boys. Many boys, they say."

I stared Zek right in the eyes. "How about Gaby, Vanel's wife?"

He volleyed my stare right back at me. "Could be, yes."

"Gaby's having a birthday party on the yacht. Are you going?"

"I'm not invited, Johnny."

"I didn't ask if you were invited, I asked if you're going."

He made a jack-o'-lantern smile. "It would be good party. You going?"

"I'm invited. I have a hunch I'll be seeing you there."

Viktor was on his knees. Even on his knees he was a big man.

I gave Zek a friendly wave, started off, and then stopped and turned as if I'd suddenly remembered something.

"Alex. Does the name Joel Pardee mean anything to you?"

"No. Who he?"

"A cowboy. He worked at the Jack Tar Hotel. He was helping me track down Boris, but he disappeared."

"Maybe Boris take him back to Russia," Zek said, the grin on his face indicating that he was pleased with his answer.

"Maybe you're right. I think Pardee and Boris are in the same place."

Zek twisted his head toward Viktor, and started reeling off something in Russian.

As I was ready to hop onto the dock I spotted a woman approaching—Kim Lee.

"I've got to hand it to you, Alex. You know how to get all the pretty girls."

Lee hesitated for a moment when she spotted me, then continued on. She had the silky, athletic moves of a dancer.

"Well look who's here," she said, as she put a hand on the gunwale.

Viktor scuttled over to help, but I waved him away, put my hands on Lee's waist and hoisted her aboard.

"Going for a sail, Kim?"

"I have business with Mr. Zek."

On cue, Zek came over and shook her hand. "I have those rug samples you wanted."

"Rugs," I said. "I thought that Henry Mar was the rug man."

"I'm redoing his office," Lee said. "The new...manager will be coming to town soon. I want it to be completely redone for him; nothing of Henry's will remain."

"Who's the new man?"

"Feng Sha," Zek said, his answer drawing a withering look from Lee.

The name meant nothing to me, but the information might give me some leverage with Bob McCard or Charlie Ledegue.

"Well, I'll let you two get along with your work," I said.

"Come to cabin," Zek said to Lee with a wave of his hand. "I show you rug samples."

"Be careful not to sit on any guns," I advised her before climbing onto the dock.

# CHAPTER 41

I checked the ivory-handled Derringer before dropping it off to the crime lab for a fingerprint test. The gun had no serial number, just a stamped letter M, which I assumed meant it was manufactured in Mexico. Finding Joel Pardee's Derringer in the *Krùto's* galley probably meant that Boris had delivered Pardee to the boat, dead or alive, and that Zek had taken care of disposing of Pardee's body.

Zek, being who he was, couldn't resist holding onto the Derringer. Would Zek miss the little gun? Think that I had taken it? Or just figure that Viktor had stuck it in his pocket or some drawer with a dozen other guns?

Before I could get properly settled behind my desk, I got a call from Bogus Bob McCard. "Johnny, I found Boris. Come on over to 2812 Green Street, it's close to the Russian Embassy. Park at least a block away. We don't want too many cop cars in the area."

The house on Green Street was three stories of apricot-colored stucco topped by a clay-tiled roof.

McCard was waiting for me by a wooden gate that led to a neat garden of well-trimmed shrubs and flowering margarita trellised archways.

"This way, Johnny O."

I followed McCard through a doorway that lead to a curving stairway.

We hiked up two floors, McCard humming all the while.

"Home sweet home," Bob said, as he opened a heavily varnished mahogany door.

The room was painted the color of biscuit dough. The furniture consisted of upscale steel and leather office equipment.

There were electric cords coiled around the floor, and a circular table covered in green felt, like a gaming board, that held a half-dozen or more cardboard coffee cups, piles of photographs, camera lenses and a magnifying glass the size of a pancake

Venetian blinds shielded the windows. An assortment of cameras with telescopic lenses perched on tripods, lined up like sniper-rifles, all pointed at a building some hundred yards away—the Russian Embassy.

The Embassy was a red brick building the size of a small hotel, the roof a maze of antennas.

"How the hell did you get your hands on this place, Bob?"

McCard settled himself into a black leather Barcelona chair and beamed a smile up at me. "Luck. The owner likes local cops, hates the feds. He was screwed royally by the IRS."

He struggled to his feet, walked over to the window and scissored the blinds open with his fingers. "We don't get a full view of the front door, but all the real action takes place right there, on the west side. The garage. They move their cars in and out at all times of the day and night."

He leaned over the felt table, shuffled through a stack of eight-by-ten black-and white photographs, slipped one free and handed it to me.

"That's Boris, isn't it?"

I studied the picture. It showed the inside of the Embassy's garage and the rear end of a Lincoln sedan. Standing alongside the sedan was Erik Gromov, the Assistant Consul General, and number one KGB man in California, according to FBI agent Charlie Ledegue.

Gromov had his hand held out to a medium-sized man with dark hair.

"Here. Take a better look," McCard said, passing me the magnifying glass.

It was definitely Boris. There was a date and time stamp on the bottom of the photograph. The date was yesterday's, the time was 11:14 P.M. That was just about the time I was wading through the crowd at the Bullpen, searching for Boris and Polina.

"There's no doubt about the time, is there, Bob?"

"None at all. That's the only shot we got of him, and I don't know when he left the Embassy, or even if he did leave. The car's windows are tinted black, so we can't see who's inside the damn things, but the Ruskies don't take chances. They like to hide people in the trunks of their cars, or cover them up with blankets while they're lying on the floorboards, and we can't follow all of them."

I ran the magnifying glass slowly across the photo. "Mind if I keep this?"

McCard tugged at his lower lip and let it snap back. "I kind of do, Johnny. I can't compromise this operation."

I could understand that. "Just keep it available for me, Bob."

"Sure, and if Boris is spotted around the Embassy again, I'll give you a call."

"Thanks. Do you like champagne, Bob?"

"It's not my favorite, but my wife loves it."

"Good. I've got a case of Dom Perignon that should make her happy."

McCard smiled widely. "You don't have to do that, Johnny."

No, I didn't have to, but the champagne had come from Alex Zek, and using it to help put Zek and Boris into jail seemed like a good idea.

"Got a phone I can use?" I asked.

"On the table by the window. Help yourself. I'm going to make some coffee."

I dialed Nika's number. I'd pictured Polina sitting by the phone: upset, mad, worried, and scared, wondering when James was going to call. She answered on the first ring.

"That was a stupid stunt you pulled at the Bullpen," I told her.

"Do you still have the diamond, James?"

"Yes, but the price has gone up."

"Do you have it close to you? Could you place your hand on it quickly?"

"Yes, I could do that."

"Well, then hold it between your fingers, drop your pants, bend over and shove it up your ass!"

There was the brief sound of hysterical laughter before she slammed down the receiver.

# CHAPTER 42

"You're right. Polina must have gotten a hold of another fake diamond," Francie Stevens said, as she stood on her toes to shove a box of files into her closet. She dusted her hands off and gave me an amused look. "Either that or the great Stalin Blue caper has been called off."

I'd been using Francie as a much-needed sounding board. "Polina might be in the mood to call if off, but I don't think anyone else is."

"Let me put my brand new defense attorney slippers on," she said, "and let's pretend that Boris is my client. Tell me, Inspector, do you have any proof whatsoever that my client was involved with the death of..."

"Vanessa the Undresser."

"Was there any evidence found at Ms. Undresser's home to link my client to the murder?"

"No."

"Were there any witnesses to place him at the scene at the time of the murder?"

"No."

"So, Inspector, why are you harassing my client?"

"Vanessa claimed that he had raped and assaulted her, shortly before her death."

"Ms. Undresser was a man, a transvestite and a prostitute, and you took his word for all of this?"

"I did."

"Were there any witnesses to the alleged assault?"

"No."

Francie smiled. She was enjoying this. "And since the unfortunate death of Ms. Undresser, has anything come to light that would implicate my client in her death?"

"Nope."

"And the second alleged assault, perpetrated on another transvestite—"

I'd had enough of being a piñata for Francie's legal questions. "Wanda. And Wanda did not make out a complaint, and is no longer available for interrogation. Boris was reported to have been carrying a silenced pistol, but I have no proof of that, even though I believe it was he who took some shots at me in the St. Francis Yacht Club parking lot. So, brand new defense attorney, I have nothing to charge your client with at the moment."

"God, I hope all of my cases are as easy as this. How about dinner? I don't feel like going out, and I don't feel like cooking. That leaves Chinese takeout or pizza."

"Make it pizza." I'd never found a drink or a bottle of wine that went well with Chinese food, and I was in the mood for an adult beverage.

After Francie had called in the order and hung up the phone, I said, "Vanel is throwing another party on his yacht, on Wednesday night to celebrate his wife's birthday."

"Gaby's very beautiful, but she doesn't appear to be very bright. You told me that she's having an affair with Alex Zek. How could a woman get in bed with that man? Do you think her husband knows about the affair?"

"According to Zek, Dimitri Vanel is not up to performing in the bedroom, and he doesn't seem to mind if she sees other men. I'm pretty sure Gaby and Trower are also fooling around."

"I saw Trower at the party. He's attractive, but Vanel isn't a stupid man. From what you tell me, he's dealt with some tough people in the past. He has to know what's going on with his wife, yet he's flaunting the Stalin Blue diamond around, seemingly begging for someone to steal it, or at least try, and he's putting his daughter in danger by letting her hang around with Polina."

"Polina and Nika are cousins. Both Zek and Vanel hinted that Polina is a bit of a nymphomaniac."

Francie moved her head in a quick, negative gesture. "Do you know what the definition of a nymphomaniac is? A woman as obsessed with sex as the average man. Still, Vanel's attitude doesn't make any sense to me. None of this does."

"I agree. Do you want to go to the party?"

"Are you kidding? I'm not sneaking onto that boat again."

"We're invited."

"Thanks, but no thanks. There will just be a crowd of people I don't know, mixed in with a bunch of drunken men I want nothing to do with." She paused, and dimpled her cheeks. "I'm not talking about you, of course."

"I have a hunch that there will be an attempt to steal the Stalin Blue during the party."

"That's another reason for me to stay away."

"There's a good chance that Steve McQueen will stop by."

She moved in close and wrapped her arms around my waist. "What time will you be picking me up?"

"About six." I buried my lips into her neck. "Tell me, what is it about McQueen that gets the ladies so excited?"

"It." she murmured. "He's got *it*. Paul Newman has it, so does Clint Eastwood, but McQueen, he has a whole lot of it."

This was all news to me. "How about Robert Redford?"

"Too pretty."

"John Wayne?"

"Too old."

"Brando?"

"Had it, lost it." She leaned back and ran her hand down my forehead and over my nose. "You've got some of *it*, Johnny. The pizza won't be here for an hour or so. Do you want a drink, or should we just...relax?"

"Does it have to be a choice? We could do both, you know."

She patted my cheek lightly. "See. I told you you had *it*."

# CHAPTER 43

"I like your Mary Janes," Francie Stevens said, pointing a long red enameled fingertip toward my feet.

"My what?"

"Your Mary Janes, the shoes with the bows. They're cute."

I resembled a roadhouse waiter in my rented black tuxedo and patent leather shoes with small bows that matched the clip-on tie that was hanging under my chin.

Francie was wearing a lettuce-green-colored dress that glided over her body like a thin sheet of water.

We were standing in line waiting to board the *Dégager* for Gaby Vanel's birthday party. The weather had cooperated; the city was going through what the locals called a spring heat wave, with temperatures close to eighty during the day, cooling off some ten degrees at night.

I nodded toward a dark green Ford GT Mustang fastback parked a few yards from the gangplank.

"That's Steve McQueen's car. He's already here."

Francie grabbed my arm and gave it a tight squeeze. "I want to meet him, Johnny. Just for a few seconds."

The line moved quickly—beautifully gowned women in ages ranging from thirty to seventy accompanied by men in a variety of tuxedoes and dinner jackets, mostly black, but there were a sprinkling of white, a few powder blues and even one pink jacket. There were also several traditionalists in top hats and tails that got me humming Fred Astaire tunes.

Misha, the young man who'd been guarding the gangplank on our last visit to the *Dégager,* was back on duty. He gave me a wink and waved us aboard. The wave opened his jacket far enough to reveal a holstered revolver on his hip.

The food tables were much the same as last time: beef, lobsters, shrimp, et al. The same redheaded pianist was playing show tunes and waiters with trays held at chest level were dishing out drinks and hors d'oeuvres. Déjà vu all over again, in the immortal words of the great Yogi Berra.

"Over there," Francie said.

Over there was near the bar, where Dimitri Vanel, Gaby, Nika, and several middle-aged men had surrounded Steve McQueen, who was wearing a brown cable-knit cardigan with a shawl collar.

Alan Rickeby was in the mix, talking to a gray-haired gentleman who had banker written all over his face.

"Let's get a drink," I said, leading Francie over to the bar. She kept her eyes on McQueen as I ordered her a vodka martini.

Rickeby spotted me and gave me a wide smile.

"Hang on," I told Francie.

"Johnny" Rickeby said, "Our dropping by turned out to be a damn good idea. Steve wants to make a flick about the French auto race, Le Mans. We're having trouble with the financing and Mr. Vanel thinks he can be helpful, he knows some French bankers and knows the terrain."

Rickeby patted my shoulder. "Thanks a lot."

"Alan, see that gorgeous woman in the green dress at the bar?"

His eyes narrowed. "She wants to be an actress?"

"No. She's an attorney, and a damn good one. She's also my date, and she'd really like to meet Steve."

"Consider it done. What's her name?"

"Francie Stevens."

He glanced at his watch, which was the same blue-faced model I had on my wrist. "Steve has to get out of here in about twenty minutes. Send Francie to me and I'll take care of her."

I waved Francie over and left her in Rickeby's hands, then

started mingling. I found Alex Zek in deep conversation with one of the waiters. Deep Russian conversation.

Zek was in his disco-ball mode—a gold-colored tuxedo jacket with wide lapels ribboned on the edges. His jacket hung open and was probably too tight to button. The shirt was pleated and ruffled. His Elvis pompadour was shellacked in place.

"Where's Viktor?" I asked.

"I couldn't get him on board. Vanel is very uptight about party." He leaned in close. "The waiters are all armed, Johnny"

I headed for the bar, wondering if Boris would have the nerve to show up for the party.

Francie and McQueen were chatting away, their faces only inches apart.

Gaby Vanel was sipping champagne from a long goblet while flirting with Trower. She was wrapped in an ice-blue strapless dress that magically stayed in place just above her nipples. Around her lovely neck, dangling from a gold chain was the Stalin Blue diamond.

Trower had passed on a tuxedo; his bulging-pocket Safari jacket actually appeared as if it had once been on a safari.

The ship's horn sounded. McQueen gave Francie a friendly peck on the cheek and then slipped through the crowd much like his Mustang weaved through traffic cones.

Francie was all aglow. "Everything go well?" I asked.

"Yes, and Steve really likes you, Johnny. He said you did just great in the scene they filmed with you at the Hall. Shame on you for not telling me about that."

The *Dégager's* engines revved up and the boat began backing away from the dock.

"And you didn't tell me we were going out on the water," Francie said, a tinge of panic in her voice.

"Is that a problem?"

"I get seasick very easily."

"The bay's like glass tonight and this is a big boat. You won't have a problem."

Boy, was I wrong about that.

We cruised out to the Golden Gate Bridge, U-turned between the towers, and then sailed back into the bay.

Zek caught me as I was at the bar getting another drink for Francie.

"We going to Vallejo, then turn around and come back to the yacht club dock. What do you think of Gaby tonight? Good enough to eat, huh?"

"Right. Just don't get the Stalin Blue caught in your teeth."

Zek liked that one—liked it so much he slapped the back of the guy standing next to him hard enough to make him spit out some of his drink.

I found Francie talking to another beautiful woman—Kim Lee. Both ladies were about the same height, thanks to Kim's stiletto heels, both slim and sexy. Kim's bright red cheongsam style dress had a slit from the Mandarin collar all the way down to an area where I remembered seeing a bellybutton.

They were smiling at each other, laughing, and I wondered if I was the cause of that.

"Here you are," I said, handing Francie her martini.

"Thanks. You know Kim, don't you, Johnny?"

"Oh, we have met several times," Lee said. "Francie was telling me about her career change. An attorney at Mr. Riordan's law firm. It sounds exciting."

Francie and Kim. They were already on a first name basis.

"Need a drink, Kim?"

"No, thanks. There's someone here who you should meet. Feng Sha, who has taken Henry Mar's position. He's around somewhere."

I edged away and bumped right into the bulky frame of Erik Gromov. Bumped him hard enough to set a few of the medals on his chest swaying back and forth like a pendulum bob on a grandfather clock. He was talking to a tight-faced Asian man in his forties with a skull-close haircut.

Gromov mumbled something in Russian and the Asian gave me what we used to call a stink-eye look when I was a kid. I trekked up to the top deck. The younger crowd was in good form—dancing, necking, drinking, and smoking weed. There were no sexual aerobics—yet. And still no sign of Boris.

Nika was standing by herself, looking lonely.

"Hi," I said to her. "I told you I'd do it."

"Do what?" she asked as she blinked her eyes rapidly. She was wearing a man's style one-button blazer, with no shirt or blouse underneath. If that one button popped open, she was going to show the world her double-breasted birthday suit.

"Steve McQueen. Remember at the last party? I told you I'd get you to meet with him."

More blinking. "Oh, I remember now. You're Russ Cortig's friend."

"Where's Polina?"

"I don't know," she said vaguely.

Her fingers toyed with the blazer's button. "I guess I should thank you for getting Steve to come to the party."

"You already did, Nika. What do you think of Gaby wearing the blue diamond tonight? I'm afraid someone might steal it right off of her neck."

That thought seemed to please her. "Gaby's such a bitch."

She waved to someone—a youngster with glazed eyes and shoulder-length frizzy hair.

"Sallllong," she said, as she brushed past me.

It took me a few moments to translate that one—so long?

The yacht kept a slow steady pace as it slid through the Raccoon Straights, past Angel Island, under the Richmond-San Rafael Bridge, slowing down a bit to give the party guests a view of San Quentin Prison, then up to San Pablo Bay, reversing course when we neared Vallejo.

Most of the guests were well aware of the sights and

sounds of the Bay, and paid little attention to anything but the food, drink, and the opposite sex.

The alcohol had performed its purpose—loosening everyone up. Ties were undone, jackets abandoned, speech slurred, hands patted fannies, and that was on the main deck. I stayed sober and kept an eye on Gaby and the Stalin Blue as she paraded around as if she was the queen of the ball, and in a way, I guess she was.

Francie moved in to talk to Gaby, and Kim Lee soon made it a threesome.

I hadn't seen Dimitri Vanel since he'd been talking with Steve McQueen, and Trower had also disappeared.

Nothing much happened for a while, other than rich people were dancing, drinking, and eating expensive food with other rich people.

I was feeling jittery, butterflies were fluttering around in my stomach, and my Mary Janes were biting my insteps.

Francie had moved on and was now chatting with a trio of infatuated gentlemen. I saw her reach into her purse and pass out some of her new business cards.

Kim Lee kept her voice low and humble when she finally introduced me to Feng Sha. He was the tight-faced Asian I'd seen with Gromov.

"Kim has told me all about you," Sha said. "I welcome the chance to get to know you better."

"How is Henry Mar getting along?" I asked, drawing a gasp from Kim.

"As well as can be expected," Sha said. "He won't bother you or your family again." His voice was soft, low-keyed, but it had a steely insistence. "We have wiped that slate clean."

Alex Zek moved in to join the conversation. He was telling Sha something about a rug when the *Dégager's* engines made a booming sound. The boat turned sharply to starboard and the lights went out.

There was a period of nervous silence, and then a woman's voice let out an ear-splitting scream.

Choruses of shouts and screeches joined in, then, after what seemed to be a minute or so, the lights flickered back on. Gaby Vanel was still screaming, her hands clutching her bare neck. Her topless gown had been ripped down to her waist.

"The Blue," she wailed. "My diamond. It's gone!"

It was strangely silent, everyone focused on Gaby.

Dimitri Vanel was nowhere in sight.

There was another booming sound, the lights went out again and the yacht made loud groaning noises, like a large animal in great pain.

Everyone was screaming. One voice seemed to carry over the others. It was shouting "We're sinking!"

# CHAPTER 44

I'd been in panic situations before: shootouts, bomb scares, big fires. On those occasions people did the first thing that came to mind—which was to run. But on a crowded yacht there aren't many places to run to.

I parried the swinging arms of men and women while searching for Francie. The boat drifted around rudderless, out of control. Another loud shout, this time with a Russian accent: "Man overboard!"

The lights came back on. I found Francie holding onto the piano for dear life.

I took off my jacket and wrapped it around her shoulders. She was shivering, her teeth chattering in Morse code.

"We'll be okay," I told her, just as the *Dégager* hit bottom and shuddered to a stop.

Through the maze of confused party goers I spotted Alex Zek, calmly smoking a cigar. He had a bottle in one hand. He waved the bottle at me and pushed his way over to us.

"Relax, Johnny. We've run aground. When all of these idiots have stopped bumping into each other, we can climb onto dry ground, it's low tide."

"Where the hell are we, Alex?"

"Treasure Island. Appropriate, no? What do you think happened to the diamond?"

"I don't know. Was that you that hollered *man overboard,* Alex?"

"No." He made clucking sounds with his tongue. "Not good falling into Bay, even when water is calm. Currents very strong. Can take body out to Farralones, make dinner for white sharks."

"What happened? It sounded like an explosion."

"From engine room, I think. I know boat hit a buoy. Good captain never do that. Maybe Vanel was at wheel."

Zek handed me the bottle. "Is Wyborowa vodka, from Poland, better than Russian. I think your lady needs a drink."

Francie took a swig from the bottle. Her shivering had stopped, but she still seemed scared.

"Get me the hell out of here, Johnny," she said.

The yacht had landed sideways, with the portside facing land, which allowed an easy exit down the gangplank to the rocky eastern shoreline of Treasure Island, a man-made landform of about one square mile, roughly midway along the Bay Bridge. It's shaped like a thumbprint and was originally built for the 1939 World's Fair.

The night air was filled with sirens: fireman, cops, ambulances, all racing to the scene. The air was also filled with a lot of grumbling. Dimitri Vanel's guests were making it known that they were not at all pleased with the way the cruise had ended.

"I'm going to sue the bastard" was one popular phrase. Several women were complaining about their ruined dresses and shoes.

I picked up Francie and carried her through a foot or so of cold salt water. She felt better once her feet touched solid ground, and I half expected her to start handing out more business cards.

The emergency vehicles seemed to all arrive at the same time; the way buses do when you're waiting for one.

I could see Trower arguing with a tall man in a windbreaker and a captain's hat. Gaby Vanel was cloaked in Trower's safari jacket. She was sobbing, her makeup sliding down her face like Pagliacci, the sad opera clown. There to blot the mascara away with a handkerchief was Alex Zek.

The only ones that seemed to be taking it calmly were Erik Gromov, Kim Lee, and Feng Sha. It was as if they'd been expecting the disaster to take place.

Misha, the *Dégager's* dock guard, came by, clipboard in hand.

"Names, please," he said nervously.

"O'Rorke. Have they identified the person who went overboard?"

"No. I'm checking the guests now." He paused and took a deep breath to compose himself before adding, "No one can find Mr. Vanel."

The once stately and dignified yacht was a sad sight— scarred and tilting on its side. A Coast Guard helicopter was searching the water for the missing person. If it turned out to be Dimitri Vanel, there would be hell to pay.

"I'll try and sneak you out of here, Francie. I'll be stuck talking to cops for hours."

"No," she insisted. "I'll stay." She shuddered involuntarily. "But I want to go somewhere warm."

Somewhere warm ended up being the back of a San Francisco Police Department black-and-white patrol car. I knew the two cops, and they opened up the trunk and provided me with a black windbreaker with SFPD stenciled in large white block letters on the back.

There was a blanket to help warm up Francie. I was able to borrow a pair of rubber boots from a fire rig. I had to peel off my water soaked Mary Janes.

More and more state and county agency vehicles rolled onto the scene. There was some civil service in-fighting as to just who had control of the area, and the problems therein.

These stalwart civil servants weren't fighting so that they could take charge; they wanted the *other* departments to take over. "It's your problem not mine" was the general theme.

Treasure Island and the waters leading to the city shoreline definitely belonged in the jurisdiction of San Francisco.

But, according to a Coast Guard commander, when the *Dégager* had first run into trouble it had struck a buoy anchored in waters controlled by Alameda County. The boat was now safely aground and was no threat to navigation.

I saw Trower pushing his way through a trio of Alameda County Sheriff deputies in an attempt to get back on the boat. I flashed my badge at a sheriff and said, "It's okay. He's with me."

"I don't need your help," Trower told me, spit flying from his lips.

"If you want to get back on board, you do."

Trower grunted, and then heaved himself up the gangplank.

He was a trained assassin and an all-around hard-ass jerk, yet I felt a little sorry for him. He was in charge of security and he'd lost the Stalin Blue, the *Dégager* was beat to hell, and his boss Dimitri Vanel may have gone overboard.

"Let's work together on this, Trower. Where were you when the lights went out and the diamond was taken from Gaby? "

"There was a problem in the galley, a small fire, then there was the first explosion." He slammed the palm of his hand against his forehead. "Shit, shit, shit."

"Let's check out the boat," I suggested.

We did just that—every room, every nook and cranny of the yacht. The engine room smelled of smoke, electrically caused smoke, like the smell when the ballast of a fluorescent light fixture burns out. The big engines were coated with white powder from $CO_2$ extinguishers. The main salon was a mess of broken glass and abandoned jackets and shoes. When we were in the wheelhouse, Trower did some more swearing, and then draped himself over the spoked captain's wheel, like some Inquisition prisoner waiting to be whipped.

"You must be happy, O'Rorke. I'm totally fucked. After this I'll be lucky to get a job guarding a library."

"Quit whining, and let's find out what happened. Come on, it was a setup, wasn't it? The lights going out, the diamond disappearing, and then things got out of hand."

Trower stood up, rolled his shoulders, and bunched his fists. In other words, he was back to normal.

"What are you talking about?"

"I figure that Vanel set it up. Maybe with your help, maybe not. It was supposed to be like a magic trick—now you see the Stalin Blue, and now you don't. Where is it? Who took it? Gaby? She seemed to be in shock after the lights went back on. So what was the game plan? Vanel had to hide the Stalin Blue, at least until the *Dégager* hit the shore of Treasure Island. Or was that part of the screw-up? Was the boat meant to sail back to the St. Francis Yacht Club?"

Trower opened his mouth and then snapped it shut.

"Let's try another scenario then," I said, circling to Trower's left so that I was out of range of his right hand. "The real Stalin Blue was never onboard; it's back home in Vanel's safe. Gaby was wearing a fake, so all whoever ripped it off her neck had to do was toss it into the bay. But then someone decided to change the plan. He dumped Vanel into the water, too. Who was it, Trower? It had to be someone who knew all about the scam."

"You don't know what the hell you're talking about." He swung around and pounded his fist onto the ship's compass, shattering the glass.

A San Francisco fireman, his white helmet indicating that he was the battalion chief in charge, stormed into the room.

"Everything okay in here?" he asked.

"Yeah, fine," I said.

"The boat's clear, no one was left onboard." He turned his flashlight toward Trower. "Your hands bleeding pretty bad. There's a first aid rig outside."

I left Trower brooding in the wheelhouse. Come morning the insurance company representatives would go over the *Dégager* inch by inch in attempts to determine what caused the yacht to go out of control and to plow into Treasure Island.

Buses and limousines streamed in to take home the party guests, after they reluctantly provided their names and addresses to the cops and the Coast Guard.

Alex Zek's tugboat made an appearance, hovering fifty yards offshore.

Francie Stevens had had enough—she'd finessed a ride in one of the limos.

There was still no sign of Dimitri Vanel.

The emergency services jawed things over until well after one in the morning. All involved agreed to make out their reports and "coordinate efforts as events evolve."

Several SFPD officers were left to guard the ship.

Zek rolled his pant legs up and waded out in the bay, where Viktor was waiting for him in a rowboat to take him out to his tugboat, which was anchored nearby. Had Viktor heard about the grounding of the *Dégager* on the radio? More likely Zek had used a police or Coast Guard phone to let the giant know about the incident. Either that, or Zek had had Viktor trailing the yacht, just waiting for it to run aground. Or waiting to pick up the supposed man overboard. Or waiting to run him over with the *Krùto's* propellers.

Trower hopped into a stretch limousine with the still sobbing Gaby, and Nika, who was bundled up in one of the yacht's orange lifejackets.

Which left me hitching a ride by hanging onto the back end of a fire engine to get back to the St. Francis Yacht Club.

I guess just about every kid has wished they could take that ride at least once in their lives. Well, it's cold, windy, and you have to hang on damn tight if you don't want to fall off when the rig hits a bump, which it did quite often, perhaps for my benefit. Once was enough for me.

# CHAPTER 45

It was a little after three in the morning when my head finally hit the pillow. At ten to six the phone rang, it was Communications, telling me that my presence was requested by Sausalito Detective Duane Garant. A body from the *Dégager* had been picked up in the waters off Stuart Point, near Angel Island and taken to the Fort Point Coast Guard Station, in the San Francisco Presidio, not far from the south tower of the Golden Gate Bridge.

"That's him, isn't it?" Detective Garant asked me.

"Him" was Boris Jakov's corpse, dressed in a soggy black tuxedo. His body was lying face up on a metal-framed rescue-gurney.

We were standing on a pier that led out into the bay from the Coast Guard Station, which was a collection of clapboard buildings with shingle roofs painted that distinctive red-lead color that the Guard used on the hulls of its ships. The pier was some sixty-yards long, and there were four small cutters tied to mooring whips, bobbing with the current.

The Guardsman's duties included picking up jumpers from the bridge and victims of boating accidents. Boris was lying directly under a wooden sign the size of an opened newspaper that had been nailed to the boathouse at the end of the pier. On the sign were stenciled images of human figures, male and female, the type they put on restroom doors. A number was printed alongside each figure to signify the victims plucked out of the bay waters since January. Boris would bring that number up to seventeen.

"How did you find out about the body?" I asked Garant.

"The night duty sergeant notified me. He said that there

was an all-out search going on for a man overboard from the yacht owned by Dimitri Vanel. You told me that Boris was after Vanel's daughter, so I thought it was worth checking out."

"Has he been searched?" I asked.

"No. I'm waiting for the coroner to show up."

I bent down and began patting down the corpse. "I know the coroner's crews; they have no problem with me searching the victims."

"It'll be my coroner. The body was found in Marin County waters."

"Too late now." I moved Boris's hands and began going through the pockets of his tuxedo. They were empty except for a roll of bills held together by a rubber band. He had a leather holster of a type I'd never seen before—with a compartment for a pistol, and alongside, one to hold a silencer.

I two-fingered the gun from the holster. It was a Makarov semi-automatic—a Russian-made spinoff of the German Walther PK. The silencer was the screw on type—all very neat and professional.

I went through his pockets again. He wasn't wearing a belt, suspenders, or a cummerbund. I then checked his socks and shoes; anyplace that might be hiding the Stalin Blue.

"What are you looking for?" Garant asked.

"I was on Vanel's yacht last night. A priceless blue diamond was stolen, right off his wife's neck."

"You were there."

It wasn't a question, it was an accusation.

"You must have seen Boris," he said.

"No, I didn't."

"Someone must have seen him," Garant said.

"You'd think so, wouldn't you? What's your next move?"

"Fingerprints. If I can match Boris's fingerprints to the unknowns from Robert Alverson's Sausalito cottage, I can pretty much wrap up the case."

"Good idea." I said. My knees made popping sounds as I got to my feet.

"You're leaving?"

"Your coroner, your case, Duane. And you're doing a good job."

"Thanks," he said, zipping up his jacket. "I'll keep you in the loop."

I headed back down the dock. The rising sun had copper-plated the clouds hanging above the East Bay hills. There was just enough of a breeze to wrinkle the blue gray water.

A Coast Guardsman in his mid-twenties wearing dungarees, a chambray shirt, and a blue knit watch cap was waiting for me with a mug of coffee in his hand. His last name, Molder, was printed above the pocket of his shirt. An unlit cigarette hung from the corner of his mouth.

"You the cop?" he asked.

"I'm one of them." I introduced myself and we made a trade, one of my cards for the mug of coffee.

"There are donuts inside, and the cook would be happy to make you some ham and eggs."

"The coffee's fine. I'd like to talk to the men who pulled the body from the bay."

"That would be me. My partner went off duty about twenty minutes ago."

"How'd you find the body?"

"We were out searching since about midnight and figured from what they told us about the position of the boat, by Treasure Island, and the currants at that time that the body would have headed toward Alameda, maybe Berkeley. No luck, so we just kept moving around."

He jerked a thumb at the cutters tied to the pier. "We were all out there a long time. Coming home I spotted the body close to the shore of Angel Island. He must have been a pretty smart fella. He had cinched his hand to his belt and then tied the belt to a piece of flotsam. That's what kept him afloat."

"Flotsam?"

"A pretty good size log, cedar or oak, I guess. They float pretty good. I saw the man's gun—couldn't miss it."

"There was no ID; no wallet, just a roll of money."

"I didn't touch anything. Just saw the gun and then we took him right back here."

"I believe you. Tell me, have you ever seen anything like that before, a man using his belt to tie himself to a piece of wood?"

"No, like I said, he must have been pretty smart, huh?"

"Either that or he had some help."

I went home and tried to make up for lost sleep, but I was too juiced up—adrenaline was surging through my veins and my feet wouldn't stop tapping.

I called the Coast Guard headquarters, and spoke to Commander Ben Staves, who was in charge of their investigation. Obviously he'd heard all about the body being found by Angel Island, but it was a John Doe as far as he knew.

I gave him Boris's name and some information on his background. In return I was told that Dimitri Vanel's body had not yet been found, and that their preliminary investigation indicated that the *Dégager's* engines had been tampered with. "A low-powered explosive device, big enough to put the engines out of commission, but not big enough to sink the yacht."

I gave up on getting back to sleep and drove to the Hall of Justice. It was time to type out a CYA (cover your ass) report on the grounding of the *Dégager*. My name would be all over the reports from the fire department, the Coast Guard, and whichever law enforcement agencies ended up with the mess.

It took me more than an hour, and when finished it was a piece of fact and creative fiction that might be worth presenting to Steve McQueen as a movie script. All it needed was an ending.

Another police agency called to get into the action, FBI agent Charles Ledegue.

"Johnny, I've heard that the man you're interested in, Boris Jakov, has been—"

"Pulled out of the bay. Yes, I know, Charlie. I was going to call you."

"The story going around is that Boris tried to steal that blue diamond from Dimitri Vanel, and the two of them struggled and ended up in the water."

"Where did that story come from?"

"Hold on."

I heard the shuffling of papers, the squeaks from Ledegue's chair, then he came back on line and said, "A Sausalito cop, Detective Garant. He was on TV. My secretary saw it."

"He's the investigating officer," I told Ledegue.

"Garant mentioned in the interview that he was working with you, and that you were onboard Vanel's yacht last night."

"That was nice of him," I said between clenched teeth. "Your buddy Gromov was also at the party. He was getting chummy with Feng Sha."

"Who?" he said in the innocent voice of an altar boy.

"The man who has taken over Henry Mar's job. I've got to go, Charlie. Thanks for the call."

In a rare moment of self-restraint, I hung the receiver up rather than throwing it through the nearby window.

I was seething, near foaming at the mouth when I noticed a big shadow approaching my desk. The big shadow belonged to a big man, Raleigh Trower.

# CHAPTER 46

Trower was still wearing his safari jacket. He'd obviously missed his morning shave, and there were traces of dried blood on the bandage on his right hand.

He ran his eye around the room. Several of my fellow inspectors were watching him closely, with good reason. Trower was even angrier than I was.

"Is there somewhere we can talk privately?" he asked.

I fast-walked Trower down the corridor to the wide, concrete walled outer stairwell. There were open slots in the walls, like gun ports in an old castle, affording a narrow view of the downtown area. No one really used the stairs, it was an elevator world in the Hall of Justice, and they were usually jammed with an eclectic mixture of cops, attorneys, and their clients: hookers, burglars, rapists, armed robbers, a murderer or two, en route to court. You can spend an interesting hour or so just riding the elevators.

"They're trying to screw me," Trower said, sticking his left hand through the wall slot as if wanting to feel fresh air.

"Who?"

"Gaby, Nika. Everything is my fault. They tried to kick me out of the house, but I told them no way, not until Vanel is found. If he's found. He could be in Switzerland or South America, with the Stalin Blue in his pocket."

"Why would he do something like that?"

"Because he was in deep shit, money wise. He owed some people in France a lot of money. I mean big time money. And they're not the kind that you fuck with. And then there are his old Russian buddies. When you came to the house and gave me that photo of that punk, I had no idea who he was, but when I showed it to Vanel, he knew *exactly* who he was—Boris Jakov, one of Arkadi Kusmenko's thugs."

"Vanel recognized him right away?"

"Right away. He knew Jakov was working for Kusmenko. Kusmenko wants the Stalin Blue. There was no other reason for Jakov to be in San Francisco."

"Vanel acted pretty casual when I showed him the photo," I said.

"Polina had already clued him in. She had seen Jakov at some party in the Haight. She knew him from Moscow. Her mother and father did business with the Russian Mafia—stolen paintings, and icons, stuff like that. Jakov wanted Polina to help him get the Stalin Blue. Of course, she dumped to Vanel right away. The fact that a cop had Boris's photo and that he was suspected of a murder, shook Vanel up. I don't know all the details, but somehow Polina set up a meeting with Jakov."

"So what happened to Vanel? He couldn't have just jumped overboard and swam home."

"Don't count on it. He's a long distance swimmer. He liked to brag about swimming right past the Kremlin in the Moscow River, in winter, when he was a kid."

Vanel jumping off the yacht and swimming to safety somewhere didn't feel right to me. I'd noticed several party goers, along with some caterers and delivery people leaving the boat before sailing time. And I hadn't seen Vanel since the beginning of the party when he and some businessmen had huddled with Steve McQueen. He could have just grabbed a coat, got a hat, left his worries on the yacht and disappeared with the Stalin Blue.

I had to find out just how far I could trust Trower, so I said, "Why do you pretend that you can't speak Russian, French, or Cantonese?"

"Who says I can?"

"A spook I know."

Trower got that "I want to kill someone" gleam in his eyes, but he quickly calmed down.

"It was part of the employment agreement with Vanel. He wouldn't have hired me if I wasn't fluent in Russian and French. The Cantonese was sort of a bonus. I acted dumb and listened into some very interesting conversations, especially between Alex Zek and Gaby."

"Like what?"

"The two of them were making plans to steal the Stalin Blue at the party. I told Vanel, but he told me not to worry about it."

"And nobody caught on that you spoke Russian?"

"Polina did. I don't know if she just figured it out, or if Vanel told her."

"What do you know about Boris being on the *Dégager* last night?"

"Not a chance," Trower said.

"I saw his body. It was found floating out by Angel Island. He was wearing a tuxedo."

"A tuxedo. That was a nice touch. Something Vanel would have thought of."

"So you're telling me that Vanel killed Boris."

"He looks soft, but he's a tough cookie. He could have hired someone. Or Polina could have done the killing."

That surprised me. "Polina wasn't at the party last night. At least I didn't see her."

"She wasn't there, and neither was Boris. He had to have been killed earlier, and then dumped into the water."

Some of what Trower was telling me made sense, some of it didn't.

"Someone else could have thought of the tuxedo," I said.

"Like who?"

"Alex Zek."

Trower rubbed the bandage on his right hand. "Zek's at the house now, all over Gaby. If Vanel does turn out to be dead, there's going to be a real war between Gaby and Nika."

"What about those valuable paintings in Vanel's den. He wouldn't leave without them."

"Maybe he already has. Those are mostly copies, he kept the originals in his safe. The same thing with the diamond. Gaby was wearing a duplicate of the Blue at the party."

"Vanel had a duplicate?"

Trower seemed surprised at the question. "You think he'd trust that bitch with the real thing? I saw Vanel fiddling with two blue diamonds in the safe before the party."

"Then the real one could still be there."

"Could be."

"Who else has the combination to the safe?"

"Just Vanel. Gaby, Nika, and Zek, they're digging through his desk for the combination." Trower tapped his forefinger on his temple. "They won't find it. He kept it in his head."

"What do you know about another man—mid-thirties, reddish hair, speaks French? Polina called him Maurice. He was on the yacht the night Stalin's daughter was there."

"Maurice Bernier."

I asked Trower to spell the name out, and then said, "Have you seen him recently?"

"Bernier stayed over at the house for a couple of nights. He, Polina, and Vanel spent some time together in the swimming pool and in Vanel's office. He claimed he was a jeweler, from Paris. I heard them talking about the duplicate.

"There's another player in this, O'Rorke, some Brit who uses the name James. He somehow swiped a duplicate from Polina. She went through the roof. She wanted to send me after him, but Vanel wanted me close to home."

"Did Polina ever find this James guy and get the duplicate back?"

"No. Bernier came through with another duplicate."

Good old Maurice Bernier, who had been standing next to Polina on Broadway just before Danny Higgins swiped the fake Stalin Blue from her purse, the one that was now in my coat pocket. Was that when Maurice delivered the first fake diamond? How many damn fakes were there?

Trower said, "Polina and Vanel are very tight—a lot of whispers and hushed conversations between the two of them. They're related, but I wouldn't be surprised if Vanel was screwing her."

"Why are you telling me all of this?" I asked.

"You're a hard-ass cop, and I hate cops, but you remind me of guys I worked with in the commandos. I could trust them when the going got tough."

"Why would you want to trust me?"

He stuck his hand through the wall slot again, wriggling his fingers as if he was waving goodbye to someone. "Like I said, they're trying to make me the fall guy for all of this. For once in my life I'm clean. But that could be hard to prove when push comes to shove. I may need your help."

"Why should I help you?"

"Because I've got the safe's first combination number. Thirty-six."

"How did that happen?"

Trower shrugged and seemed a trifle embarrassed. "I've watched Vanel open the safe hundreds of times. When he was drunk, I'd help him place paintings or jewelry and statues inside, and I was able to see the starting number. So I'm thinking that you might know a safecracker, or someone who could come up with the other three numbers."

"Are you okay in here?"

"Sure, sure," Danny Higgins said, settling into a straight-back wooden chair in the Fraud Detail's interrogation room. There was just enough room for two chairs and an oak table, the top of which was scarred with cigarette burns, penknife graffiti and coffee stains. The walls and ceiling were perforated acoustical tile.

Danny took off his hat with the feather in the band and propped it on his knee. "Not like I ain't been in these things before."

"This time you're just a visitor, helping out an old friend."

"Jeez, Inspector. I don't know. The safe you're talking about, how many numbers on the dial?"

"A hundred, Danny; zero to ninety-nine."

"And it's a four number combination, right?"

"Right. I've got the first number, thirty-six."

"That leaves the other three numbers, and each one could be anything from zero to ninety-nine, so you've got a hundred times a hundred times a hundred, which gives you a million different safe combinations. What I'm telling you is that you don't have a chance without the entire combination. What kind of safe are we talking about?"

"A Mosler."

"Wow," Danny said. "Is the safe in a building or a house?"

"A very big house in Hillsborough."

"The owner lives there alone? He's married?"

"Married."

"Separate bedrooms?"

"I'm not sure, but it's a possibility. His teenage daughter lives there also. The owner is missing, quite possibly dead. There are a number of people at the house right now, searching through his office for a slip of paper with the combination."

"Wasting their time," Danny said confidently. "Odds are that he's got the combination written down somewhere, but, if he's got any brains, nowhere near the safe—but somewhere fairly close. No matter how smart the guy is, he picks numbers that mean something to him. Like his birth date, his wife's, kids', anniversary date, an old address, so if you find a list of numbers and one of them is thirty-six you might get lucky.

"Look for the combination somewhere in the bedroom or bathroom, that's where most people hide them. Otherwise you've got do some drilling. Every safe has some weak points. And if that fails, you're left with brute force and explosives."

# CHAPTER 47

Francie Stevens phoned to let me know that she'd been busy fielding calls from some of the partygoers she'd given her business cards to, one of which was Gaby Vanel.

"Gaby's concern was what would happen if her husband's body doesn't turn up."

"What did you tell her?"

"The Presumption of Death Law goes into effect after seven years. There are exceptions, but that's the general rule."

"What are the exceptions?"

"It's complicated, Johnny. And besides, I shouldn't be discussing it with you. Mrs. Vanel may hire me to represent her."

"From what I've heard, Vanel's daughter Nika is the odds on favorite to inherit everything. Did Gaby tell you that she'd signed a divorce settlement agreement?"

"She did. A lot will depend on what Mr. Vanel stipulated in his will."

"Where is the will?"

"Mrs. Vanel believes the will is in her husband's safe. She doesn't know who he used as an attorney."

"I'm going out to the house now, Francie. I'll let you know what I find."

"That would be nice, but remember, when and if she signs a retainer agreement, I'll be bound in the utmost good faith in protecting her."

Alex Zek's black hearse, the red Jaguar convertible I'd seen Gaby driving, and the chocolate-and-cream Rolls Royce were parked in front of Dimitri Vanel's mansion.

I nosed the unmarked alongside the Jag. The front door was wide open and I could hear the sound of loud voices coming from inside the house.

Viktor was the first one to spot me. He was standing in the hallway with his legs spread wide and his arms crossed over his chest.

"You," he said.

I couldn't argue with that. I skirted around him and moved toward Vanel's office. The gang was all there, at least those who were still alive. Zek was dressed in dirty jeans and a sweatshirt. He was sticking close to Gaby, who was wrapped in her version of mourning clothes—a sleeveless little black dress, a black pearl necklace with matching earrings, and black-framed sunglasses with smoky lenses.

She had a black silk scarf tied around her neck. I'd gotten a good look at that lovely neck after the diamond went missing. There were no scratches, and having had a gold-cable necklace ripped off like that should have left scratch marks.

Nika was wearing ripped jeans, a butter-yellow cashmere sweater and had a daisy-flower headband holding her hair back. Her eyes were glazed and her lips were chapped. She was sitting in her father's desk chair and had a tall glass in her right hand. The liquid was clear and there was a slice of lime floating between the ice cubes.

There was no sign of Polina, and Nika seemed lost without her.

Trower still hadn't shaved, but he'd switched from the safari jacket to a khaki colored commando sweater, the type with leather shoulder and elbow patches.

Vanel's desktop was littered with papers, the drawers pulled out, their contents spilled on the floor.

Zek gave me a "what are you doing here" stare, and then said, "Johnny O. Any news on Dimitri?"

"No. But Boris Jakov's body was found in the waters by Angel Island."

Zek waved that away. "We know that. I was out on bay all night and morning. I talk to Coast Guard peoples. Boat was..." he fumbled for the right word, and then said, "Sabotaged," said it slowly, as if he liked the way it sounded rolling off his tongue.

"By who, Alex?"

"Coast peoples don't know yet." He twisted his head in Trower's direction. "Someones who knows of boats and bombs."

Zek didn't realize he was describing himself.

I walked into the room where the safe was located, Zek right on my heels. The sheetrock around the Mosler had been chipped away in spots, the cement floor speckled with chalky white dust.

"The coroner is going over Jakov's body, Alex. The preliminary report is that he was frozen a little more than he should have been."

"What does that mean?" Gaby asked.

"That he may have been murdered, and put into a freezer before he was dumped into the bay."

"Is crazy," Zek said irritably. "Bay is ice cold. Man freeze if in there couple of hours."

"True, but he doesn't get frostbite."

Zek wasn't buying it. "Water freezing. Jakov fell from boat."

He was right about the freezing. I had made the frostbite up.

"No one saw Boris on the *Dégager*," I said.

"Maybe he have on disguise," Zek said. He put his index finger under his nose. "Fake mustache, makeup. Water wash it off."

Zek had done his homework—he had all the answers, so far.

Gaby came over and touched my arm. She removed her sunglasses, revealing thick, dark Cleopatra-style eyeliner.

"Do you think there's a chance that they will find my husband?"

"There's a chance, but the longer he's missing, the less chance there will be."

Her eyes started watering, and she put the glasses back on. There was no way to tell if the sadness came from the probable loss of her husband or the seven year wait she'd have to go through before she got her hands on all of his money—all of the money that Nika didn't beat her to.

I made small talk with Zek and Gaby for a few minutes, then went over to say hello to Nika. She mumbled something. I got a whiff of her drink—the distinctive pine-tree-juniper berry odor of gin.

"Where's Polina?" I asked her.

Nika shook the ice in her glass. "She left a note, saying she had to go back to France for a few days."

"That was bad timing."

"Maybe she won't come back."

"That would be a shame," I said. "The two of you seemed to be good friends."

"Friends. I don't have *any* friends."

She spun the chair around and dropped her chin to her chest. A lonely little rich girl with no shoulder to cry on at the moment.

I headed over toward Trower. His eyes were bloodshot and narrowed down to slits. He needed a shower and some sleep.

"I spoke to an expert on cracking safes," I told him. "Basically, the only way we'd be able to get into the Mosler is if we come up with the full four number combination. Can you get me Vanel's records: birth date, Nika's too, those of all of his wives, his son, and old addresses and phone numbers?"

Trower's lips molded into a half smile. "You think Vanel

would be stupid enough to use numbers like that for the safe?"

"My expert says that that's what people do, whether they're as smart as Vanel or not, and the most likely place they'd keep a copy of the combination is in their bedroom. Did he and Gaby share a room or—"

"Separate rooms, at opposite sides of the house."

"Is there a way I can get into his room without anyone seeing me?"

"Meet me out front in about five minutes, I'll show you the way."

Trower took off. I saw him purposely bump into Viktor's shoulder as he passed him in the hall. Trower was itching for a fight, and if Viktor had any brains—a debatable proposition—he'd stay out of the big ex-soldier's way.

I went outside and propped my butt on the Jaguar's fender. It had that washed and waxed every day glow, so I wasn't worried about dirtying my pants.

Trower came out and waved me over. He took me around the north side of the house. There were six or seven sleek black Dobermans housed in a large steel mesh kennel. They started barking and scratching at the mesh with their paws.

We entered the house through an unlocked door and I followed Trower up a carpeted staircase to the second floor.

He led me to a set of double-doors wide enough to wheel a grand piano through.

"This is Vanel's room. Gaby's is down the hall, and around the corner."

"What about Nika and Polina?"

He nodded his head to the ceiling. "Third floor."

"Who's Vanel's attorney?"

"He is. Vanel graduated from law school at Lomonosov Moscow State University. That's how he first got in with the mob back there."

"Where would his will be?" I asked. "In the safe?"

"Will?" That seemed to amuse Trower. "You speak any French?"

"Not really."

"Vanel liked to spout it when he was feeling a little superior to the rest of us. One of his favorite lines was '*Quand je mourai, c'est la fin du monde.*' When I die, it is the end of the world. You won't find a will."

"You mean that Vanel would just let his family slug it out for everything?"

"That's exactly what he'd do."

"What about you?" I asked. "Vanel must have been paying you well."

"He was. I salted some away." Trower dragged a deep breath into his lungs, his shoulders rising and falling with the effort. "Jobs like this, you always have to figure they're going to end in a sudden way."

He stood there uncertainly for a few seconds, moving from one foot to another before saying, "I figure you've got less than an hour before they start getting restless downstairs."

Trower turned on his heel and strode off, head up, ramrod stiff, as if he was back in the commandos preparing for battle.

I entered Vanel's bedroom and closed the doors behind me. The first thing I saw was an ebony Steinway grand piano.

The room was huge. One entire wall consisted of book shelves. There was one of those rolling ladders of the type used in libraries to help you get to the top shelf.

The rest of the walls were pale-gray silk, the carpet and over-sized upholstered chairs were a similar shade of gray. A coffin-shaped coffee table covered with glassware and a vase filled with a profusion of colorful gladiolas sat in front of a white stone fireplace with a crusader-style cross chiseled on its front.

There were no paintings on the walls, but there were clusters of canvases leaning against available wall space and the chairs. I fingered through dozens of them—not recognizing the artists. For the size of the room, even with all the clutter, Vanel could have put in a lot more furniture. Hell, he could have put in a couple of bowling lanes.

A door at the back of the room opened up to a smaller room, some thirty-by-forty feet.

The room was all pale gray—the walls, carpets, the drapes. There was just one painting on the wall, an oil of Vanel, his shoulders leaning forward, his head held up high, one eyebrow raised, the thumbs of both hands sticking out of the pockets of his suit jacket. It was the style of painting you'd see hanging on the walls of men's clubs or in the offices of bank presidents.

Vanel's extensive wardrobe hung neatly in built-in closets. His suits were arranged by colors, as were his shoes, sweaters and shirts.

An open door revealed a bathroom, which was worth seeing. Cream-colored marble floor and walls, a sunken tub, a shower built for at least two, a toilet sitting next to a bidet, and a mirrored medicine cabinet which held an array of upscale toiletries and a dozen or more prescription medicine bottles.

The drawer in one of the bedroom nightstands held a collection of lubricants, several boxes of condoms and one pair of bikini style panties, bright red in color.

I stretched the panties out between my fingers. The size marker showed XS. Extra small. It didn't appear as if it could stretch around Gaby's sumptuous rump.

Polina? I thought. Nika? I didn't like that thought.

The bed had a pole-supported canopy, into which was set a large mirror to reflect the activity below. I flopped down onto the bed and stared up at my reflection.

I could search this damn room for days and not find the safe's combination.

Where would *you* hide it? I asked myself.

Where *you* wouldn't find it.

Then I'm wasting my time.

You've been doing that for too long, my reflection seemed to say.

# CHAPTER 48

I had lunch with Francie Stevens the next day at Clown Alley, a burger joint just a block from her new office. She picked at her cheeseburger in between wide smiles. She had retained her first client, Gaby Vanel, and was pleased with my news that Trower didn't believe Vanel had made out a will.

"That should make it easier for me. I advised Nika to hire an attorney. She told me she'll wait a few days, until she hears from her cousin, Polina."

"Polina's a mystery woman. She's involved in this mess somehow, Francie."

"This is all going to end up in court. I don't want to do anything to jeopardize Mrs. Vanel's position." She picked up a french fry and dipped it in a mound of ketchup. "Tim thinks this could be a really big case."

Tim, as in Tim Riordan, her new boss.

"He's right. I talked to an Alameda County Sheriff Detective. They're handling the criminal investigation. There are no new developments on the search for Vanel's body, and Misha Turov has gone missing."

"Who?"

"Misha. The young man who was guarding the *Dégager's* gangplank when we went to both of those parties."

"Is anyone else missing?"

"Not that I know of."

Francie rummaged around in her purse and pulled out a newspaper. "Have you seen this?"

The *Chronicle's* headline read: STEVE MCQUEEN LEAVES YACHT PARTY SHORTLY BEFORE THE BOAT CRASHED INTO TREASURE ISLAND.

You had to read through several paragraphs before finding Vanel's name and the news that he was missing.

"The investigation's going to be a nightmare for the sheriff, having to interview all of those high-powered guests, including the Russian Ambassador, Alex Zek, Kim Lee and her new boss, Feng Sha."

Francie gave another fry a ketchup bath before plopping it into her mouth.

"Lee seems...nice," she said, when she was finished munching on the fry.

"Nice? She's the number two hoodlum in the bing kong tong, and they're a rough crowd. Drugs, prostitution, loan sharking, you name it, and her manicured fingernails are deep into it. I saw her climbing aboard Zek's tugboat the other day."

"Lee and Zek. Now there's an odd couple."

The waitress came with the check and Francie snatched it from her hand.

"I've got an expense account now, Johnny. This one is on me."


When I got back to my desk, Captain Candella grilled me on the Vanel fiasco, asked how the *Bullitt* filming was going, and then let me know that comedian Woody Allen was making plans to make a film, *Take the Money and Run*, with a lot of the shooting to be done in the city and at San Quentin Prison. The mayor wanted to be sure that Woody was treated right.

While I was going over the Allen proposal the phone rang. It was Sausalito Detective Duane Garant. He sounded chipper—a word that suited his mood and his preppy image.

"I've got the autopsy on Boris Jakov. His demise will go down as death by drowning. There were no matches with the prints from Jakov to those found at Robert Alverson's cottage. My chief has told me to wrap up the case. A man like Jakov would certainly have worn gloves."

"So Boris is going down as the murderer."

"Yes. Don't you agree?"

"You've done a thorough job, Duane. It was nice working with you."

Something had been bothering me for days, something that I kept shoving to the back of my mind.

"Duane, you never told me just where you found Inspector Cornell's fingerprints at Alverson's cottage."

"In the bathroom, under the toilet seat. His right thumb and index finger."

There were two bathrooms at the cottage, one off the kitchen the other in the master bedroom.

"The toilet near the kitchen?"

"No. The bedroom. Why?"

"Nothing. The guys were just kidding him about it, you know how cops are. I hope we can hook up on a case again, take care."

I hung up and slowly got to my feet. It was time to go to Cookie's.


I got back to the Hall at twenty-to-five, stopped at my desk just long enough to retrieve a pint bottle of whiskey that was half empty after my last visit to see my father, then headed to the Sexual Assault Detail.

Ed Cornell was still there, a big grin on his face, his feet up on his desk, a cup of coffee in one hand.

I wriggled a finger at him. "Come on. We have to talk."

The grin vanished. "Johnny O. Everything all right?"

"Everything's fine. But this is private."

He reached for his coat, which was draped across the back of his chair.

"You won't need it, Ed. This will only take a couple of minutes."

His holster was on his hip, but it was empty, his gun in the desk drawer.

I kept quiet while I lead him to the outer stairway, the same one where I'd spoken to Trower.

"What's up?" Cornell asked, as he lit up a cigarette with a throwaway lighter.

"You lied to me, Ed."

He tilted his head to one side and narrowed his eyes. "What are you talking about?"

"Robert Alverson. Vanessa the Undresser. Boris Jakov was too smart to follow Vanessa over to Sausalito, and then kill her. She was a minor annoyance to him. I talked to those three witnesses you had back your alibi up at Cookie's—a bread driver, a longshoreman, and an insurance salesman. Not a single cop. They admitted they'd lied, Ed. Said they did it because you told them it was a joke on some punk Sausalito cop. You killed Alverson, Ed. Tell me exactly what happened."

He flicked the cigarette away and pushed a hand out toward me.

"Fuck you, I—"

I grabbed his arm, yanked it hard and kicked out at his right knee. He tottered back and forth for a few seconds and then went tumbling down the cement stairs.

He was lying on his back, hugging his knee to his chest.

"You scream and I'll knock all your teeth out, Ed."

I unscrewed the cap from the pint of Jim Beam and poured a stream of the whiskey over Cornell, then picked him up by the shoulders and hurled him down the stairs again.

He tried to crawl away. I jammed the tip of the bottle into his mouth and held his nose. He started coughing and crying.

"You told me you were never in the bedroom, that you'd just had coffee in the kitchen. Your prints weren't found in the kitchen, where they should have been, but you left two prints, under the toilet seat in the bedroom bathroom. You screwed Vanessa, and then you killed her while she was in the hot tub. Snapped her neck like a chicken's, just what Vanessa told you Boris had threatened to do. Then you ripped apart the bedroom to make it look like the killer had been in a rage."

I kicked him in his already damaged knee. "Why, Ed? For God's sake, why?"

He held up a hand in front of his face. "It...it was an accident, Johnny. Vanessa was all dressed up when I got there, she looked pretty hot. We had a few drinks and...things happened. Later she got undressed, got rid of the wig, the makeup, and went into the tub. God, she...he was really ugly. An ugly man. He started needling me, you know—big tough cop getting a blow job from a guy. He was drunk."

Cornell wiped some blood from his mouth away with the back of his shirt sleeve. "So was I. I mean I was blasted. I must have had six or more shots of Wild Turkey. Alverson kept needling me, said he was going to put the word out to everyone that I was a fag, if I didn't find this Boris creep. Said he was going to tell you. Tell everyone."

"So you murdered Alverson."

"No, no. I mean I didn't want to kill him. I just wanted to shut him up. I grabbed his head and he tried to get away, and that's when it happened. I swear to God it was an accident. I swear it!"

Accident, homicide, manslaughter, whatever you called it, Cornell was going to walk. Sausalito was happy with pinning the murder on Boris Jakov and two fingerprints under the toilet seat wouldn't make a court case, unless Cornell confessed, and he wasn't going to do that to anyone but me. I could read his eyes. He was running everything through his cop's brain, no proof, no case—coercion by a deranged fellow policeman.

I poured what was left of the whiskey over him.

"After you get out of the hospital you're going to turn in your badge."

"Hey, you can't—"

I kicked his knee again then shoved him down a few more stairs.

"You do that, Ed, or I'll burn you on this. You'll lose your job, your pension, and your wife and kids will find out just what kind of a man you really are."

I used a payphone on the third floor to call for an ambulance. "A policeman fell on the stairs of the Hall of Justice. I think he's drunk."

I had the Fraud Detail all to myself when I got back to my desk. Everyone had gone home for the day. The phone rang. I half expected it to be someone asking about Cornell.

"Hey, O'Rorke, this is Sergeant Boswell."

It took a moment for the name to click in; Boswell, from the Harris County Sheriff's Office in Houston.

"Listen, O'Rorke, Joel Pardee's mother, Laverne, passed away about six months ago, so as far as I know he doesn't have any family or good friends down here." A pause, a laugh, and then, "Or anywhere else, I guess. Have you found him?"

"He's still missing."

"What do you figure happened to him?"

"I think that he was murdered, his body cut up for shark bait and thrown into the Pacific Ocean."

"Who the hell would do that to Joel?"

"I think that it was a couple of Russian gangsters, but I can't prove it. One of them is dead."

"And the other?"

"Isn't."

"Okay," Boswell said wearily. "Listen, Pardee wasn't a real cop, and he was a pain in the ass, but as a deputy he did a few good things. He found some kids that got lost in brush country and probably would have died if Pardee hadn't rode along. Another time he pulled some young'n out of Buffalo Bayou. Got off his horse and went in the water after him. So what I'm saying is Pardee was one of us, you know what I mean?"

*One of us.* "I'll do my best to find out just what happened, Sergeant."

"Thanks. Let me know if you get it done."

I opened the middle desk drawer and ran my finger across the Derringer that I was sure—but couldn't prove, had belonged to Pardee. The crime lab hadn't been able to pull any identifiable prints from the gun, there were just too many overlapping and smeared prints.

Guns. Have we talked about guns? The range master at the Police Academy told all of us new recruits that if we were ever in a situation where someone was holding a .45 automatic on you, and that if you were at least twenty yards apart, turn around and run away, because the power of the bullet was too much for the gun's frame. "You're lucky to hit the side of a barn with a .45 from that distance."

He also didn't have much use for the weapon of choice for plainclothes cops at the time—snub nosed revolvers. Their stopping power was nothing like that of a .45, and the accuracy wasn't a hell of a lot better.

The Derringer was a whole different story. No accuracy and no power, but it had a kicker. While the .45 could blow a hole the size of a baseball in someone, the Derringer's small .22 cartridge entered a human target and then kind of meandered around, traveling the path of least resistance. Thus you could shoot someone in the leg, and the bullet might cruise up to the heart.

I had one case when a man accidentally dropped a Derringer to the floor causing it to fire. The bullet entered his calf and ended up in his brain.

I started to put the gun back in the desk drawer, but at the last second decided to slip it into my coat pocket.

It had been a sloppy mistake for Zek to leave the gun in the *Krùto's* galley. Maybe he had made some other sloppy mistakes.

# CHAPTER 49

I sat in the unmarked, drinking coffee from a thermos and keeping a wary eye on Alex Zek's tugboat. The hawser lines securing the boat to the dock cleats made occasional loud creaking noises. Other than that, the night was dark, still, silent, save for an occasional siren wailing in the distance.

I watched intently for a good hour. No lights of any kind showed in the tug. It was time to get out of the car and commit a felony or two.

I hooded my flashlight, climbed onboard the *Krùto* and hurried up the ladder to the bridge deck. The wheelhouse was located directly over the galley. Its wooden door was as scarred and battered as I'd hoped it would be. I slipped my burglar tools from my waistband: a small crowbar, a screwdriver, and a putty knife.

I was no Danny Higgins, but like most cops, I'd learned how to gain entry through most any door.

I got down on one knee, jammed the crowbar under the bottom of the door, then stood up and pushed my shoulder into the door while pressing down on the crowbar with my foot. The heavy door didn't move much, but just enough. I worked the screwdriver and putty knife into the latch and within half a minute was rewarded with the sound of the lock clicking open.

I stepped inside, closed the door and relocked it. I could make out the ship's spoked wheel, two chrome-handled throttles, and a marine ship-to-shore radio. There were gauges and a compass, a battered leather captain's chair with a footrest, and an ashtray overflowing with cigar butts.

I took the narrow interior stairwell down to the lower

deck, coming out in a passageway just aft of the galley. I stood statue-still with my eyes closed for several seconds, listening for anything unusual, like snoring sounds coming from Viktor or Zek.

All was quiet. I moved slowly. The door to Zek's gun room was unlocked. I washed the flashlight beam around the room. There were enough weapons for a small army: a few dozen rifles resting in racks running from the floor to the ceiling, pistols of every shape and size dangling from their trigger guards, and shelves filled with boxes of cartridges.

Mixed in with the weapons were an impressive number of fishing rods and reels.

I went back to the passageway and cautiously entered the *Krùto's* sleeping quarters. "Sleeps four, fucks eight" was the quaint way that Zek had used to describe the arrangement.

There were four bunk beds bolted to the walls, all of them in disarray—sheets hanging out, blankets jumbled up.

The floor was littered with men's clothing: pants, jackets, shoes, underwear. In the mix was one black lace bra that had Gaby Vanel's measurements written all over it.

I pawed through the clothes, hoping to find one of Joel Pardee's cowboy boots or his horsehead belt buckle.

No luck. I moved on down the passageway. One door opened to a bathroom with all the standard fixtures. I then came to a stainless steel door with a heavy cargo door latch. It took some effort to open the latch.

It was a freezer, and the interior light went on automatically. I stepped back and said something loud and obscene. Staring up at me from the freezer floor were the monstrous heads of four great white sharks, their jaws spread open to reveal rows of sharp, pointy teeth.

The sharks weren't the worst of it. Hanging by his roped hands from a ceiling hook, his shoes dangling inches from the floor, was a dark-haired man in a white shirt.

I stepped inside and swiveled the body around. It was

Misha Turov. His black eyes were wide open, his eyebrows and lashes laced with ice. There were no visible wounds, no bullet holes, no knife scars, and no blood on his clothing.

I shuddered, partly from the freezer's icy stale air and partly from thinking that Misha had been hung up alive and allowed to freeze to death.

I backed out of the freezer and closed the door. All I needed to do now was call for backup, arrest Zek and then do a thorough search of the tug.

I was making my way back to the front of the boat when I heard voices and the barking of a dog.

Peeking through the galley window I saw Viktor climb aboard the *Krùto*, followed by Zek. The slim figure of Kim Lee made a graceful leap to the deck, and then said, "Someone lift the dog."

Someone was Viktor, who leaned over the gunwale, and hoisted a large white dog onto the tug's deck. Claw.

Viktor started undoing the mooring lines as Zek and Kim Lee, with Claw at her side, made their way to the galley.

I backpedaled as fast as I could, opened a door toward the rear of the boat and slithered into the belly of the engine room.

They were here to pick up something, I told myself. A rug, drugs, whatever. Pick it up and then get off the boat.

Loud chugging noises and then the full roar of the *Krùto's* twin diesels brought that prayer to an end.

The noise was deafening. I covered my ears with my hands, kept a sharp eye on the engine room door and took stock of my position. I was outnumbered three to one; four counting Claw, and outgunned fifty or a hundred to one. Make that two. I had my Colt .38 caliber snub-nose revolver, and Pardee's Derringer. Five bullets in the Colt, two in the Derringer.

So I was outmanned, outgunned and starting to get sick from the noise in the engine room.

The noise only got louder as the tugboat backed away from its berth and headed out to the bay.

I tried to figure where Zek was heading. Out to the Farralones to drop Misha in with the sharks? But why bring Kim Lee along for a burial at sea?

I focused the flashlight on my TAG Heuer watch. It was twenty minutes past midnight. I waited a long, ear-cupped ten minutes before the engine noises drove me to opening the door.

The passageway was empty. There was music coming from the galley area: Tom Jones wailing "Delilah."

I reentered the sleeping cabin and locked the door after me. The starboard porthole-style window gave a view out to the north. We passed Alcatraz, then Angel Island and a few minutes later the tug glided by the north tower of the Golden Gate Bridge.

Next stop, the Farralones?

No, we sailed by those miserable islands and the water got a little rough. Unlike Dimitri Vanel's classy yacht, the *Krùto* had a round bottom, which caused it to roll with every wave, which caused my stomach to roll with every wave.

Suddenly the engines slowed down. Straining my neck around the porthole I could see the outline of a big ship, a freighter, come into view.

Zek or Viktor, whoever was at the wheel, brought us up alongside the bigger ship.

I slipped out of the cabin and found a door leading out to the port side of the boat. I sucked in fresh air and watched as the tug nosed closer to the freighter, which was a grimy, rust-streaked vessel with the name *Genoa Maru* painted on its bow.

I could see at least a half dozen Asian seaman leaning over the freighter's railing, some thirty feet above us.

Kim Lee strode out into the middle of the deck with a loudspeaker in hand and began yelling out orders in Chinese.

Within minutes a crane boom swung into view and a cargo net attached to a steel cable was slowly lowered from the *Genoa Maru* down to the *Krùto's* deck.

Viktor crabbed over and undid the cable hook while Kim Lee continued her conversation through the bullhorn.

The cable hook made clanging sounds against the freighters side as it was hauled upward. Then there was a long horn toot from the freighter, followed by three shorter toots and the big ship began moving away.

Zek came out to join the party, slapping Viktor on his back and then pulling in Kim Lee for a big hug.

Viktor pulled out a knife and cut the netting, letting loose bread loaf sized packages wrapped in aluminum foil and duct tape. China White heroin? It had to be China White.

Zek lifted up the stern cargo hatch and he and Viktor began tossing the packages into the ship's hold.

Kim Lee stood close by, a clipboard in her hands, counting each and every package.

I headed back to the relative safety of the cabin with the bunks and plotted out my next move. Hide and wait until we docked, then catch Zek, Viktor and Kim Lee off guard, disarm them and call for help by using the radio in the wheelhouse? Lee might have a crew of thugs waiting at the *Krùto's* home berth to unload the heroin. I couldn't let that happen.

The trip home went by in agonizing slowness. When we were abreast of the Mile Rock Light House, a couple of miles west of the bridge, I opened the cabin door slowly and edged out into the passageway. No noise, other than the hum of the twin diesels. I unholstered my revolver and crept forward.

Growling sound, from behind me. I spun around and saw Claw. He started barking.

"Claw, Claw," I pleaded, holding out my left hand in his direction. "Good boy. Remember me? Good boy."

The dog remembered me enough to stop barking and sit on

his haunches. What was it Kim Lee had said? "Pet him now and he will be your friend for life."

I moved slowly, until I was close enough to pat his forehead. Claw responded with a tongue lick.

I coaxed him into the cabin with the bunks. He was all right with that until I closed the door, then he started barking like the Hound of the Baskervilles.

The barks brought Viktor. His jaw dropped when he saw me. He was unarmed, but he lumbered my way, like the Mummy chasing after Abbott and Costello.

I pointed my gun at him, but it didn't seem to make much difference. When he was within a few feet, I told him to stop.

He kept coming. A man the size of Viktor, you shoot him in the chest, the stomach, the shoulder, you might not stop him. I aimed at his knees. Two shots.

He screamed and dropped to the deck, grabbing his legs and cursing.

When I tried to get past him, Viktor reached out with one bloody hand for my crotch. I pounded the butt of the gun against his skull, but that only seemed to make him madder. I pounded his head four more times and he finally let go of me.

All of the commotion had not gone unnoticed.

Kim Lee peeked into the hallway. She had an automatic in her hand—a big gun, a small hand, but even a missed shot and ricochet could do me in.

I dropped down behind Viktor's unconscious body as she let off a string of shots that hit the metal walls of the passageway and careened around like pinballs.

The next time her head came into view I got off a shot of my own. I missed, but it caused her to duck back into the galley.

I pushed my way through the door leading out to the port side of the boat.

There were seconds of pure nerve-racking silence. My chest was heaving, sweat was running down my face. Then a series of shots from an automatic weapon—a dozen or more of them.

I figured Zek had come down from the wheelhouse and was inside, raking the passageway with an AK-47. Zek had all the ammunition in the world. I had fired three times, and, with the chamber under the hammer empty for safety sake, had just two bullets left.

I dropped down to my hands and knees and scuttled forward, toward the door leading to the galley.

More shots—these coming from the stern of the tug.

I got to my feet, pulled the galley door open and dove inside.

Kim Lee was standing rigidly, a pistol in her right hand.

"Drop the gun, Kim."

She hesitated a moment, and then opened her fingers and the weapon clattered to the floor.

I started to reach for it, just as Zek arrived and let go with a clip of bullets. I crawled under the table, aimed in his direction and fired off my final two shots. Stupidly, I kept firing. Panic does that to you. Zek heard the clicks of the gun's hammer hitting the empty cartridges.

He started laughing. "Johnny O. You out of bullets. Get out from under there. Let's have a drink."

I didn't have much choice. I crawled out from under the table, and slid my gun across the floor.

"What the fuck you doing here?" Zek asked, zeroing the barrel of the AK-47 in on my head.

"Give me that drink, and I'll tell you."

He flicked his head toward the sink. "Help self. But don't be stupid, huh."

I grabbed a bottle of Polish vodka and swallowed a double shot.

"I found Misha Turov in your freezer, Alex. Why didn't you get rid of his body earlier?" I asked. "Like you did with Boris."

"Too busy. No time yet. Misha was helpful to me on yacht, with making engines stop, but he get nervous after Vanel go missing. Too nervous. I feed him to sharks soon."

I could see Zek's mind whirling around. Why not make it a double meal for the sharks—Misha and Johnny.

"Who was the thief, Alex? Who ripped the diamond from Gaby's neck?"

"Was me, and I didn't rip it. Used wire cutter on necklace. No want to hurt her."

Such a thoughtful, considerate man.

"Gaby was in on it with you."

"In, yes. She knew Vanel was going to dump her, so I told her we get diamond and I split money with her."

"But it was a fake diamond."

"Yes. Cocksucker Vanel. He give her fake to wear. I find out later it no good piece of shit."

"Where do you think the real one is now, Alex?"

"Vanel. Son bitch he has it. Or maybe Polina, little niece he was fucking has it. Or maybe is in safe."

"Or maybe I have it," I said.

Kim decided to join the conversation. "He's stalling. Kill him."

"Go to wheel," Zek told her. "Steer for dock."

"No. I want you to—"

"My boat, I'm boss," Zek screamed. "Go to wheel before we hit something."

Kim Lee didn't like it, but she followed orders, after bending down and scooping up her automatic.

"I hate woman telling me what to do, Johnny. She pretty, but a bitch."

"She's your new partner, isn't she, Alex? All of that China White you picked up must be worth a lot of money."

"Is true. But she just along for ride. I deal with Feng Sha." He gave me a wink. "He think she bitch too."

I took another nip of the vodka, gauging the distance

between us, and the chances of my throwing it at Zek before he plugged me. They weren't very good.

"Why did you kill Boris?"

"He stupid, Johnny. Okay be stupid in Moscow, but not here. He make trouble. He say he like America, want to stay, be my partner, kill peoples for me and for Gromov. He want to kill you."

"I saw Boris's body, Alex. There were no wounds. How'd you kill him?"

"Gromov and me get him drunk. Put some pills to sleep in his cabbage soup. He go sleep, I put him in freezer. No pain that way."

"Boris was friendly with Polina. I found someone who saw the two of them meeting on Polk Street."

"Boris think he could scare Polina. She not scare." Zek scratched the barrel of the AK-47 under his chin. I could hear his whiskers bristle. "Is nice talk, Johnny, but, sorry, I can't let you off boat."

"You have to, Alex. I've got the Stalin Blue."

He wagged his ugly head. "No. Is what you call, nice try. No, you—"

"I have it, Alex. I got it from Trower."

"Trower? Dumb solider? You full of it, Johnny."

"No. Trower's been running rings around you. All of you, including Vanel. He speaks fluent Russian."

That didn't sit well with the Swine. "Trower understand Russian?"

"Yes, so he understood everything you said to Gaby, and he passed all of that information onto Vanel. He knew about the two of you and your plan to heist the diamond on the yacht. Trower watched Vanel for months, learned the combination for the safe, and got the real diamond after Vanel gave Gaby the fake."

Zek lowered the barrel of the AK-47 a few inches. "And then what? Trower just give you diamond? Bullshit."

"He didn't give it to me willingly. I had to kill him." I put the vodka bottle down on the sink and then moved my hand very slowly toward my pants pocket. "That's why I came onboard tonight. I don't give a damn about Misha. I wanted your help in selling the Stalin Blue. You have the right connections."

I carefully, slowly, removed the fake Blue from my pocket and held it out to him.

"Son of bitch," he said, lowering the machine gun's barrel further.

I tossed the stone in his direction and he caught it with his left hand.

While he was scrutinizing it, I took Joel Pardee's Derringer from my other pocket.

Zek had to know I was lying, had to know that I was making all of it to save my life, but he was mesmerized by the blue stone in the palm of his left hand. And he still had the AK-47 in his right hand.

"It's the real Blue, Alex. Bring it to your lips. It'll be icy cold."

He started to do just that, and I said, "Drop the machine gun, Alex."

He dragged his eyes away from the stone. When he saw the Derringer in my hand he gave out one of his belly laughs.

"Recognize it, Alex? It belonged to a man named Joel Pardee, a hotel cop. Who killed him? You or Boris?"

"Was Boris. I told you he stupid. Brings dead body to my boat. Johnny, drop little gun. Is no good. If this is real diamond—"

"You'll kill me anyway, right?"

A shoulder shrug. "Would I do such a thing?"

He started to bring the barrel of the machine gun up. I shot him in the chest, then jumped forward, jammed the Derringer's muzzle against his neck and pulled the trigger.

Zek's eyes popped and he sagged back, bumping up against the stove. There was a look of shock on his face—not pain, just shock, as if he'd been bitten by a bug. Then he collapsed to the floor.

I wrestled the AK-47 away from Zek and made my way over to the narrow stairway leading to the wheelhouse. I started up the steps, saw Kim Lee sitting in the captain's chair, one hand on the wheel, the other on her automatic.

She fired as soon as she saw me, the first bullet whizzed by my head, the second caught my left shoulder. The AK-47 dropped to the stairs as I stumbled backwards. Another shot followed. I slammed the stairwell door shut, and stumbled down the passageway. I had that soft, nauseating feeling in my gut, the kind you get when you know you're hurt bad.

I needed a weapon. I made it to Zek's gun room and picked a Colt .357 magnum with a four-inch barrel from the wall. The shotguns and rifles were tempting, but my left shoulder and arm were useless, which left the long weapons out of the picture. I could see the outline of the cartridges in the Colt's cylinder, meaning it was loaded, like most of Zek's weapons.

I peeked cautiously out of the door into the passageway. I should have noticed right away that something was missing, something big. Viktor. There was a trail of blood leading back toward the bathroom.

Maybe it was the smell of my blood that caught Claw's attention. He started barking again, and pounding his body against the cabin door.

I leaned against the wall and slid my way toward the galley. The bathroom door opened and there was Viktor, lying on the ground, a seaman's knife in his right hand. He lunged out, the tip of the blade ripped across my left ankle. Then Viktor flopped back into a pool of his own blood and lay motionless.

I left him there, bleeding to death, while my own blood was streaming down my arm and ankle.

Where was Kim Lee? Still behind the tug's wheel? She could have come down and finished me off easily, but why take the risk? All she had to do was get the *Krùto* home to its berth where there would no doubt be a gang waiting to unload the heroin, and take care of me.

The stairwell leading to the wheelhouse was a death trap. I'd be an all too easy a target, which meant climbing up the bridge ladder, something I wasn't sure I could do.

I humped my way back to the galley. The wheelhouse was directly overhead. I cocked the .357, pointed to the ceiling where I thought the captain's chair was positioned, and pulled the trigger. The recoil knocked me to the floor.

I got into as comfortable a sitting position as I could and fired off another round, then another.

There still was no change in the boat's speed or direction, but drops of blood started trickling down through the bullet holes I'd made in the ceiling.

The revolver felt like it weighed fifty pounds, but I kept a tight grip on it as I crawled to the door leading to the wheelhouse. I went up step by step on my elbows and knees. Kim Lee was lying back in the chair, her beautiful head lolling to the left side. Her gun was lying next to the marine radio.

I struggled to my feet, leaned over and grabbed the radio microphone.

I barely heard the click of the switchblade knife opening. Kim Lee slashed the blade across my back. She hissed something in Chinese at me before I was able to jab the barrel of the Magnum into her chest and pull the trigger.

Through the wheelhouse window I could see we were approaching a familiar sight—Treasure Island, where Vanel's yacht had been beached. The microphone was dangling from its cord. I picked it up and used the word that I'd remembered from all of those WWII movies, when Errol Flynn or John

Wayne were about the crash their airplanes or torpedo boats. "Mayday! Mayday!"

Then I stumbled to the floor and passed out.

# CHAPTER 50

The only one to get off of the *Krùto* unscathed was Claw, and he nipped some fannies and legs before the police were able to subdue him and send him to the SPCA.

Viktor somehow survived, but he'd lose one of his legs.

While recuperating in the hospital, I found out why people just don't like cops. I was interviewed by local departments, state agencies, the Coast Guard, and the feds around the clock.

An Alameda Sheriff detective threatened to charge me with homicide for the deaths of Alex Zek and Kim Lee, and they were willing to throw in an attempted homicide on Viktor. Three different federal agencies tried to tie me in with the China White found on the *Krùto*.

The question most asked was: "Why were you on board the tug boat?"

My ace in the hole was Misha Turov. I explained I'd received an anonymous tip that Misha was onboard the tug, went to investigate and through no fault of my own, went out to sea with Zek and his crew.

Good old FBI agent Charlie Ledegue helped save my bacon by backing me up regarding my sterling character and our conversations regarding Russian agents and Chinese gangs.

Still, the questions kept coming. I was being treated like a criminal when I thought I deserved a raise and the keys to the city.

It took about two weeks for the cops to get tired of grilling me.

My shoulder was going to take longer than that to heal. Months, quite a few months, and there was some question as to whether I'd ever be able to return to full duty. I still had my private entertainment security management gig, taking care of the likes of Sinatra, Bob Hope and Judy Garland when they came to town, but I was longing to get back to real police work.

It had been a long, rough summer. Bobby Kennedy was assassinated, the Tet Offensive came to an end in Vietnam, the Republicans nominated Richard Nixon for president, a coup d'état put Saddam Hussein in charge of Iraq, there were riots at the Democratic Convention in Chicago, and Dimitri Vanel's mutilated body had washed up on a beach. Not a San Francisco beach—Santa Teresa Beach in Costa Rica.

Vanel had been put through the wringer before hitting the water. Much of his skin had been sliced off, his arms and feet removed, as well as his penis, which was inserted into his anus—a typical Russian Mafia sendoff.

The finding of Vanel's body paved the way for Francie Stevens to broker an agreement between Gaby and Nika Vanel, though there wasn't as much as hoped for to divvy up between them. Vanel had borrowed heavily on both his home and yacht. A Mosler company safe expert had opened his safe. There were several nice pieces of jade, a small stash of cash, and several paintings that were worth in the high hundred thousand dollar range.

The only person not heard from was Polina Popov, aka Morel.

The Stalin Blue never surfaced, but something awfully close to it did.

Marty Rothman called me to his office and over a few shots of Israeli scotch told me that a large blue diamond was to be auctioned off at Christie's in London.

He showed me the brochure Christie's had put out. "It's the Stalin Blue, Johnny, I'm sure of it. It's been shaved and polished, and has lost a carat or two. A perfect job, I couldn't have done any better myself. They're calling it *Le Régent,* but it's the Blue."

"Who's the seller?" I asked.

"A very well-known person in the auction world." Rothman's eyes twinkled. "Mr. Anonymous."

My father had passed peacefully in his sleep, and I'd come into a little money from the sale of the house on Diamond Street. I decided to use some of it to fly to London and check out the new blue diamond.

Rothman was able to get me a pass to the auction. Christie's was packed with a mixture of men in expensive suits, and women in furs and designer dresses.

There were also several Arab sheiks in white robes and headdresses.

The seating arrangements consisted of rows of rather ordinary wooden chairs. A phone bank, manned by a dozen or so suits-and-ties took up one wall.

A handful of paintings, statues, and tapestries went down before the blue diamond made an appearance—on a cart, wheeled in my two young men wearing black aprons. The stone was sitting on a white silk pillow. The room hushed. This was what they had all been waiting for. A carousel slide projector flashed images of the diamond on a screen behind the auctioneer, a dapper fellow in his thirties who had one of those British accents that sounded like he was trying to talk while yawning. The bidding started at five hundred thousand and quickly moved upwards.

I strolled around the back of the room where dozens of those who were too late to grab a seat waited their turn to place a bid.

I spotted a young woman wrapped up in a red Audrey Hepburn style coat that buttoned up to her throat. She wore Audrey's style of hat too, also red, one of those cute ones with a strap under the chin that looked it belonged on a polo player. Her eyebrows were different, her makeup expertly applied to accent her cheekbones, and she was chewing on the stem of a pair of eyeglasses.

It was Polina. She was so intent on the auction prices, which had reached nine million dollars, that she didn't notice me sidling up to her.

"It was too bad about Dimitri," I said.

She arched an eyebrow and begged my pardon.

"Dimitri Vanel, Polina. He died the hard way. Did you help? I don't mean by actually cutting his penis off, but by calling someone in Moscow to let them know that Vanel was in Costa Rica."

Her response was a frozen stare.

"And how about Nika? You left her holding an empty bag. I thought you cared about her, you being her cousin and all."

"*Va te faire de fourte*," she said, before pushing me away and hurrying through a door guarded by a rent-a-cop wearing one of those silly Sam Browne gun belts that always remind me of suspenders.

Later, I leaned that Polina's French translated to the old, vulgar, go do something to yourself that you can't really do.

Shortly after Polina had disappeared, Maurice Bernier, the man Trower described as a French jeweler, the one I'd pounded to the ground at the Bullpen, showed up and slipped through the same door. He'd put on some weight, re-styled his hair, and the wounds I'd inflected on his face during our scuffle had healed, but I was sure it was him.

I didn't bother trying to follow them; there would be doors leading outside or to other hiding places in the building. Polina and Bernier were obviously preferred customers, to be treated with great respect.

You get that kind of respect when you've just sold a blue diamond for twelve-point-five million dollars—1968 dollars.

I was certain that the two of them had gotten away with murder and grand theft, but there wasn't a thing I could do about it. They'd pocket the millions from the sale of the diamond and vanish.

I thought briefly about calling Moscow and dropping the dime on Polina to Arkadi Kusmenko, but there had already been enough gruesome killings.

The Stalin Blue seemed to have some kind of a curse about it. Everyone who owned it ended up dying violently. It was hard not to root for the same thing happening to Polina.


Steve McQueen's hair was long and curly. He'd flown to San Francisco from Mississippi where he was filming a comedy based on a William Faulkner novel, *The Reivers*.

There was a party at the St. Francis Hotel after the premier showing of *Bullitt*. In addition to McQueen, Jacqueline Bisset, and Don Gordon were there.

Francie Stevens was in attendance, lovely as ever in a backless ruby-red dress. She gave me a nice wave, with her left hand. On the third finger of that hand was a large diamond, five or more carats—an engagement ring from her boss, attorney Tim Riordan.

Fred Breen, Sergeant Sunshine, was wearing a blue suit that looked like it had been ironed on him. His face had a special glow to it that I didn't think had come from the sun. He came over and flashed his teeth at me.

"Not a bad flick, Johnny. But they should have given me at least one line."

I shouldn't have done it, but I couldn't resist. Just as I had years ago, when we were in the Police Academy, I tapped the edge of my nose and said, "Fred. You've got a pimple."

He did an about face, and went in search of a mirror.

Steve McQueen was friendly and gracious—taking time to talk to all of the cops who'd helped him during the filming of *Bullitt*, including yours truly.

"Johnny O," he said, "I couldn't have made the movie without you. How'd you like it?"

"It was great." Which was the truth. The story held together, the San Francisco hills were photographed beautifully, especially during the spectacular car chase, and McQueen had done a hell of a job at projecting a cool, dedicated cop.

"Just one thing was missing, Steve. Me." My scene had made the cutting room floor.

He gave me a lopsided grin and a pat on the shoulder. "That's show biz, Johnny."

Jerry Kennealy has worked as a San Francisco policeman and as a licensed private investigator in the City by the Bay. He has written twenty-two novels, including a ten-book series about private eye Nick Polo, two of which were nominated for a Shamus Awards. His books have been published in England, France, Germany, Japan, Italy and Spain. He is a member of Mystery Writers of America and Private Eye Writers of America. Jerry lives in San Bruno, California, with his wife and in-house editor, Shirley. He is currently working on a new Nick Polo novel.

# OTHER TITLES FROM DOWN AND OUT BOOKS

*See www.DownAndOutBooks.com for complete list*

By Anonymous-9
*Bite Hard*

By J.L. Abramo
*Catching Water in a Net*
*Clutching at Straws*
*Counting to Infinity*
*Gravesend*
*Chasing Charlie Chan*
*Circling the Runway*
*Brooklyn Justice*

By Trey R. Barker
*2,000 Miles to Open Road*
*Road Gig: A Novella*
*Exit Blood*
*Death is Not Forever*
*No Harder Prison*

By Richard Barre
*The Innocents*
*Bearing Secrets*
*Christmas Stories*
*The Ghosts of Morning*
*Blackheart Highway*
*Burning Moon*
*Echo Bay*
*Lost*

By Eric Beetner and
JB Kohl
*Over Their Heads*

By Eric Beetner and
Frank Scalise
*The Backlist*
*The Shortlist (\*)*

By G.J. Brown
*Falling*

By Rob Brunet
*Stinking Rich*

By Dana Cameron (editor)
*Murder at the Beach: Bouchercon
Anthology 2014*

By Mark Coggins
*No Hard Feelings*

By Tom Crowley
*Vipers Tail*
*Murder in the Slaughterhouse*

By Frank De Blase
*Pine Box for a Pin-Up*
*Busted Valentines and Other Dark
Delights*
*A Cougar's Kiss (\*)*

By Les Edgerton
*The Genuine, Imitation, Plastic
Kidnapping*

By A.C. Frieden
*Tranquility Denied*
*The Serpent's Game*
*The Pyongyang Option (\*)*

By Jack Getze
*Big Numbers*
*Big Money*
*Big Mojo*
*Big Shoes*

*(\*)—Coming Soon*